Now
and Always

Also by Lori Copeland

Morning Shade Mystery Series
> A Case of Bad Taste
> A Case of Crooked Letters
> A Case of Nosy Neighbors
> Child of Grace
> Christmas Vows

Brides of the West Series
> Faith
> June
> Hope
> Glory
> Ruth
> Patience
> Roses Will Bloom Again

Men of the Saddle Series
> The Peacemaker
> The Drifter
> The Maverick
> The Plainsman

Stand-Alone Titles
> Monday Morning Faith
> Simple Gifts

LORI COPELAND

Now and Always

ZONDERVAN®

ZONDERVAN.com/
AUTHORTRACKER
follow your favorite authors

ZONDERVAN®

Now and Always
Copyright © 2008 by Copeland, Inc.

Requests for information should be addressed to:

Zondervan, *Grand Rapids, Michigan* 49530

Library of Congress Cataloging-in-Publication Data

Copeland, Lori
    Now and always / Lori Copeland.
       p. cm.
     ISBN 978-0-310-26351-7
     I. Title.
  PS3553.O6336N69 2008
  813'.54—dc22

                                             2007051420

Printed in the United States of America

---

08 09 10 11 12 13 14 • 21 20 19 18 17 16 15 14 13 12 11 10 9 8 7 6 5 4 3 2 1

In loving memory of my brother
Danny Lee Smart
September 8, 2007
Blessed by God
Loved by family

Now
and Always

Prologue

No one could say exactly how he got five hundred birds in one car.

Electronic carnival lights flashed myriad colors. Loud music blared from rides with names like The Octopus, The Whip, Flying Scooter, and Dodgem Cars.

Nine-year-old Katie and her friend, Essie, stood transfixed, rounded eyes focused on a sideshow where a ten-foot-tall man proceeded to load crates of canaries in a compact car and then folded his legs and nimbly climbed inside behind the wheel.

Another man with a bullhorn promised even more amazing feats, and he gestured the carnivalgoers inside for an astonishing thirty-five cents.

The girls moved on, pausing minutes later in front of the gypsy tent. If a picture was worth a thousand words, this attraction was worth every penny of twenty-five cents.

Katie glanced at Essie and Essie nodded. Here was a real, honest-to-goodness gypsy with stringy, long black hair, witch's fingernails, and evil— *very* evil eyes.

Squirming, Katie knew that Grandpops and Tottie would kill her if they knew what she was doing. Essie's parents weren't religious like Katie's folks. They'd forked over fifty cents to each girl and told them to "have fun." One turn on the Ferris wheel would have eaten their fifty cents, but for twenty-five cents they could have their future told and still buy cotton candy. The nine-year-olds paid the admission price, parted the tent, and entered the dim interior.

There she sat, big as life.

Katie's foot struck the metal folding chair, and she sucked in her breath and dropped onto the cool hardness.

The gypsy focused on them, running her hands over the crystal globe, evil eyes bright with supernatural knowledge. Katie studied the soothsayer, feeling a bit evil herself. Grand-pops said evil powers belonged to Satan. She shouldn't be here. It was wrong, clearly against God's teachings. But she had one question, one burning question she needed answered, and chances were she'd never again have an opportunity to ask it.

The old woman eye's settled on Katie. "Little one. What do you wish to know?"

Katie's mind went blank as a sheet of paper. What did she want to know? What did she want to know? Her mind was as vacant as the little boy, Ralphie, in *A Christmas Story* who wanted a Red Ryder BB gun.

The Knowledgeable One waited.

Katie couldn't think. She couldn't breathe! She sank deeper into the folding metal chair.

"Eh? Speak up!"

Katie couldn't talk. God had rendered her speechless and with good cause.

Essie edged forward. "I know what I want."

The old woman's eyes switched. "And what is that, little one?"

"I want to know if I'll get married when I'm old."

"Married?" She cackled. "Married, you say." She moved her hands over the top of the ball, leaned, and peered closer. "Ah ... yes. I see."

Essie slid forward in her chair. "What? What do you see?"

"A handsome man, indeed, very handsome. Fair of color, fair of hair. He will come into your life most unexpectedly, and you will know immediately that he is the one and only." She looked up, revealing a yellowed grin.

Essie sighed blissfully. "I knew it."

Katie's brain still refused to function. Her mind screamed for answers! She'd spent twenty-five cents; she deserved an answer!

The gypsy began to fold a black velvet cloth over the magic globe. She was through. Katie grappled for coherent speech. *She's through. Say something*!

"Wait!"

The woman fixed evil eyes on her. "You had your chance. Now move on."

"No. Wait." Katie swallowed, then blurted, "I remember my question!"

The mystic snorted, uncovered the ball. "What is it?"

"Will I get any taller?"

There. She may go to hell, but now she'd know, even if Grandpops would skin her alive for consulting an evil power. She'd shot up five inches in the past year, and by golly she couldn't tolerate any more height. She was taller than every boy in her class, and the girls were starting to call her Giraffe.

The gypsy eyed her. "That's your question? How tall will you get?"

Katie swallowed. "Yes. How tall will I be?" If the gypsy said seven feet she'd die, right here in this tent on this cold metal folding chair, and pray nobody ever told Grandpops, Grandmoms, or Tottie where she was when it happened.

The mystic sighed and then quickly ran her hands over the top of the ball. "How tall will—what's your name?"

"Katie. Katie Addison."

"How tall will Katie Addison grow?" The old woman leaned and peered inside the clear ball. "I see. You will grow very tall—"

"How tall?"

"How tall do you want to grow?"

"No taller than I am. In fact, I'd like to shrink if you can do that. I have another quarter." She fumbled in her pocket, but the old woman stopped her.

Her gaze returned to the ball. "You will grow no taller than six feet."

Katie felt color drain from her face. Six feet. A giant. A big, old, ugly giant.

"But take heart, my child. Your forever love will come along early in life, but you will not recognize him. It will take many years and many trials to distinguish him from other men, but when you do, you will live happily ever after." She reached for the velvet cover and draped the ball, and before Katie could blink, she'd disappeared through a colorful beaded curtain.

Katie gaped at Essie, astounded. "Did you hear that? I'm going to be a giant."

She nodded. "I heard. Sorry—but you have pretty hair."

The girls got up, exiting through a maze of thick electrical cords. Music blared. Screams came from The Octopus, and the smell of popping corn filled the air. Everything seemed so normal, but Katie's life was over.

Essie shouted above the confusion. "Want some cotton candy?"

Numb, Katie nodded, putting one wooden foot in front of the other. She might as well eat until she burst. No man was ever going to want her. Her conscience pricked her. This was God's punishment for going to a gypsy.

One

Very few things distracted Katie Addison when she was on a mission, but the sight of three dead horses strewn across the winding road stopped her in her tracks. Her jeep skidded and veered to the right before stopping. Motorists set out flares. The highway patrol began the process of diverting traffic around the gruesome sight.

Putting a tissue over her nose, Katie exited the jeep. Thick smoke covered the area from the fire burning on the ridge below Devils Tower. Wildfire had broken out in the thirteen-hundred-acre park, and crews had been battling it all day. A suffocating haze blanketed the landscape.

Confusion reigned as Katie threaded her way through curious onlookers and fellow travelers who'd stopped to help. Her eyes focused on the black skid marks, and it didn't take a sleuth to see that the overturned truck and stock trailer had veered to the center and jackknifed, blocking most of the road.

Blowout? Deer blocking the road?

The long, white trailer lay on its side in the ditch. The sides were enclosed, and the top was lined with openings for ventilation. The terrified screams of trapped horses, kicking and lunging, trying to break free, sent a shudder up her spine.

She'd lived on a ranch all her life, and while she wasn't a vet, she knew almost as much as anybody about animals. She took care of her own — three dogs, three cats, a goat, and an aging Appaloosa. She'd sewn up more than one wire cut by lantern light.

Katie approached Sheriff Ben O'Keefe, who was trying to redirect traffic. "Is the driver hurt?"

"Don't know. An ambulance is on the way."

Katie strained to see what was going on through the chaos. Men worked to open the truck's passenger side door while others were trying to break into the mangled trailer. Katie observed the work and then impulsively raced to help, her former mission forgotten.

Working her way around the overturned trailer, Katie tried to peer through the narrow slits in the side wall. It was nearly impossible to count the heaving flesh trapped inside, but she estimated three, maybe four horses down, kicking and struggling to get out. Men worked feverishly to reach the injured animals, but the enclosed trailer defeated their efforts. The back door hung by one hinge, but the divider separating the back compartment from the front was jammed, making it almost impossible to reach the injured. Apparently the dead animals had been thrown out when the trailer jackknifed. Some had been hit by cars, judging from the damaged autos scattered along the roadside. A portly man collapsed against the overturned trailer, breathing heavily and wiping sweat from his forehead. The cloud of smoke cast a stifling blanket, hampering rescue efforts.

Katie eased into the back of the overturned carrier, working her way cautiously to the crumpled and jammed divider. Her stomach seized at the sight of tangled limbs and the sound of the injured horses' screams. There had to be a way to free them before they sustained more injury. A bay kicked frantically, lunging against the divider. Blood spurted from a nasty shoulder gash.

"There, boy, take it easy," Katie crooned, trying to calm the horse.

A shout and the wail of a siren heralded the arrival of emergency vehicles. Katie focused on the arrival of an ambulance, two firetrucks, and a couple of police cars, sirens blaring. Paramedics hit the ground before their vehicle fully stopped, racing to the truck cab. Firemen approached the overturned trailer, openly assessing the bedlam. Katie wanted to scream at them to move faster, but she knew they needed to determine what would be best for the horses' sake. Someone brought a Sawzall. Was it strong enough to slice through the metal trailer? Rescue workers were already using the Jaws of Life to cut through the truck cab and reach the driver pinned inside.

The screech of metal cutting metal sent the horses into a panic. Firemen sliced through twisted metal. Whining saws died away, and Katie eased to maneuver into line to help remove the animals. But a burly captain stepped in front of her.

"Sorry. You need to step back out of the way."

"I can help. I've doctored animals all my life."

"You could get hurt in there. If you want to help, you'll stand back and let us work."

A tall, rawboned woman with short salt-and-pepper hair ran toward them. "I'm a vet." She was allowed to pass to the scene of action.

A couple of men cautiously approached the trailer. Katie held her breath as they tried to untangle the downed animals.

Finally they led the bay out at the end of a rope. One by one, the horses were removed. Frightened, shying at every noise, the trembling animals were led to safety. Two were limping and all were bleeding from numerous wounds. A stock trailer rattled up, restoring alarm. The men leading the horses spoke calmly, guiding them gently forward. One horse couldn't get up. "Broken legs and internal injuries," someone in the crowd murmured. The vet administered an injection. After a short time the thrashing body went limp, and the horrible sound of an animal in agony was stilled. The carcass was dragged out and loaded on a flatbed trailer.

The woman vet glanced at Katie, her color drained. "Those horses look like someone took a baseball bat to them. It's a shame to allow this to happen in a civilized nation. Someone ought to do something about this disgrace." A fireman called her, and she moved away to join him.

What disgrace? Accidents happen.

A news reporter held a microphone to the fire chief's mouth, and Katie shamelessly eavesdropped. "How many horses were saved?"

"Four. At first we thought we only had four in the trailer, but when we got inside, one was down and buried under the weight of the others. Eight horses in all were involved."

"Are the remaining ones going to be all right?"

"Can't say." The chief lifted his hat for ventilation. "You'll need to talk to the vet — looked to me like most of them were hurt pretty badly. They got tossed around when the trailer overturned."

Attendants strapped the truck driver to a body board and loaded him into the ambulance. A stench of oil and spilled gas, of blood and sweat and death, hung over the scene of the

accident like a thundercloud mingling with the sharp, stinging scent of smoke.

Devils Tower loomed in the distance. The national monument formation jutted out of the smoky Black Hills landscape,
looking almost surreal with the smoke billowing around its
base and the flickering flames skirting the ridge. Katie knew
several northern plains tribes called it Bears Lodge and considered it a sacred worship site, but it was probably best known
for the role it played in the late seventies movie *Close Encounters*. Today the tower, the smoke, and the tragic wreck sent a
shiver of apprehension rippling through Katie. She breathed
a quick prayer.

*Father, be with the driver and with these helpless animals.
You can work miracles, and it looks like the victims could sure
use one.*

"The driver will be lucky to get out of this alive."

Katie turned to find Warren Tate beside her. Warren
owned the ranch two miles to the south. Except for the seven
years he'd recently spent on Wall Street, he'd been a fixture in
these parts. Katie and Warren had gone to school together, and
known each other most of their lives. Warren had returned
from New York a few weeks earlier, but this was the first time
Katie had bumped into him. She smiled. "I'd heard you were
back. Welcome home!"

The former classmate removed his hat. "Katie." His eyes
skimmed her. "You're looking good."

"Thank you. So are you." The latter was an understatement. He looked terrific! Gone was the gangly, acne-prone
teenager. In his place stood a self-possessed, darn good-looking
man. Rumor had it he'd graduated college summa cum laude.

Shortly afterwards, he left the state to make his fortune in New York on the stock exchange.

Warren's gaze focused on the frantic scene. Katie eased closer. "It's so tragic. Does anyone know how it happened?"

He inclined his head toward the distorted wreckage. "The driver hasn't regained consciousness."

Katie's eyes scanned the highway where the rest of the carcasses were being loaded on the flatbed trailer. "It's a miracle anything survived."

Warren lifted his Stetson and ran a hand through thick black hair. Katie had to admit that the years had worked to his advantage. He'd bloomed. His odd-colored eyes, a dark green hue, had been a distraction during his youth, but now they enhanced his features. In high school he'd been the bookish sort, not particularly handsome and certainly not part of the in crowd. He hadn't been a partyer. She'd liked that about him, but others called him a geek. Well, world, Warren Tate was anything but a geek now. He was a couple of inches taller than her own six feet, which made it nice to stand beside him. It hadn't been easy in high school when she had towered above him and most boys her age. Her gaze shifted to his ring finger. Empty ...

Maybe Warren was like Katie, content to wait until Mrs. Right came along, though rumor also had it he'd been involved in a pretty nasty breakup prior to leaving the Big Apple.

Katie didn't have time to brood about her own lack of social life, much less Warren Tate's. Taking care of Grandpops until he died took time, then establishing the shelter ... She glanced at her watch. "Oh, granny's skirts! I was due at the airport fifteen minutes ago!"

Warren turned to look at her. "New guest?"

Katie nodded. Everyone around knew that she took in battered women, but the town kept the information to themselves. Little Bush was a close-knit community, loyal to a fault, and the Addisons had been part of the community as far back as anyone remembered. It wasn't a large community, though it had grown since Katie graduated from high school. A couple of factories had moved in, and a few hometown boys made good, investing time and money into the community. Quite a few mom-and-pop businesses had sprung up, and the chamber of commerce boasted a healthy number of members. The town still had most of the original buildings, reminders that Little Bush was an old town with roots going back a long way. But there was still a hint of wildness, a feel of the frontier that outsiders sometimes found intimidating. If they wanted something more, Sundance and Gillette were a short drive away, and Cody, if you really wanted an outing.

Katie's Grandpops, old man Addison as the locals called him, was a crusty Little Bush councilman before he died six years ago. Paul and Willa Addison, Katie's maternal grandparents, had raised Katie from an infant when their daughter had been shot and killed by her jealous husband.

Because of the abuse in her background, if mistreated women needed protection, Katie gave it, and Little Bush enforced it. Katie had been young, but she still remembered her mother's dying screams. They had been seared into her memory, and she vowed she would protect helpless women — with her own life if necessary — when she grew up.

Katie's thoughts returned to Warren. "What happens to the surviving animals?" She stepped back, allowing an emergency worker to pass.

He shook his head. "Overheard someone speculate they were on their way to the slaughterhouse."

Katie's jaw dropped. Slaughterhouse! She knew these things happened, but ... slaughterhouse?

"Why?"

"Why? Greed, of course."

Katie had heard that animal byproducts was a huge business, but to see evidence of the cruelty turned her stomach. Sure, she was accused of taking in every stray that wandered her way, and if her house and yard were any indication of her being a pushover, she couldn't argue with the accusation. But horses, innocent animals, on their way to becoming glue or paste, or whatever they did with them, appalled her.

"How can they do that? The survivors. Where will they go? Who is going to take care of them till they heal?"

Warren shrugged. "If the rumors are true, they'll continue to their destination. If not, then I really don't know. Maybe they'll go to the humane society. I can't really say."

"I want them."

Warren glanced over. "You want them?"

"Yes. I want them if all that awaits them is the slaughterhouse. Who do I talk to?"

He shook his head, a grin shadowing the corners of his mouth. His clean-shaven features hadn't changed much over the years; his youthful complexion had cleared, but faded acne scars still shadowed his cheeks. Wall Street's pressure had done a job on him, folks said. Made him cynical. Sick of life. He pretty much stayed to himself, only going into town for groceries and supplies every couple of weeks.

He shifted. "I see the years haven't changed you."

"Meaning what?"

"Meaning you're still a bleeding-heart trying to take care of the whole world."

Katie shrugged. "And that's a bad thing?" That was most people's problem; because they couldn't take care of everything, they quit trying to take care of the things they could. Katie believed one person's efforts, regardless of how puny, made a difference, and she tried to live her life accordingly.

Katie's cell phone rang and she punched the on button. "Yes, this is Katie. Oh. Hi. Yes, I meant to call you this morning about the feed bill. I'll have the payment to you by morning—yes, in the morning. No later, Sue." Katie flashed a lame grin in Warren's direction. "Yeah, can't really talk now. Thanks for calling." She clicked the off button and resumed the conversation with Warren without missing a beat. "I really have to go. Who do I see about getting the animals?"

"You've got room for four near-dead horses?"

"I've got a barn and pasture. I'll make room."

Shaking his head, Warren focused on the activity. "I haven't acquired injured horses on their way to the slaughterhouse, but I suppose if I was planning on it, I'd start by consulting Ben O'Keefe. Most likely he can trace the owner's name, maybe talk to the people at USDA or the humane society."

"Ben?" Her eyes tracked the sheriff, busy trying to redirect traffic. "You think he'd help?" Not likely. She and Ben had been at sword's point since the night all those years ago when he'd failed to show up for their high school prom. The man had stood her up. She didn't hold grudges, but neither had she necessarily treated him cordially since that humiliating evening so long ago. She wasn't sure he would be overly eager to help her, though lately he'd been teasing her about dating. As if she'd date a man she couldn't trust. She hadn't stayed single all of her thirty-six years by practicing stupidity. Like Warren, she'd known Ben most of her life, but the two boys — at least at the time they were boys — were as different as rain and fire. Warren, though a nerd, had always been kind, courteous, with dark complexion and dark eyes, while Ben had rugged features, ruddy complexion, and unruly curly red hair. Feisty features — maddening features when she was sitting in a prom gown waiting for the man to show up. Warren's voice broke into her thoughts. "You'd have to pay the person who owns them something, I suppose — though if they're injured enough, he might pay you to take them off his hands."

Katie shrugged and scribbled down the information on a notepad. "Thanks, Warren. Good to see you back."

"No problem." He tipped his Stetson. "I suppose your lady guest has an escort with her?"

Ah yes, this woman would have high security. Katie had been reluctant to take this particular case. She wouldn't have if a college schoolmate-turned-judge hadn't pleaded with her to give the woman temporary shelter and anonymity, the latter being of utmost importance. Elections were coming up, and if word spread that the party candidate was married to a wife beater, the party could lose a Senate seat. Katie's shelter only held three — no more than four women at the most, and with this celebrity arrival the house was full.

"She's with an escort. I'll phone and tell them I'm running late." Katie turned to thread her way through the onlookers and emergency vehicles. "Oh!" She whirled and cupped her hands to her mouth to be heard above the crowd. "Hey Ben?"

The sheriff was immersed in the rescue efforts, and she had to yell twice before she got his attention. "Yo?"

"If I get permission to take the horses to the ranch, can you haul them for me?" She knew he had all sorts of stock trailers, big and small. She'd had one several years back, but it was out of commission now, and it only hauled one horse.

Katie wasn't surprised when Ben's usual edginess with her flared. "Katie Addison, before you can take care of the world, you'd better take care of yourself!"

"Yada yada! Can you haul my horses?"

Eyes the color of cool summer ponds met hers. Katie held her breath. Even she realized the audacity of her request. Why would this man give her the time of day when she probably wouldn't have reciprocated? But he could easily say no. And he never gave up on asking her for a date. Two weeks ago, they happened to land side by side in stadium bleachers at the local Legion high school ball game, and he tried to entice her, or she supposed. "Want to get a hot dog afterwards?" constituted his idea of a date. She had refused, yet her pride had not kept her from eating half of his bag of popcorn.

Warren trailed Katie. "I'll haul them for you."

She turned. "You will?"

If he was being polite, the geek-turned-prince was too much of a neighbor to retract the offer. He nodded. "If you manage to get the horses, give me a call."

"Thanks!" She tossed him a salute, then cupped her hands and called to Ben. "Never mind!"

He barely glanced her way as he continued to divert traffic.

Katie bolted for the jeep. Her guest's plane had landed over thirty minutes ago.

Inside the vehicle, she turned the ignition key, her eyes catching sight of the gold bracelet Grandpops had given her his last Christmas on earth. The thin chain had one tiny charm that read, "Expect a miracle."

She'd need a miracle to get those horses, but she was going to try like blue blazes to pull it off. How hard could it be? Adopting horses on their way to doom?

Where would she get the money if the owner required cash?

Starting the jeep, she decided she'd see if Ben would help her locate the horses' owner before she started worrying about finances.

❧

Warren turned and watched Katie drive out of sight. She hadn't changed an iota over the years. Blonde hair still worn in a chin length cut, hazel eyes, taller than most women. She was easily still the prettiest girl in Little Bush, and still determined to save the world. Katie had been the champion of the underdog since kindergarten. He'd admired her for her faith in people back then, but years spent trying to survive in the real world had taught him that very few cared about anything except advancing their own agenda. Apparently Katie Addison hadn't learned that yet. In his opinion, bad choices run in families. Katie's mom and fraternal grandmother had been involved with abusive men — Katie's mom had died at the hands of one, and Katie was determined to keep her private women's shelter open when obviously money was tight.

What did it take to shake her faith? A Wyoming tsunami?

Warren glanced at the disappearing jeep. If it was possible, he'd get those horses for Katie. Not because he had any interest in her personally—he'd had his fill of females, especially independent females, which described Katie Addison to a tee.

But horses were a different story. For horses, he would compromise his convictions to stay far, far away from females. All females.

Two

Katie swerved around a slow-moving pickup, trying to make up time. The airport wasn't equipped to handle large aircraft, but private planes and commuter jets came in regularly. She braked and slid out of the jeep, her leather soled boots clicking on the pavement. It wouldn't be hard to recognize her newest guest. Clara Townsend's face was plastered on Katie's TV screen every day, a dozen times a day. Calm and poised, the politician appeared level headed, confident, and a far cry from most guests at the shelter. Why would a woman with Clara's apparent intelligence put up with an abusive husband, and how had she managed to avoid the knowledge going public? The violence could be a recent occurrence, maybe even a onetime incident. Or the abuse could just now be surfacing.

Understandably, the knowledge that Neil Townsend was a wife batterer would affect the election. People expected a woman to be tough enough and hard enough to make it in a male-dominated world. The scandal of the abuse and potential divorce could very well cost Mrs. Townsend the election. Katie had seen Clara's husband, a former campaign advisor, on TV and didn't care for him. He was a fat cat, flashing a large diamond pinkie ring. Television lights reflected off his shaven head, and he snarled and snapped at anyone who crossed him. He reminded Katie of a sleazy pit bull. How could a woman like Clara, a respected senator, put up with the man? No, not man. Katie refused to classify men in general with an abuser. There were too many good men in the world, but a few tarnished the name.

Katie strode into the terminal searching for a woman with flame red hair wearing a power suit. No one immediately met that description or resembled Clara Townsend. Had Clara and her escort grown tired of waiting for her and left, or had they actually come in the first place? Katie's eyes skimmed the near-empty terminal. She didn't want to inquire if Mrs. Townsend's private plane had arrived, since her presence in Little Bush was to remain quiet—and she was probably traveling incognito. Katie stifled a sigh of exasperation and glanced at her watch again. Where was she? Tottie would hold supper only so long.

A slender female with long black hair approached, followed by a couple of casually dressed men wearing dark glasses. Katie noted the ugly green bruises on both sides of the woman's oval-shaped face, injuries that makeup failed to conceal. The politician paused in front of her, removing a pair of jewel-rimmed sunglasses.

Katie suddenly remembered her appearance. She'd been dashing around in smoke, helping to free the horses, and climbing through wreckage. She smelled of smoke, sweat, and blood. A smear of black grease marred the once pristine surface of her white shirt.

The woman's eyes narrowed. "Addison?"

Katie nodded. "I'm Katie Addison."

"Clara Townsend." She flicked a gloved hand in the men's directions, and they picked up a half dozen bags.

This poor woman looked nothing like the suave, polished Senator Townsend Katie saw on the national news every night.

The woman lifted a dark, bruised brow. "You're late."

"I ... there was an accident."

Townsend brushed the explanation aside. "My time is valuable. In the future, be prompt." She stepped ahead of Katie and headed toward the exit door.

Speechless, Katie viewed the stack of bags occupying the men's arms. "Mrs. Townsend ... I ... your room ... The shelter can't accommodate that much luggage. One bag. House rule. You'll have laundry facilities ..." Her words trailed off as she hurriedly fell into step with the entourage that wasn't listening to her. She might as well be a vending machine offering bags of trans fat.

"I never go anywhere without a complete wardrobe." Townsend shoved her way through the glass doorway and outside to the parking lot, where she paused.

"You do now." Katie stopped beside her, appalled at her manners. She didn't want to cause trouble or bring unnecessary stress to the politician, but rules were rules. Besides, Tottie would have fits if Katie let this woman drag in six bags, and if Tottie wasn't happy, nobody was happy. House rule number one.

"You'll have to clear that with my people." Clara's eyes searched the parking area. "Where's my transportation?"

Katie scooted around the baggage-toting men. This was turning ugly. *Way to go, Katie. Alienate a guest first thing. Real diplomatic.* She inclined her head to the jeep sitting on the

first row. Her lips firmed. She towered above the petite politician who was wearing three-inch boots. Katie felt like a giraffe
in flats with an attitude. "One bag, Mrs. Townsend. House
rule."

The woman's tone was anything but compliant. "Surely
you're not serious."

"Yes, ma'am. I surely am." Katie flashed a smile. Judge
Amy would throttle her if she failed to protect this woman,
but she had a feeling the woman was going to be hard to
control.

Clara stared at her for a full minute before heaving a sigh
of disgust. "All right, one stinking bag."

Well, it doesn't have to be stinking, Mrs. Townsend.

The men began to organize her bags into one full of the
essentials, and Clara, lips pursed, snapped, "I will require a
private room and bath."

Katie bit back a snort. *Yeah, right.* The shelter women were
going to love this one. They'd eat Townsend alive, especially
Meg. Young, tough Meg, fresh off the streets, single and pregnant, could hold her own with anyone except the boyfriend
who'd beat her so badly he'd put her in the hospital for a long
stay. By now the entourage reached the jeep, and Clara peeled
off the black wig, leaving her natural short-cropped, flame red
hair standing in spikes. She glanced at Katie, her eyes daring
her to say something. "It's hot and it itches. But it served its
purpose. No one noticed me."

Why, not a living soul in Little Bush—a town of three
hundred—would think anything was amiss if they spotted two strange men wearing dark glasses and juggling six
designer bags between them, stepping out of a private jet with
a large *T* emblazoned on the tail stabilizer. "To err on caution's

side, I'm going to ask you to wear the wig until we reach the shelter."

The woman didn't like the order, but Katie was relieved when the politician put the wig back on. The men loaded her bag in the jeep and stepped back.

Clara stared out the window as Katie wheeled out of the parking lot and headed back to the shelter. "How far are we from civilization?"

"This is as civilized as it gets." Katie drew a deep, appreciative breath and nearly choked on the smell of smoke coming through the open window. "Fresh air and wide open spaces."

The woman turned to stare at her. "You're kidding, right? What do we do to keep from going mad?"

Katie made a right turn onto the highway. "We have books and television, hiking trails, and of course, I encourage our guests to help with chores. Make their beds, help with laundry, kitchen work."

Clara snorted. "In your dreams."

Katie mentally sighed and shifted into third gear. How far off was that election? Less than four weeks? Thank you, Lord. Until tonight Katie had been undecided in the Senate race, but her mind was suddenly crystal clear. She couldn't remember offhand the name of Clara's opponent, but whoever it was, he or she had just gained another vote.

Katie Addison's.

Three

Well, then those people just need to acquire a taste for soy products!" Katie slammed down the receiver, seething. Oh, Ben was glad to help, only he was taking his own good time locating the horses' owner.

"Whoever owns those animals are making a hefty profit," he'd pointed out with the aplomb of a terrorist. "You really think they'd give them to you instead of selling them for meat?"

That's when she'd said the European market needed to acquire a taste for soy products, which made Ben snort.

Taking a deep breath, Katie drummed her fingernails on the counter, Grandpops's voice ringing in her head. "It's a crying shame, just a crying shame." Life's setbacks were either the government's fault or a crying shame with him. Katie must have gotten her faith from Grandmoms. She never recalled a time when Willa complained about anything. Everything was just fine. Really good. Couldn't be better, happier, or healthier. The roof could be caving in and she'd be praising the good Lord for rain. The day they buried Grandpops, she was stricken with grief, but she commented several times about what a pretty day it was for December. Wouldn't get many more of these, she predicted, until spring. Then she blew her nose and wiped her red eyes and lived another four years before she joined Grandpops in heaven.

Those beautiful horses had been on their way to a slaughterhouse. Katie cringed to think what would have happened if she hadn't come along when she did.

She sat and started snapping green beans. Rules and regulations—the world was full of them. She snapped a bean and tossed it into the pot. What harm would it do to take the four surviving horses and nurse them back to health? Once the animals' health was restored—if it could be restored, local children could come to the house and ride on Sunday afternoons—*no, think clearly, Katie. You run enough risk by giving private riding lessons. You can't invite more outsiders here because of the women, but you could nurse the horses back to health and place them in a rehabilitation farm.*

Another bean hit the pot. There were compassionate farms that would care for the horses until someone was found to adopt them. Katie's earlier call to the humane society had proved a dead end. They had no knowledge of the horses and suggested they were owned by a private party. She'd called Ben back, and he assured her that he was putting a trace on the vehicle. He'd promised to get back to her by noon. When she'd asked where the injured horses were, he'd said they were being taken care of. She didn't want to think what that might mean. She went back over their earlier, brief conversation.

"Call me the minute you hear anything, Ben. Promise me?"

"Katie, don't get your hopes up on a bunch of injured horses. American horses are killed every day so their meat can satisfy the palates of overseas European diners. And Premarin sure isn't helping the cause. Horses are abused every day to harvest artificial hormones for women. As far as I'm concerned, women have too many hormones the way it is."

"These horses aren't going be somebody's dinner if I can help it."

"Where would you put them? Your barn can't hold more than five or six animals."

"The four surviving horses and my Appaloosa make five, so I'm okay. I also have ten acres, you know."

"Your ten acres are full to overflowing with strays, and you're constantly telling me you're broke."

"I am constantly broke, but I've learned to live with it, and I can take care of those horses until they're ready to be moved. They don't need to end up in a slaughterhouse."

"That's all you need. A big feed bill."

"You just help me get the horses, and I'll worry about feeding them."

"What time is it, anyway?"

Katie dropped a bean in the pot and glanced up to see Clara Townsend framed in the doorway. The politician focused on her. Smoke rolled from the cigarette dangling from the right corner of her crimson lips. Katie stared — aware that staring was rude. But this woman's face was plastered on the television in commercials hourly — or a replica of this woman touting Townsend for Congress! The smooth talking, baby-kissing politician that belted out welfare reform, lower taxes, and revamping Medicare looked nothing like this — person.

Katie's gaze dropped to her watch. "10:15."

Clara stared back through a trail of roiling smoke. "a.m.?"

Katie nodded, still puzzled by the politician's radical change of appearance. She'd let her new guest sleep in this morning. By the time she picked her up at the airport, argued over luggage and the lack of a private bathroom, and returned home, it was late. Tottie had been in her nightgown watching the news when they arrived. A dim lamp burned in the study window. Clara said little on the drive, chain-smoking incessantly. Katie should have stated the shelter's rules, but last night the woman had looked so drained, she decided to wait until morning.

Last night, the bruises had been less visible beneath heavy makeup. Now with her face void of artifice, it was easier to see the huge shiner beneath Clara's left eye. The fading bruises were far worse than Katie had first expected. She knew little about the politician's story, other than that the woman was married to an abusive husband. Who knew how long the abuse had existed, but however long, Clara and her political machine managed to conceal the troubled marriage until this last incident. Now she was in a heated congressional race to win back her seat, and until the seat was sewn up, it was up to Katie to keep her safe and the ugly secret intact.

Katie didn't like the assignment. Lying by omission wasn't something she'd ordinarily condone, but the election was only a month away, and Clara clearly needed help regardless of her political aspirations. When the ballots were counted, Clara would have to decide what she wanted to do about her marriage. Until then, Katie would do her best to protect her. Katie turned to pour a cup of coffee, and Clara stopped her. "Do you have any gin in the house? I could use something to take the edge off."

Katie's eyes flew to Grandpops's picture sitting on the kitchen shelf, halfway expecting him to leap from the frame and give the politician a scathing lecture on the evils of drink. Grandpops was a teetotaler, and he had no sympathy for the devil brew.

"Liquor isn't allowed on the premises."

Clara brows shot to her hairline.

"Nor smoking," Katie added.

The cigarette drooped. The politician slowly reached up and extracted the butt. "You must be kidding."

"I never kid." Katie raised her brow. "Get rid of the cigarettes."

Four

Before lunch, Katie gathered the women in the living room for their biweekly group session, planning to lay groundwork for community harmony. She had a feeling Clara and Meg would strike sparks if allowed to do what came naturally.

Clara sauntered in and took the most comfortable chair, clearly at odds with her surroundings. The others entered and sat down. Meg, whose straight, long hair hung like a dark curtain, was wearing jeans ripped at both knees and a T-shirt that bared her stomach. Heavy with baby, she dropped onto the sofa. Katie sighed and looked away. It was a waste of time talking to Meg about her clothes. She would listen and then repeat what she'd already said — "I didn't have anything else to wear." The butterfly tattoo on her right bicep looked particularly garish today.

The girl was barely twenty with a lot of baggage. In life experience, she was a hundred years old. She grew up with an alcoholic father and had been on her own since she was fourteen. She'd shared some of her childhood and was trying, with Katie's help and a lot of prayer, to accept and believe that her father's drinking hadn't been her fault. Confrontational and outspoken, Meg had an inferiority complex that she tried to cover up with an attitude. Katie had a feeling the girl thought that she didn't deserve to be loved, so she took what was offered, and what was offered was abuse. Her significant other had used her for a punching bag.

Janet, short, plump, with a halo of blonde curls, wore jeans and a dark blue shirt with the sleeves rolled up. She was the most helpful of the three, always underfoot, always trying to lend a hand whether it was wanted or not. Her husband was a professor in their local college, a pillar of the community, a deacon in the church, and an abuser at home. Katie had a feeling that Janet had spent so many years trying to be the perfect wife, she didn't know how to relax and just be Janet.

In their late night talks, Janet admitted she was an enabler, helping her husband cover up his behavior and not holding him accountable, either in church or at home. She had a heart as big as the Grand Canyon, always offering help. She drove Meg crazy trying to mother her.

Mousey little Ruth was scared of her shadow. Even her manners depicted a frightened soul. She wore her nondescript brown hair scooped up in a ponytail and always sat quietly, wearing a blank expression. She seemed sad, holding herself a little withdrawn from the others. She'd had to leave a child behind. Ruth never spoke of the accident that put her child in the hospital. The courts ruled the fall accidental, but her husband had kicked her out of the house, refusing to let her see their young daughter. When she went to the police with her story, she was given a court-appointed lawyer who was fighting her case, but for now she sought protective shelter at Candlelight. Katie stood before them, four wounded females seeking to put their lives back together. The rules written on the paper were trivial compared to the problems they faced, but there had to be behavioral guidelines. They eyed her expectantly, so she took a deep breath and began.

"I know you're familiar with the rules, but I thought we should go over them one more time."

Meg jerked her chin toward Clara. "She was smoking on the side porch this morning."

Clara shot her a haughty glance.

Meg's expression plainly asked, *You think you're special?*

Katie cleared her throat and continued. "Without some guidelines, we'd all be stepping on each other. So let me quickly reiterate Candlelight Shelter's policy. No alcohol, either on or off the premises."

Clara's expression tightened.

"No smoking — either in your rooms or outside. Some, including me, have allergies, so we should be aware of each other's needs and try to support one another. Secondhand smoke is harmful to Meg's baby. Let's try to remember we are a family, a caring and supportive family."

"I can't smoke because you have allergies?" Clara's brows rose. "Well boo-hoo."

Meg shifted her position on the sofa. "Really, Mrs. Townsend. Must we spell it out for you? No booze, no smokes, no hassle. Got it? You might be Queen on the Hill, but you're nothing here. You're just like us."

Katie sighed. So much for family unity. She should just let Meg read the rules and be done with it. She seemed to be doing fine with passing them on. Katie tried again. "Each of you is asked to limit your calls to lawyers and emergencies. Phone calls from the house line will be monitored. No cell phones, and email access is forbidden. You are free to go outside, but you are limited to the house property. If you need something that can only be provided outside these grounds, you will tell Tottie or me, and we'll arrange to accommodate you."

Clara made some sort of unimpressed sound in her throat but otherwise remained silent. The woman was abused; she wasn't stupid nor did she want her location announced to the world.

"It really isn't so bad," Ruth suggested softly. "We're all here for the same reason, and the rules are for everyone's welfare."

Voices agreed. Except for Clara. Was she getting this? Could Katie ever penetrate the icy wall the woman—or her circumstances—had erected around herself? Katie didn't want to embarrass her by singling her out, but she had to be a team player or leave. The consequence of failure to abide by the rules sometimes was a matter of life or death. How could she impress on Mrs. Townsend that this was not a luxury spa with breakfast in bed and seaweed wraps?

"Clara, because you are so recognizable, you run the biggest risk of being spotted. I suggest that you wear a hat any time you venture outside. Your hair is a most becoming shade, but easily spotted." Katie smiled warmly, praying to break through the woman's brittle veneer. "Would you like to tell the others a little about yourself?" Katie always encouraged the women to share, to let them know they weren't in this fight by themselves.

Clara shook her head.

Smiling, Katie made the introductions. "Clara is our celebrity, ladies. She's running for political office."

"I thought I recognized you!" Janet, always the cheerful one—not to mention the only one in the room who looked interested, gushed. "I see you on television all the time! What are you running for?"

"The county line," Meg cracked.

Clara sent a steely glance. "I'm running for the office of the United States Senate."

"That's *you* on those icky commercials?" Meg's flabbergasted expression was as authentic as butter. "You're that slick-talking chick who's going to solve the world's problems, cut my taxes, and make my kids rich if we just give you a chance? What happened? Your old man didn't agree?"

"Meg," Katie cautioned.

Janet reached over and laid a hand on Clara's arm. "You'll get used to her, honey. Meg speaks her mind, but she's got a good heart. Don't feel bad about being here at Candlelight. The Lord knows we may all be different, but we have one mutual problem we share." Janet's gaze singled out Meg. "We're a sisterhood here. Some of us speak our minds, and others sit back and live and let live. But one thing you can count on. We're here for each other, and as God is our witness, we have taken a stance. No one, no one will ever strike us, try to strangle us, or try to verbally or physically abuse us. We stand united, and you're one of us."

"Look." Clara shoved out of her chair. "Don't think me rude, but keep your pacts and sisterhoods to yourself. This is not something that I will allow to happen to me again. I'm here until the election. November 8, I'm out of here." She left the room.

Silence lingered like a bad air.

Finally, Katie cleared her throat and said. "And the most basic rule—love your neighbor as you love yourself."

"Ha." This came from Meg.

"Perhaps a study course on servanthood would be helpful," Janet supplied.

The young woman rolled her eyes.

"Can't we all just get along?" Ruth had said little, but Katie knew dissention unnerved her. Ruth had been verbally abused as a child and had grown up to marry a man just like her father. Withdrawn, unable to trust easily, she shrank from any kind of confrontation. Her eyes roamed the others, bearing a pleading expression. "Isn't life hard enough without us picking each other apart?"

Katie agreed. "Ruth makes an excellent point, ladies. I realize that Clara may seem harsh and unfeeling, but we need to allow her time to adjust, make friends at her own rate. She'll come around," she predicted.

If she didn't, the shelter only had a month to deal with the situation.

The steel band beneath Clara's assumed indifference was a brittle front. Katie was sure the woman wasn't as unconcerned or as boorish as she appeared. Her circumstances were humiliating. Instead of being on the campaign trail, she was hiding away and depending on pretaped ads to excite her constituents.

Meg struggled to her feet and pulled her T-shirt down, although it wasn't possible to conceal the bare stretch of skin covering her protruding abdomen. Katie made a silent vow to buy that girl some larger shirts. Longer too. One more thing she needed extra money for.

The women filed out, and Katie acknowledged that the next month was going to be a struggle, to say the least.

Father, you've given me a path to follow. To the best of my ability, I'm following it, but money is a problem, Lord. You know that. If I'm to keep the shelter open, I pray you will intervene and show me the way.

The guests knew nothing about the shelter's precarious lack of funds. Years ago those who knew about the shelter kept it running with donations, but these days everyone had a hand out, and contributions had slowed to a trickle. Given the women's situations, most didn't have access to funds in hiding. Katie had never applied for state financial help; her establishment couldn't comply with government rules and regulations. Candlelight Shelter was an act of love, not a business. She took only special cases, ones that Amy recommended.

Katie figured she could hold out another month. One month. Like Clara's destiny, four weeks and the shelter's fate would be decided. If the money situation worsened, she'd have no choice but to close the facility and sell the property. Her heart ached at the thought of selling Grandpops's land, but sometimes life didn't offer many choices.

Was it possible that Clara, the coarse, ill-tempered woman who opposed almost everything, had the same dinosaurs bumping around in the pit of her stomach that Katie had right now? After all, the woman had been in the spotlight for years; now she cowered in a small corner of Wyoming, fearing the public's reaction to her plight, terrified of the very source that could send her back to fame and fortune.

The phone rang and Katie lifted the receiver, still thinking about Clara.

A raspy voice came over the line. "You're in the wrong business, lady."

"What?"

"Someone's going to get hurt, sticking your nose in where it doesn't belong."

"Who is this?"

"A friend. Send those women back to their husbands and quit sticking your nose into everybody's business."

Anger surged through her. "You listen to me—"

"No, you *listen* to me. Heed this warning." The anger spawn from the voice chilled her, though the late afternoon heat had turned vicious. "*Close* the shelter before you get hurt."

"Listen—"

The line went dead. Katie took a deep breath before hanging up the receiver. *Idiot.* She was surprised to see her hand tremble. Prank call? No, there had been too much venom in the voice. Someone … a man … didn't like her shelter, and wanted the facility closed. *Relax, Katie. He has a wife or girlfriend here, or had sometime in the past.* Well, she wasn't closing the shelter. Had the call shaken her? Of course. She wasn't stupid—stubborn maybe, but not stupid. She couldn't tell Tottie or the women about the call; it would unnecessarily frighten them. This wasn't the first nor likely the last of these kinds of scare tactics. Suddenly Katie's skin crawled. She'd had similar calls, but not in many years. *Phone Ben.* No, she didn't want to involve him. Besides, he hadn't bothered to call about the horses. *The call was nothing. Prank. Forget it.*

An alarm went off in her head. *Townsend.* Had he discovered Clara's location so soon?

Of course his sources would be unlimited. Campaign aides are notorious for providing information to the person with the deepest pockets.

No, she better call Ben and err on the safe side. She picked up the phone. Seconds later, she was dispatched through to the sheriff.

"Ben? Katie."

"Hell freeze over?"

"Very funny. I just got a prank call, and I thought you need to know about it."

His tone sobered. "Regarding the women?"

"In a way. Of course he didn't give his name, but a man's husky voice demanded that I close the shelter and mind my own business."

"You didn't recognize the voice, anything about the caller?"

"Nothing. I'm sure it's a prank. I get them often, but I haven't had one in the past few months. My newest guest is high profile. It could be her abuser or one of his cronies."

Ben didn't ask the new guest's name. She knew that he knew better. "I'll keep a closer eye on the shelter for the next couple of days. I wouldn't worry. There are all kinds of crackpots running loose."

"Thanks."

"Just doing my job."

"Of course."

"I hear the café has good chicken and dumplings on Saturday night. Care to join me?"

"Thank you, but I have a date, and I'm sure he'll be prompt to show up."

"Ouch. Isn't that grudge getting a little heavy? It's been twelve years."

"What, are you talking about the prom?" she teased, though the thought stung.

She hung up, her mind still on the prank call. She had to hope that if Neil Townsend was behind the prank call, he was just blowing smoke. Otherwise, the next month, the shelter was in for a bumpy ride.

Five

A miracle occurred. Katie got the horses. Not through Ben, but through Warren's efforts. The original owner agreed to let Katie nurse the animals back to health before they were sent back to California.

She stepped from the shower and spent a few minutes combing conditioner through her hair before applying a light touch of makeup. House rule number four was that guests were to keep up appearances. She had found a volunteer to conduct Bible classes every other day, and in her spare time Katie was helping them brush up on computer skills. She hoped that by the time they were ready to leave, each one was mentally and spiritually stronger and had a chance at finding a good job.

The women were allowed to sleep in as long as they were at the table for breakfast at eight o'clock. She sniffed at the scent of frying bacon hanging in the air. Tottie was up and cooking. Katie was blessed to have her help with the shelter, but then Tottie had always been an important part of her life. She would be lost without the older woman's common-sense approach to everyday problems.

Katie glanced at the stack of envelopes she had tossed on the dresser last night, most of them bills. There had to be a way to get on top of her financial problems. A budget, maybe, something to keep track of income and outgo? Steady funding—but where would it come from? Katie didn't have a clue how to start. She sighed. So many things to think about and so little time to get things done.

A rattling, clanging racket sent her hurrying to the window. She lifted the curtain to see a truck with Warren Tate behind the wheel pulling a red stock trailer up her driveway. His farming skills weren't rusty; he put the trailer in the right spot on the first try. Hard to believe a Wall Street honcho could be so proficient.

Giving herself a final inspection in the bathroom mirror, she smoothed her hair and assessed her jeans and the rose pink T-shirt. She didn't know why she should bother. It was just Warren, but now he was, well ... different. Some smart female would snap him up. Somehow the thought dimmed her excitement, but only for a moment. Her horses were here!

She ran down the stairs and out onto the side porch. The sun was coming up, its late summer warmth spreading over the barnyard. A sleepy bird rustled in the branches of the old lilac bush. Katie approached the late model pickup, smiling as Warren shoved the transmission into park and got out of the truck.

"Morning." He flashed a half-smile. "I didn't know if you'd be up this early." He wore denims, weathered work gloves, and a blue-and-white checked shirt. The rolled-up sleeves revealed bronzed forearms with a dusting of dark hair, clearly stating that he was a working man.

Nope, nothing sissy about the nerd anymore.

Katie tried to imagine him in a three-piece business suit, carrying a leather briefcase, and to her surprise, she realized either image fit. She was going to have to ditch the *nerd* vision.

"Good morning. I see you brought my horses."

He lifted his Stetson, running a hand through his still-damp hair. The gesture must be habit, she decided, because she'd noticed him doing it before.

"Yes, ma'am." His eyes skimmed the trailer where the four surviving horses awaited a new home. "Where do you want them?"

"Put them in the barn. I want them close where I can doctor them for a while, give them time to get acquainted with the place before I turn them out."

He opened the gate and urged the horses to unload. Katie watched through the gaps in the metal doors where she waited in case they made a bid for freedom. She needn't have worried, though. These horses weren't ready for normal activity. Two had a limp and all had lackluster coats. Every horse had various cuts from the trauma of being overturned in the trailer and the struggle to get out. It was a wonder they weren't all killed. Poor guys. They'd had a rough week.

Katie helped Warren settle the animals in separate stalls. Once they were shut inside, she filled buckets of fresh water, and he sat them inside each compartment. She paused, studying the old barn with its fragrance of hay, dust, and a hint of fall carried by the morning breeze. Of course now it smelled of horse, a comforting scent. Grandpops and Grandmoms had built the faded red structure together fifty-six years ago. Although the outside hadn't been painted in years, the building was sound and provided protection from cold winter winds. Right now, it offered shelter of another sort to four injured animals. Grandpops would have been proud.

Sweet Tea watched from her stall, ears pricked forward. She nickered softly trying to get Katie's attention. "What's the matter, old girl?"

Katie patted the horse's nose as Sweet Tea stretched her neck, sticking her head over the gate. "Don't you want company?"

Sweet Tea whickered softly and tossed her head. "Selfish." Katie picked up a bucket, dropped in a scoop of oats, and extended the offering. There was plenty of grass in the pasture, and recent rains had greened them up. But Sweet Tea was a little territorial, even with the dogs and cats. Four strange horses probably put her nose out of joint.

Warren called. "She yours?"

"Sort of—actually, she belongs to the shelter. The women like to come out and tell her their problems, and believe me they have—"

Her cell phone interrupted them.

"Yes? Oh ... yes." Katie glanced at Warren and then away. "Really? Oh my goodness, that's the second time I've done that. I'm sorry ... Yes, sure ... I'll get a check in the mail immediately, and I'll ... Well, sure, I could run it by the office this afternoon. Right away; thanks for reminding me."

She clicked off and without missing a beat continued the previous conversation. " ... real problems. Isn't it odd how some women continue to attract the wrong kind of man?" She picked up a pitchfork and tossed a flake of hay over the rail to Sweet Tea. "But then, I suppose you wouldn't know much about abusers. Your folks were good people."

She hadn't meant to emphasize the difference in his background and hers, but facts were facts. Warren had been one of the lucky ones. Safe, steady home life with parents who loved and protected him. Not everyone had it that good.

She moved outside the barn to give the other horses hay, then returned. Warren leaned against a stall, watching her work. "I know people can be core rotten."

Katie turned. "Core rotten? What an odd thing to say."

He shrugged. "You know, people who are mean down to their very souls."

She considered the observation and then shrugged. "I'm sure there are plenty of people like that, but I know a lot more core good ones. More good than bad, actually. I believe, when it comes right down to it, there's good and bad in everyone, and it only takes the right circumstances to bring out either trait."

She felt strangely at ease confiding in this man. He'd grown up here and knew her past. Everyone in Little Bush knew her mother and fraternal grandmother were victims of abuse. Katie's mother had died at the hand of her father, and she could be bitter and unforgiving, but instead she felt a need to help the abused, do what she could to set them on a new road, free of fear and abuse.

Warren's expression softened as the tight lines around his mouth relaxed. "Why do you do it, Katie?"

She stopped to think for a minute, not bothering to pretend she didn't understand what he meant. His was a familiar question, one she often defended. "It's a way to give back, I guess. God's been good to me, and I want to pass it on."

His eyes motioned toward the house where the women were. "Do you have much success?"

"Sometimes. I try to give them some tools to help them start over with a new life, and sometimes they do. But sometimes they go straight back to their abusers." She thought of Meg and her abusive boyfriend. Scars dotted the young woman's back, but still she thought about going back, giving him one more chance. *He was really a great guy*, she would say. *When you knew him.*

Warren shook his head. "Why would they do that?"

"They all have a reason. Some have left children behind. Some have no job skills, no way to earn a living; they're scared of being on their own. Some don't believe they deserve any better. For the most part they're beaten down, their self-worth nonexistent. They're convinced that they can't get by without the man who kicks them around. And some of them have deep convictions about divorce. They believe divorce is sin, that what God has joined together no one should put asunder."

"That is in the Bible," Warren said.

"I know it is. But it's also in the Bible that husbands are supposed to love their wives just as Christ loved the church. If the men in these situations would do that, there wouldn't be a problem."

She folded her arms on top of a stall, watching as Sweet Tea meandered over to check out a black-and-white tomcat cutting across the lot. "Some of the women go back, thinking they need to for the children's sake. I asked one woman why she was going back, and do you know what she told me? She said even an abusive father is better than no father at all."

Warren pushed off the railing. "That's sick."

"To you maybe, but you lived in the original Beaver Cleaver family. When you came home from school, supper was bubbling on the stove and bread rising on the kitchen counter. I never saw your parents when they weren't well groomed, and they were always in church on Sunday mornings."

Katie's cell phone rang and she reached for it. "Yes? Oh, Jan. What's up?... I didn't sign the check? No, it's just an oversight. Don't shut off the electricity, Jan. I'll drop by before noon and sign the check. I promise ... Thanks a bunch. It won't happen again."

She sent Warren an apologetic glance, realizing this was the second time today he had caught her in an awkward situation. Embarrassed, she tried to explain. "Uh, things are a little tight right now, but it will ease up soon."

"And you took in four horses? How are you going to feed them? The agreement for you to keep the horses is that you have to foot the bill."

Her chin rose to a defiant angle. "I'll manage."

The phone rang again, and she shot him a glance of pure frustration. "Hello? Oh, Mr. Brown ... Yes, I know the premium is due. The bill is on my desk ... Yes, I just overlooked it. I'll get it in the mail tomorrow ... Yes, I know I can't afford to be without insurance. Thanks for reminding me."

She turned off her phone and sighed. Warren looked her, his expression questioning. She shrugged. "All right, things are more than a little tight. They squeak."

"Anything I can do to help?"

"No, I can work it out." She thought about what she had just said. No, she couldn't work it out. She'd been trying, but the money just vanished in thin air. Too little income, too much outgo, and she was dismal at keeping track of everything. If she kept on like this, there was a chance she might lose everything Grandpops had worked all his life to build. And the shelter would have to close. She couldn't imagine what else she would do. Helping these women was her ministry, her way of serving God ... it was her life. Warren was known to be a shrewd financier, and she couldn't let pride stand in the way of her getting help.

"On second thought, there is something."

"Sure. What can I do?"

"I admit I'm not good at figures. Remember back in high school that math wasn't one of my best subjects?"

"That's the understatement of the year. Mr. Johnson hated to see you coming into his class."

"Did you really mean it when you offered to help?"

He hesitated, and she was afraid he would retract the offer. But he nodded. "Sure, what do you need?"

"I'm not sure—I know I need a steady source of funding—but I think I need a budget too. A workable one."

"Workable one?"

"You know, one I can live with."

❧

Warren lifted his hat and released a breath. What had he got himself into now? Judging from the phone calls she'd been getting, she didn't have a clue how to handle money, and chances were she wouldn't be willing to buckle down and make the needed changes in her lifestyle to get her finances under control.

She was looking at him now like he was the answer to her prayers. He'd helped people with financial matters often enough to know they seldom appreciated being told what to do, particularly when it went against what they wanted and old habits.

A horse whickered, and Warren watched as Katie went from stall to stall, petting the injured animals and talking softly to them. She had a heart as big as Devils Tower and a whole lot softer. In school she hadn't made any effort to run with the popular crowd, picking her friends from the ones left standing on the sidelines. She'd befriended him. He'd not fit in with the jocks, the kids with money and cars. He'd been the nerd, the one left out, but Katie hadn't seemed to mind.

He stepped in to assist her when she tried to calm a mare. "These are the best conditions they've had since they left home."

"I'm thankful the owner agreed to let me care for them."

"The original owner didn't have anywhere to keep them. She'd had to sell out when her husband died, couldn't keep up with the work required on a ranch. She thought she'd sold to a private party; it turns out the buyer was purchasing for a slaughterhouse. The owner is relieved that they'll have a good home, but she'll reclaim them once they've healed."

Warren couldn't blame the owner for taking Katie's offer. The horses had basically been stolen from her. She'd lost the stock that had died with no chance of reimbursement. Katie took care of people and animals. He sighed. Now he was going to agree to help her work out a financial plan.

The back door opened, and Clara sauntered out in their direction. Her bruises were less evident today, but what was she thinking, making herself so public? She was supposed to stay out of sight, not arouse curiosity. The foolish woman didn't have a clue who Warren was. He could be a reporter for the Little Bush *Banner* for all she knew. Katie was going to have to have another rule discussion. Apparently Clara was used to doing things her way, making the rules fit what she wanted. Clara paused, lighting a cigarette. She gave Warren the once-over.

He politely doffed his hat. "Just dropped by to deliver Katie's horses, ma'am."

"What horses?"

Katie took her arm and turned her toward the house. "They're in the barn. Why don't we go inside and have a cup of coffee?"

Clara shrugged off Katie's friendly embrace. "I want to see these horses."

"Oh?" Katie smiled. "You're interested in horses?"

"I don't know anything about animals, but I like them." The two women walked toward the barn and entered. Clara paused in front of a stall, studying the occupant. "What happened to him?"

"He was in an accident. They all were."

Clara turned back to Warren. "You're a neighbor?"

"Yes, ma'am—and longtime friend."

"Clara Townsend, you may have heard of me. I'm running for the Senate, and I'd appreciate your vote." She reached out to shake his hand.

"Warren Tate." He accepted her gesture. "Nice to meet you, Clara, but I'm voting for your opponent."

Clara's features froze. "Why?"

Warren shrugged. "Party policies."

"Is that sensible? My opponent will raise taxes and opposes the hike in minimum hourly wage."

"Ma'am, I make it a practice to never discuss politics or religion." He tipped his Stetson. "I'll call you, Katie. We'll set up a time to work on that budget." Warren returned to his truck, slammed the door, and drove away.

Watching his dust, Katie took a deep breath. "Clara, why are you out here?"

"I wanted to see what was going on. Why?"

"I've explained the rules. Your contact with outsiders is to be limited, not only for your protection but for the other women's safety. You just walked up to Warren and introduced yourself and asked for his vote. How do you know he won't go spreading around town that he's just met Clara Townsend?" Hadn't the woman heard a word she'd said yesterday?

"I need every vote I can get."

"Rules are for everyone. That includes you, and I expect you to at least try to follow them."

Clara flicked a cool glance and lit a Salem.

Katie's fingers itched to rip the cylinder out of her mouth and grind it underfoot. Instead, she took a deep breath, tempered her anger, and went in search of coffee.

Six

There ought to be a law against the amount of junk that came through the mail. Bills, bills, and more bills. Katie thumbed through five catalogs hawking everything from gourmet foods to designer clothes before trashing them. Her name must be on every sucker list in the country. If they could see her bank account, they wouldn't waste postage sending catalogs to this address. Neither she nor the women living here, with the exception of Clara, could afford their wares. She thought of the stack of bills waiting on her desk. Sometime today she'd have to go through them and decide what to pay and what she could put off until next month.

Janet was helping Tottie in the kitchen. The others were in the living room watching television. Katie could hear the murmur of their voices, but couldn't distinguish words. At least they weren't arguing. Clara had been a disturbing influence, the fly in the ointment. Obviously she was used to better accommodations than she received here. The food wasn't up to her standards, and while she didn't come right out and say so, Katie got the impression she wasn't impressed with the other women.

Cleo, Tottie's tiger-striped tabby cat, was stretched out on a bench next to the door, and Goldie, the one dog Tottie allowed in the house, was curled up at Katie's feet. Goldie had shown up one day, dirty, slat thin, and half starved, carrying her left hind leg. Tottie thought she'd been hit by a car. She had mended okay but still walked with a limp. Katie pitched a half-eaten cheese curl.

Janet glanced up from *Jeopardy*. "You're spoiling that animal shamelessly."

"I know." Katie pitched another curl. Goldie's gentle disposition and warm brown eyes had endeared her to everyone. The women babied her, and Katie knew she was good for them. So Goldie was free to stay in the house if she wanted, and most of the time she did.

Meg got up from the sofa and wandered to the door. She slipped outside without saying anything to anyone, but that was Meg. Sometimes she needed her space. She worried about the baby and what she would do after it came. Although it was the goal of the shelter to help the women be self-sufficient and supported, it would be hard for Meg to find a place to live, take care of her baby, and work a full-time job. Hard for anyone — almost overwhelming for someone like Meg who'd been a street urchin. Maybe they could let her live here and work in town.

The doorbell rang, and Katie got up from the table to answer it. The women stopped talking when she walked into the living room and opened the door. She knew they were wary of visitors. To her relief, Warren stood there, Stetson in hand and smiling at her.

"Have you got a minute?"

"Yes, certainly." Katie reached for a sweater on the coat hook and draped it around her shoulders before walking outside and pulling the door shut behind her. He'd stayed to himself after coming home from New York, but this was the second time he'd been here this week, and she was surprised at how glad she was to see him. They stepped off the porch and she smiled. "Let's go out to the barn. It should be private there."

As their footfalls kept pace, Katie noticed their rhythms were in sync. She had resented her height all her life, always towering over her friends and boys. The boys were the worst. She'd felt like a giraffe, tall with a not-so-graceful lope. Warren was tall enough to top her six foot height and still not be mistaken for Goliath. Walking beside him was a pleasure.

Every now and then Katie thought about the old gypsy's prediction and laughed. She had grown to the allotted six feet, but Mr. Right hadn't materialized.

They crossed the barn lot and headed for the barn. Katie guessed the surprise visit had something to do with the horses. Otherwise why would he be here?

They'd reached the barn, and Katie jerked to a stop, one arm stretched in front of Warren blocking his progress. A soft, murmuring voice, drenched with tears, drifted out to them. Katie sighed. She had forgotten Meg leaving the house. Of course she came to the barn, the one place she could let down her guard. Katie peered around the edge of the door to see the young woman standing before one of the stalls, stroking the horse's nose and talking softly. Her voice dropped to a whisper, barely audible, but Katie knew what she was saying. Meg was telling the horse about Nate, her abuser and the father of her unborn child. The horse would listen without being judgmental, and nothing said here would ever be repeated. Meg hadn't learned that she had friends yet. Nothing in her young life had taught her about trusting or forgiveness.

Katie stepped back, motioning for Warren to do the same. The animals were a blessing to the women—that is, most of the women. Clara hadn't taken to them yet, but the others seemed to draw strength from the animals that had been battered too. Even though the horses' wounds were accidental, they had been bound for a slaughterhouse, which seemed to connect them to the women.

Katie and Warren meandered away from the barn, and Katie thought of Meg, pouring her heart out to the horse. It made her sick to think the animals wouldn't be a permanent fixture at the shelter. They could be so helpful for future women who arrived here, broken and in need of comfort.

Warren turned to look back at the barn. "What was going on in there?"

"That's Meg. She's one of the women staying here." Katie proceeded to fill him in on the circumstances. "She's afraid of her boyfriend, Nate, and I don't blame her. He's unpredictable, quick to anger, and he uses his fists to solve his problems."

"Sounds like a real winner."

"Yeah, but it's a problem I hear over and over. Men who treat women like possessions instead of helpmeets. But Nate seems to be a little more out of control than most. I think Meg feels like he will eventually find her. She's afraid to go hiking or wander off by herself. Always stays close to the house and usually around other people. I have to admit, I'm a little concerned about him too."

"How so?"

"Well, I never know when one of the husbands or boyfriends might come around and decide to cause trouble. One did several years back and scared the whey out of me."

They walked on in silence. Finally, he remarked, "I don't understand why you continue to put your safety at risk."

"Because the women need help. Most have nowhere to turn—"

"Hide," he interrupted. "Isn't that what you mean? They have nowhere to hide."

"Yes, I suppose they're hiding."

"Ever stop to think that maybe they were the ones who drove their husbands over the edge?" An edge entered his tone, and Katie turned to look.

"What a horrible thing to say. No, I don't think they did a thing to deserve the punishment they got. Some might have made bad choices, but no one person has the right to strike another."

"You haven't met the women I've met."

Ah yes, the bitterness rumors spoke of. Some woman had really done a job on Warren Tate.

"*No one* deserves to be hit or hurt. Unfortunately, it seems to be a fact of life these days. Lots of women live with emotional, mental, or physical abuse. Not all relationships are made in heaven."

He shot her a cynical glance. "Very few if any are."

By the angry set of his lips and the way his eyes narrowed, Katie realized he was thoroughly ticked. Well, she couldn't judge his lack of sensitivity, but she'd seen her share of abusers. She'd had one run-in with an angry husband, and once was more than enough. Ed Mathis was behind bars, and she hoped he never got out. The day he was sentenced, she'd been in the courtroom, and he had erupted in an out-of-control frenzy, screaming that he'd make her pay for coming between him and Jana, the wife he'd driven away with his abusive behavior.

Enough gloom and doom. Katie changed the subject. "Have you thought about a shelter budget?"

She saw the set of his jaw relax. He was so uptight with the world. What had changed this man from a nerd to a vibrant, smart, yet scornful man? She wanted to reach out and touch him, assure him that life was stressful, but oh-so-worth living. Ask any woman in the shelter, and she would tell you life is tenuous, so take advantage of the years God allows you.

"Yes, I've worked up a few ideas."

They stopped by his pickup long enough for him to get a file and then walked down to the arbor swing. The clematis vines overhead had lost their blooms now and were tufted with feathery seed pods. The sun warmed her shoulders, and she caught a faint whiff of Warren's cologne. He opened a notebook and took a pen out of the cardboard file.

"All right, we're going to start with evaluating your current situation. What do you own and what do you owe?"

Katie blanched. "Why do you need that?" This was going to be embarrassing.

"It's a starting point. I've got to know what you have to work with. Now what do you own?"

"This place, my car, furniture, personal things. Is that what you mean?"

"That's it, but also stocks, bonds, and things like that. Did Paul leave you a trust fund?"

"No. He invested in the stock market and lost it all. Well, that's not completely true; he left me some money, just not very much."

"Okay. How much do you owe on loans?"

Katie did some quick calculations and gave up. "I'll have to do some research on that."

Warren frowned. "You don't know how much you owe?"

"Not right offhand. Is that bad?"

He looked like he'd swallowed a meadow bug. "Well, it's not good."

"All right, I'll total it up and call you, okay?"

"I guess it will have to be. Credit cards?"

"Two."

"How much credit left on them?"

"None." The word came out as crisp as fresh lettuce. She didn't like the direction this was going.

"None?" His eyebrows shot up. "What do you mean none?"

"They're maxed out." She met him stare for stare, mentally daring him to comment. If she knew how to manage money, they wouldn't be having this conversation.

"Both of them?"

She nodded.

Warren sighed. "Okay. How much do you bring in each month, and how much of that do you save?"

"Save? You have to be kidding." Katie sounded as exasperated as she felt. "If I had anything saved, I wouldn't be getting all those phone calls you overheard."

He shook his head. "This might be harder than I expected." He scribbled some figures in a notebook. "You do have income, I suppose."

"Yes, I have income." Not all that much, but still it helped. "I run an in-home typing business. I type medical transcripts, among other things. It isn't regular work, and I can't pinpoint a certain monthly amount. But it helps pay the bills. I give private riding lessons to one client, but I could add one more. And Tottie shares some of her Social Security with us."

"Fine. Still, you need to give me an estimated income and a fairly accurate figure of what you owe. How much do you pay for car insurance?"

Now that she did know because she had just mailed in a check. He jotted down the amount without comment. "I'll need an estimate on groceries and utilities."

Katie rolled her lower lip, thinking. "I'll have to talk to Tottie about that. What's next?"

"Looks like I will have to leave you a list of things to look up. When we get through the necessities listed, we'll start on your luxuries."

She shot him an exasperated glance. "Does the place look like I indulge in luxuries?"

"You have more than you think. How often do you eat out? Take in a movie? How about those lattes you drink?"

She narrowed her eyes at him. "Now you've started meddling. Leave my lattes alone."

"Do you have any idea what you spend on say, outside workers?"

"Not really. We do all the work ourselves here, although we pay Bobbi Weller occasionally to run errands for us. But she works for peanuts."

"Sit down and figure out how much, and then we'll allot you a realistic figure to spend on your extras."

Katie stuck out her tongue. "You know what? You're no fun."

He grinned. "What's your desk like, clean or cluttered?"

Katie envisioned the mess of unpaid bills, unopened mail, and sales catalogs. "What you'd imagine."

"Cluttered." Warren made a few notes. "Keep things cleared away. Set up files for your correspondence, and I'll find you a computer program to keep track of your income and expenses. You'll save time, and you won't be as apt to lose or forget bills under all that mess. How often do you buy groceries?"

"Whenever we run out of something." She had no intention of telling him she made two trips to town a day to get a latte. It wasn't a luxury if she was there to pick up something for Tottie.

"You're what? Three or four miles from town? How many trips do you make a week?"

She shrugged. "I don't keep count."

"Burning all that gas, and I'd guess that every time you go to the store, you buy more than you need."

Katie felt a jab of guilt as she thought of the trip she'd made yesterday for a gallon of milk and ended up with two brown paper grocery sacks full of things she hadn't planned to buy. "You could say that, I suppose."

"Buy in bulk whenever you can. It's more expensive at first, but it will be cheaper in the long run. Always make a list. Now, what about emotional spending?"

"I do plenty of that," she confessed. "Every time I'm late paying a bill and someone calls about it I get very emotional."

"That's not what I mean. Do you go shopping when you're angry? Depressed? Bored?"

"I go for a walk." She indicated the hiking trail. "I've worn out several pair of shoes working out my frustration."

He nodded, smiling. "Okay. I'll see what I can work out, but I can't do much until you get me these figures."

"I'll start to work on them right away."

He got to his feet, eyes skimming the pasture. "You're doing a good thing here, Katie, but someday, someone is going to take advantage of you big time. You're too trusting, and you could get hurt."

She stood, meeting his eyes. "It's better to be too trusting than not able to trust at all. Most people are trustworthy. It's just the few renegades who aren't."

He shrugged. "I've learned the renegades outnumber the other kind."

She watched him walk back to his pickup. Someone had broken the man's heart. He drove away, and she walked back to the house feeling pumped about the prospect of a budget. Sure she'd have to make some personal changes, starting with those lattes. She drank two lattes a day at three dollars and thirty-nine cents a cup. It would be hard to give up something she enjoyed so much, but if it helped keep the shelter going, it would be worth the sacrifice.

❄

Warren pulled onto the highway, his mind on their earlier conversation. Talk about your innocents. Katie had no idea the kind of trouble she could incur with her trust.

She couldn't stay on a budget if her life depended on it. She wouldn't last on a strict regime longer than two days, or he'd eat his hat. Paul Addison had been a good friend to his father, so it was his responsibility to take care of Katie and make her see the truth for what it was.

He pulled out to pass a slow-moving car. He'd had an experience with a woman who maxed out credit cards. His.

She had run up thousands of dollars of debt charging clothing, jewelry, and makeup before she took off with his best friend. Well, Joe was welcome to her. Chances were that as soon as he ran out of money, she'd have another sucker lined up.

After Susan left, Warren turned his back on New York, mentally leaving people in general and the business world in particular, and came back home to Wyoming. Katie had a more honorable excuse, but she was just another woman looking for a man to pull her out of a financial pit. Warren was a good enough business man to know that Katie's venture would fail. He would work with her. But she'd still be forced to close the shelter, and he'd no longer be obligated, knowing he'd done all he could do to help Paul's grandaughter.

A smile crooked the corners of his mouth. Oh, he'd make her a budget all right.

And sit back and laugh when she fell flat on her face.

Seven

Katie tipped the venti cup and finger tapped the bottom to drain the last delectable drop. Twenty-four hours would pass before the budget allowed for a second one. She and Warren had organized all her financial information, and he had laid out a strict budget for her to follow. Staying with Warren's recommended financial course wasn't easy, but for the sake of the shelter, she could do anything.

She fished Tottie's grocery list out of her jeans and skimmed the items. Parson's Market was close, but pricey. While they had an adequate selection, they couldn't begin to compare on price or variety with the larger wholesale houses. She could drive ten miles on the other side of town and shop at the Warehouse Blowout, where industrial-sized products lined every shelf. She didn't usually shop there, preferring to buy in smaller amounts, but one of the suggestions Warren made was to buy in bulk.

Thinking is first cousin to doing, and soon she was tooling down the highway congratulating herself on how proud Warren would be of her. She was taking his admonitions to heart. When he delivered the budget, she had sensed certain skepticism on his part about her ability to stick to a plan.

Well, she'd show him that Katie Addison was a woman of her word.

Ben honked and passed her on the highway. She waved back, noting the sign he carried in the front seat and now held up as he pulled even with the jeep: "Dinner Saturday night?"

She reached for the sign on the passenger seat and slapped it on her window. "Have to wash my hair. Thanks."

She needed to change the refusal; she'd used the same one for two weeks. He'd think she either had bad, overly dirty, or overly clean hair.

Another sign shot up. "Ice cream?"

She reached for her standard refusal. "Lactose intolerant."

His sign bobbed. "Cheese fries?"

Her sign. "Too many carbs."

"Ice water?"

"Not thirsty."

When she glanced over again, she stifled a giggle. The sign in the window was now one of a cross-eyed man with his tongue stuck out. The exchange was fun.

But you'd think adults could find more productive ways to use their time.

By the time Katie reached the warehouse checkout counter, she'd strained a muscle in her back unloading and loading the items onto the conveyer belt. The itemized amount totaled more than Tottie would spend in two weeks — more like two months. But there was a lot of food here. The bill would average out over a period of time; Katie couldn't expect the savings to show right away. It could also take awhile to have anything tangible to convince Warren that her marketing in bulk had paid off, but she had made a start. She pushed the cart out to the jeep, glowing. Was she good or what?

Katie loaded the bags in the jeep, packing it carefully. When she was through, there was room for more in the back seat. If she had any money left, she could have gone back for another load. Think what she could have saved. She closed the jeep door, leaving it unlocked while she pushed the cart back to the front of the store to be picked up. Lena Jackson from church hailed her, and Katie paused to talk for a few minutes. She thought she probably should have locked the jeep, but figured she could keep an eye on it. She managed to end the conversation at last and make a break for the jeep. She should have been home an hour ago. Tottie would be worried. But she had finally given in and told the trusted church friend about the strange phone call she had received the other day. Now she wished she'd kept quiet. There wasn't anything definite that pointed to a safety issue, but considering the nature of the shelter, she couldn't be too careful.

She got behind the wheel and drove out of the lot, avoiding any sudden swerves that would shift her carefully packed bounty. The envelope holding the weekly amount for jeep fuel lay on the seat. She'd burned extra gas making the twenty-mile round trip to Warehouse Blowout, but that was a minor problem considering the amount of money she'd saved on staples. Besides, gas had dropped two cents, so by her calculations, she could fill the tank and have a dollar left over for the following week. So far the budget was working like a charm. She was grateful for Warren's expertise, but she wasn't kidding herself. The budget was going to be hard to follow. But she could do it. If it meant saving Candlelight, she could do most anything.

A red light brought traffic to stop and while waiting, she leaned backward and located the orange sack. The drawstring opening gave her a little trouble, but she managed to extract one before the light changed. She peeled the round globe of juicy fruit with her teeth and bit into it. Sweet juice popped out and rolled down her chin. Fumbling for a tissue, she eased up on the gas about the time she heard the piercing scream of a siren. A glance in the rearview mirror confirmed her suspicions. Ben. The sedan with the wailing siren was on her tail now. Katie pulled to the side of the highway wondering what he wanted. She wasn't speeding. The budget said nothing about speeding tickets, but Warren would undoubtedly freak at the wasted money. She rolled her window down and waited as the sheriff approached.

He bent down, placing his folded arms on the open window frame. "Hey there. How's it going?"

"What are you doing this far from home?"

"I was about to ask you the same thing."

She reached for a sign and slapped it on the windshield.

He grinned. "I can't read it."

"You know what it says."

"Do you have dandruff?"

Dandruff? What a question. "No, I don't have dandruff."

"You sure wash your hair enough."

She slapped the sign back on her seat. The guy was impossible. He flashed an easy grin, his hazel eyes sparkling. Reddish blond hair, ruddy complexion, and a sprinkling of freckles across the bridge of his nose made him the typical, ornery redhead. "Okay, so I stopped you in hopes you'd misread my sign. Would you like to go out for dinner Saturday night?"

"You turned on your siren and scared me half to death to ask for a date? I expected a ticket at the very least."

"I can arrange that if you like; however, I'd rather take you out."

Katie really didn't want to date him, but she didn't want to hurt him either. Sure she was still miffed about the prom, but over the years she'd decided the spat wasn't worth a serious grudge. These days they had fun tormenting the other with their silly signs. Actually, thinking up new rejections had gotten to be a game with Katie. When Ben married—if he ever married, she'd miss the poster board banter. "I don't go out much because I never know when I'll be needed at home."

She could take care of herself. At any rate, there had never been any romantic sparks, and she didn't want to start something she wouldn't be inclined to finish.

He shook his head. "I admire your commitment, Katie, but you're putting your life on hold for the shelter. It's time you did something for yourself."

"And the women would do what?"

"Anytime you want to go out, I'll send a man to watch the house."

"That isn't the point. There's little I could do if trouble erupted, but I feel a need to stay close. They're insecure."

"How much of this is what God wants you to do, and how much is based on your family's history?"

Katie considered the question. "I don't know; I just know this is where I'm supposed to be right now. I don't have any idea what the future will bring, but as long as God allows me to run Candlelight Shelter, I'll do the best I can."

Ben shifted, his arm propped on the windowsill. "That's what I like about you—you hang in there despite the odds. Okay, if you won't go to dinner on Saturday, how about taking in the high school football game on Friday night? They run a mean concession stand. All the hot dogs and chips you can eat, and you can come with dirty hair."

"All the hot dogs I can eat?"

"And I'll throw in double lattes at the café later."

She gave in. He was good company, and she'd have fun. Besides he'd said the magic word. Latte. And he would be buying, so she could have more than one.

"I'll pick you up around six."

He walked to his patrol car, and she pulled out into the heavy stream of late afternoon traffic. Half a mile down the road, she slammed on the brakes to avoid hitting a steer that wandered in and was in grave danger of going to that great hamburger heaven if he didn't move his carcass.

Now dimly aware of headlights in her rearview mirror, Katie eased closer to the wheel. The dark, late model sedan hung back, but when another motorist passed, the sedan speeded up enough to force the second driver to cover the distance between both cars.

After several incidents of pass and go, doubt started to creep into Katie's mind. Was the dark sedan following her?

She steadied her trembling hands. *Be calm. You're having a lack-of-caffeine reaction, that's all.* Every sick scenario she'd seen on TV news raced through her mind. Women kidnapped and killed. Women vanished, never to be found.

Sweat balled on Katie's upper lip. The sun set early these days, and thickening shadows swallowed the cab interior, though it was barely five o'clock.

She wasn't aware the jeep had drifted over the center line until the blaring of horns jerked her back to reality. She yanked the wheel, and the jeep swerved to the right. Close call. *What should I do, God? What should I do?* Doubt no longer confused her. The sedan was right on her tail.

A sense of awful evil hung in the dusky interior. Katie realized she hadn't turned on the headlights. She could see the road in the twilight, but other drivers would have a hard time seeing her. She glanced at the odometer. Six miles to the shelter. Moments ticked by. Traffic thinned, and Katie mechanically accelerated.

The Little Bush turnoff appeared, and she suddenly served the jeep onto the off-ramp. The move caught the sedan driver off guard, and the car shot on down the highway.

Seconds later Katie pulled up in front of the sheriff's office and slammed on the brakes. Bolting out of the jeep, she shot into the office. The dispatcher glanced up as she shoved open the glass door and entered.

"Katie?" The woman removed her mouth piece. "What's wrong?"

"Is Ben back?"

The dispatcher glanced at the clock hanging behind the desk. "Not yet. He should be shortly."

Katie's heart plummeted. "Okay." Did she disturb him with a crazy notion that even she wasn't convinced happened? Traffic was heavy; the sedan could have innocently been trying to keep pace with the heavy flow.

Katie, you're losing it.

She shook her head. "No—don't bother him. I just thought of something I needed to tell him." Clearing her throat, she backed out. "Thanks."

Katie got back into the jeep, adjusting the rearview mirror. Her pulse still raced from the puzzling incident. She could have sworn that sedan was following her.

Turning the ignition, she backed out of the sheriff's lot.

But rarely was an intuition this powerful wrong.

Eight

Katie burst through the shelter's back door, slamming the screen behind her.

Tottie dropped the cast-iron skillet she held, one hand flying to her throat. "What?"

The smell of frying meat filled the air — hamburger for dinner. Katie leaned against the wooden door frame, drinking in the familiar sights and sounds, so far removed from the terror she'd experienced. She shook her head, trying to get her breath. When she could speak, she stammered, "I think someone was following me home."

Tottie reached for the ever-present ball bat. "Is someone out there now?"

"No. I ditched them and then drove to the sheriff's office."

"What'd Ben say?"

"He wasn't back yet, and I didn't want to bother him." She moved to sit down, her heart still hammering. "I didn't want to alarm him since I'm not certain I was being followed, but it sure looked to me like I was."

"How far did they follow you?"

"I'm not certain. I was too frightened to stop and look. I got out of that jeep as soon as I could slam it into park. I ran into the sheriff's office and didn't look back."

"When did you first suspect someone was there?" Tottie held her head at an alert angle, apparently listening for outside noises.

"Soon after I left the grocery warehouse. I wasn't sure for a few miles, but then the sedan crept closer and closer. I wasn't aware of it until I got onto the highway." Katie shuddered, realizing her blouse was damp with perspiration. Whatever had taken place, it had been very real to her.

Tottie placed the baseball bat beside the door and picked up the shotgun she kept in the corner. The weapon had remained there since Ed Mathis attacked Katie a few years back. "Get out of the way and open the door."

Katie automatically moved to obey. "There's no one there now. I ditched the sedan on the Little Bush turnoff."

"Never hurts to be certain."

"Where are you going?"

"Find out if someone is hiding in that jeep, of course."

Katie marveled at Tottie's casual acceptance of the situation. "Not by yourself, you're not." She wasn't exactly crazy about the idea of going out there, but she couldn't let Tottie tackle their intruder, imagined or real, alone. She scooped the skillet off the floor and followed behind.

They eased out the back door and around the side of the house, staying clear of the yard light. Tottie cautiously approached the jeep, and Katie crept along behind, holding the cast-iron skillet, comforted by its weight in her hand. If hit by this monster, the culprit would see stars for a week. Everything was calm; not a car—except for the jeep and the farm pickup, was in sight. Tottie slowly lowered the gun barrel and took her fingers off the trigger. "No one here now. But someone could have been."

"I'm certain they didn't follow me to the jail." Katie took a calming breath. "What do you think they wanted?"

"What they always want, to scare you. Most likely if someone was following you, it was one of those thugs the women are associated with."

Townsend entered Katie's mind, since Clara was the newest guest. "I'm certain they didn't follow me from town. I kept close watch."

"But you never know if they doubled back once you left the jail. You can't be too careful, Katie. You report this incident to Ben first thing in the morning."

As much as she dreaded the thought, she agreed. She couldn't be too careful.

Not when she *knew* that sedan had been following her.

Tottie led the way back to the kitchen where a boil of smoke and the smell of burned meat greeted them.

"Heavenly days!" The housekeeper bolted to the stove and jerked the skillet of hamburger off the burner.

Smoke roiled, setting off the alarm. Katie dragged a chair over and climbed up to hit the button on the smoke alarm. Meg popped through the doorway. "I smell smoke. Is there a fire?"

"No, we just scorched the hamburger."

Meg shot Katie a calculating stare. "Tottie never burns anything."

"So blame me." She figured it was her fault anyway, since she'd sent Tottie on a wild goose chase.

Nine

The women helped carry in the groceries. When everything had been laid out on the counters, the kitchen table, and the floor, Tottie stood back, hands on hips, eyes skimming the industrial-sized cans. Her expression wasn't quite as joyful as Katie had expected.

"Are we feeding the entire east continent?"

"Warren said to buy in bulk when we can," Katie defended. She picked up a mangled box of stroganoff. "This should last a long time, and I got it for practically nothing."

"Is it good?"

"I beg your pardon?" The least Tottie could do was to act like she appreciated the wealth of bounty spread out in her kitchen. Katie's knees were weak, and she realized she was still shaken from her ride home. Caffeine. She needed a jolt and fast. "Do we have fresh coffee?"

Tottie nodded, inclining her head toward the pot. She didn't look up from her survey of the pile of oversized cans and boxes. "And what are we supposed to do with all of this?"

"We'll find a place for everything. The main thing is we have it, and we shouldn't have to buy groceries for at least a couple of weeks, maybe a month. Or longer." She hoped for a ray of approval.

Tottie nudged a bag of onions with her foot. "Twenty pounds of onions?"

"They'll come in handy."

"Not unless you want onion blossoms every night. They'll rot before I can use them all up."

"Oh." Katie hadn't thought of that. "Well ... we'll put onions in everything. We can find lots of uses for them. They're supposed to be very healthy."

"Sure we can." Tottie sounded downright sarcastic. "Well, I guess I can find a place to store most of it. The rest ... we'll just manage the best we can. Did you get anything I had on my list?"

The list? Katie searched her memory, trying to remember what she had done with the list, and came up empty. "Well, no, maybe not."

Tottie shook her head and picked up a can without a label. "We can have this for dinner tonight."

Katie said. "Surprise food."

"Surprise food." Tottie's voice was as dry as stale cornbread.

A scent of cigarette smoke drifted in the open window. Katie eased the door open and saw Clara perched on the back porch puffing up a storm. She stepped back inside and shut the window. "Our politician doesn't hear well."

"Oh, she hears well, but she ignores even better. This morning I caught her using her cell phone." Tottie shoved a jumbo-sized box of Cheerios into the cabinet and reached for an equally large box of cornflakes.

"I don't understand why she behaves like that." Katie picked up a bag of potatoes, looked around for a place to put it, and then set it back down. "I know she's nervous someone will find out about this. Otherwise why would she be here? You only have to see those bruises to know she's been beaten. There's no way she would want the media to catch wind of this."

"Maybe, but the woman doesn't use good sense. She's going to bring the media down on us if she's not careful. Then what will happen to the others?"

Once the election was over, Clara would slap a restraining order against her husband and pray he took heed of the warning.

The housekeeper stared at the remaining grocery items with a helpless air. "Why would she risk her safety by making outside calls?"

"Clara's accustomed to the spotlight and to getting her own way. She doesn't know how to go unnoticed."

Tottie shoved another box of cereal into the cabinet. "I think we're too lax here at Candlelight. *No one* should know about these women."

"How could we keep something like that a secret? We've lived here most of our lives. Do you think people wouldn't notice that we always have a house full of women guests?" Katie shook her head. "Besides, the town protects us and so does the church. You know that."

"Some do. But you're too trusting. Always have been. But one of these days, someone you think you can trust will turn against us, and one of these women could get hurt because we put our faith in the wrong person. Or maybe one of us will."

Katie turned. "Will what?"

"Get hurt." Tottie slammed the cabinet door.

Katie sank to a chair. "What would our world be without trust?"

"Trust is good." Tottie's eyes filled with experience. "But trust in the proper doses. At times you appear to forget that not everyone has your heart. Now get out fresh meat and let's get dinner started."

Katie's mind raced as she took hamburger out of the freezer. She still wasn't convinced that no one had been following her. It couldn't all have been her imagination. Maybe whoever it was wanted to find the shelter. Clara's husband was almost as high profile as she was, so it wasn't likely he was the culprit. But he could have hired someone to his dirty work. Or it could have been Nate, Meg's abuser. He'd vowed to track her down, and while the man was a full-fledged jerk, he wasn't stupid. Meg could have been in touch with him. The girl was scared and pregnant, which made her extremely vulnerable.

And made the shelter even more exposed.

Ten

Katie lifted the kitchen curtain as Warren pulled into the drive. He was back with more budget crud, and she couldn't wait to tell him how well she was doing. She opened the door before he had a chance to knock, welcoming him inside. He removed his Stetson, smiling.

"Ready to get to work?"

"Eager to get started!"

Clara glanced up from the newspaper. "Ah, my missing vote. Care to sit down and talk about our differences?"

Meg waddled past. "You're wasting your time. He didn't come to see you. Katie's the draw."

Warren grinned, taking the good-natured ribbing. "That's not what I hear. I hear Katie and Ben took in the football game the other night. Rumor has it Katie downed three hot dogs and two cokes in the first quarter."

Heat tinged Katie's cheeks. "Well, really. Who's been shooting off their mouth?"

"Like I'd really tell you."

Clara pushed back from the table. "I'll let you two have your privacy."

Katie reached out to stop her. "It's just business, Clara. Warren's helping me work on the budget."

"Strictly business," Warren confirmed. "But when we're through, I'll let you tell me how you can better my life if I vote for you."

Katie led the way to her office. "That was nice of you."

He shrugged. "She's an interesting dame. Not my political party, but she's smart." He pulled a chair up to the desk. "Okay. You have some figures for me?"

Katie moved to the desk, catching movement out of the corner of her eye. A small figure made its way toward the barn. Clara. Why would she be going out there? She watched as the woman opened the door and stepped inside.

Turning away, she walked back to the desk as Warren pulled out a notebook and pen. "Well?"

She placed a sheet of paper in front of him. "Read it and weep."

He frowned as his eyes skimmed the list. Katie had a feeling he was upset at the amount she owed. Just whip out the card and it's yours. Didn't even have to write a check, so it didn't seem like you're really spending money until the bill arrived.

Warren looked up. "Where are your expenditures for the past week?"

"Right here." She handed him a second paper.

He zeroed in on the figures. "This is what you spent on groceries this week?"

She flushed with pride. "I decided to take your suggestion."

"I suggested you spend a mint on groceries? I don't remember that."

"You suggested I buy in bulk."

The frown faded into a glower. "And your point is?"

"My point is I did what you suggested, and I shopped at Warehouse Blowout. I bought industrial-sized everything—even new foods that Tottie never serves. The total bill was sixty dollars over the amount I'm allowed to spend in a two-week period, but we have enough to last us through the month." Katie thought about the burgeoning food pantry. Maybe eternity. Her gaze returned to the chicken scribbles on the pad. Warren sat across the desk, enduring her rationalizing of the first week's budget and the sixty-dollar deficit. His face was getting longer by the minute.

"So," Katie drew a pie chart. "If you add sixty dollars to the allotted hundred and thirty allowed for staples, you get a hundred and ninety. But if I don't have to shop every two weeks, if we can make the staples last, say, a month instead of two weeks, then we have enough left to pay November's utility bill."

Her calculations might be screwy, but at least she wouldn't have the dreaded overdue call from the electric company this month.

Warren slowly lifted his gaze from the writing pad, and his tone was tense. "Let me get this straight. You bought a hundred and ninety dollars worth of food you don't ordinarily eat in industrial-sized cans and boxes, thinking you can stretch the bimonthly food allowance to monthly, so you can have enough money to pay the utility bill that is already included in your monthly budget."

"Yes!" He got it. Very few people followed her reasoning. "This way, I'm sixty dollars ahead of the game! Sixty dollars goes a long way in dog food."

He pitched the pen on the table. "A bargain is only a bargain if it is needed or used. What if your guests refuse to eat the staples you purchased? If they haven't been on the table before, what makes you think it's something they would eat?"

"It's perfectly good food."

"Like what?"

"Like cans of turnips, succotash, lima beans, and corn relish. I got fifteen boxes of crushed stroganoff for a third of the original price."

"What's crushed stroganoff?"

"The boxes were crushed, not the stroganoff itself." Though, Katie realized, that might be misleading. If the boxes were crushed it only stood to reason the pasta was broken. But broken pasta wasn't a crime nor did it alter the taste of stroganoff sauce.

He flipped a page. "What happened to the gas budget?"

"Oh, that. I hit a stump when I was backing out of the drive last Monday. We've been meaning to get someone to remove it but, you know, expenses. Anyway, I wasn't think-ing, and I backed over the stump, and I must have knocked a tiny hole in the gas tank because by the end of the day the tank was empty. I took it to the garage and they repaired it." She fished in her pocket, took out a yellow sheet, and handed it to him. He couldn't be upset about this — emergencies hap-pened, and the budget allowed for crisis.

He skimmed the column.

"A hundred and fifty dollars," she confirmed, "plus the amount it took to refill the tank. But I had some gas money left from the week before, so I figure I evened out. But look. I can take the extra sixty dollars I've saved on groceries and apply that to the repair bill, and I'll only be ninety dollars short. You've allotted a hundred dollars for emergencies, so deduct that from the hundred and fifty, and I'll still just be a hundred and forty dollars short this month. And believe me, a hundred and forty dollars is pocket change compared to other months."

Bringing his hand to his nose, he pinched the end, staring back at her. "And how do you make up the hundred and forty dollar deficit?"

She touched her temple with her left hand. "I don't have a solution for that — yet."

Leaning back in his chair, Warren gave her a dark look. "Okay. You obviously can't run this shelter financially, Katie. Why do you try?"

"Because I love it."

"I love Porsches, but I don't have one because it's impractical. The same goes for you and this shelter. You haven't heard a word I've said about budgeting."

"I have," she contended. "Rome wasn't built in a day."

"Maybe not, but I seriously doubt if you can get the hang of managing money in a year, and by then it will be too late."

She frowned. The man was ruthless. She'd just spent two of the most nerve-wracking, caffeine-ragged weeks, and he was critical of her efforts?

"Obviously you've missed something. We have to start at the beginning."

A painstaking hour later, Katie rubbed the back of her neck and admitted that the budget was going to be hard to follow.

"Money, for most people, is hard to handle. We live in a microwave world. We want it, and we want it in thirty seconds." Warren pushed back and stretched, his shirt fabric outlining a taut rib cage and stomach. "You've got to stick with it, Katie. Concentrate if you hope to pull out of this. Either that or close the shelter and save yourself a lot of headache."

She bit her lower lip. Was it worth it? Of course saving Grandpops's farm and the shelter was more than worth it. Other battered shelters were available, but they weren't Candlelight. Candlelight was hers, and if saving it meant forfeiting personal comfort she'd do it.

"I can do it," she assured Warren as she walked him to his truck. Judging by the expression on his face, he thought she was blowing smoke, but she wasn't. He might have seen her around all his life, but he didn't know the real Katie, the determined Katie. But he was about to meet her.

"Horses eating you out of house and home?"

"No, but I'm a little worried about the bay. She has a deep cut on her right shoulder that isn't healing. It's scabbed over, but it's so puffy and red that I believe it's infected. I think I'll call Dr. Vincent to come and take a look."

"Vet charges," he reminded.

"Not this vet." Katie grinned. "Tottie baked fifteen apple pies for her last family get-together and wouldn't take a cent. She said she owed us one, and so now we collect."

"You're amazing. You've got an answer for everything." He stepped into the cab of his truck. "I need to get home. Got some fence to fix sometime today."

"What about Clara?"

"What about her?" Obviously chatting with the politician had left his mind.

Carefully shutting the cab door, Katie said, "I'll tell her something came up, and you'll have to visit another day."

"You don't need to tell her anything. I didn't get around to a visit." He started the engine. "She'll live."

She thought that was a little cold, even if Clara deserved it. "Thanks for the help."

"Wait until you can live up to it before you thank me."

She knew he didn't expect her to be able to stick with it, but he was in for a shock.

When Katie approached the barn, she heard Clara's voice still talking to one of the horses. The thought that tough Clara had an ounce of kindness in her brought a smile to Katie's lips.

"Hang in there, old boy. We're alike, you know. Tough old birds. We hurt; we heal. The world can't keep us down for long."

The politician's voice floated to the open doorway.

"Wounds heal, but it's the inside pain that's hard to deal with, isn't it? Who'd have thought Neil would turn so physical—so malicious. Twenty years I've spent with this man, supporting him, upholding him, up before dawn with only a few hours sleep, shaking hands at the polls, handing out doughnuts and coffee to steel workers, kissing babies, shaking hands, eating more dry chicken at stuffy fund-raisers than I can bear to stomach." She chuckled mirthlessly. "I thought I knew him. But when I tried to tell him that what he's doing is wrong, he turned on me. Struck me, then struck me again, and then it was as though all the pent-up anger he harbored toward the world came out—"

Katie cringed when she knocked over a rake and disturbed the therapy.

Clara's eyes jerked to the barn entrance.

Smiling, Katie set the rake beside the door and entered the cool barn. "Sorry to disturb you."

The politician visibly withdrew. "The animal seems to like sugar. I brought him a cube, but I'm finished feeding him." She indicated the stalls. "The horses seemed to be doing better."

"Most are. There's still one I worry about. I think I'll hitch up the trailer and take her to see a vet."

"What did you say happened to them?"

"Accident. The person hauling the horses had bought them illegally and was taking them to the slaughterhouse."

A carefully drawn brow shot up. "Slaughterhouse? Why would they do that? The horses are beautiful."

"They were intended for slaughter, and the meat would have been sent overseas. Some people consider horse meat to be a delicacy."

"That's awful. Why doesn't someone do something?"

"We're trying to stop it. There's a bill pending—"

"The American Horse Slaughter Prevention Act. I remember now."

"How do you plan to vote on it?"

Clara shrugged. "I haven't won reelection yet. If you look at the polls, I'm behind."

"You don't appear to me to be the kind of woman who gives up easily."

"I should be out there shaking hands. You can't win an election hiding away in a battered women's shelter."

Katie sensed a softening, brief but noticeable. "Then why are you here?"

Clara's face went absolutely expressionless for a minute. Then something very close to anger flashed across her taut features. "Why is any woman here?"

"Would you like to talk about it?"

"No." Her chin rose. "I have a request."

"Oh?" Something outlandish probably, but she hadn't asked for favors prior to today. "What is it you want?"

"There are certain things I'm used to, like caviar and Ca Peachio's crackers. They available here?"

Peach crackers? If they were, Katie hadn't heard of them. "I don't know." Her tastes were a bit more plebian. And caviar had never been on her list of must-tries.

"Check on that for me, won't you? I simply love them."

Katie cleared her throat. "Caviar is very expensive and the crackers ..."

"Ca Peachio."

"I've never heard of the brand, and I have no idea where I might find them. How about a box of Ritz or Town House—they're good."

"No—Ca Peachio. That's what I want. I should be allowed a few luxuries." Her tone had risen sharply, and Katie wondered if she was near breaking. No one could be this cold under the circumstances.

Caviar was a big deal on Katie's budget. A really big deal.

"Sorry, but I can't supply your request." Katie turned and headed for the house wishing she could comply. Maybe a little extra attention would bring Clara around, soften her turtle shell.

Then again, maybe not.

Katie drove into town that afternoon and stopped by the grocery store. "Hey, Jack, do you carry these items?"

He glanced at the list. "California-farmed white sturgeon caviar and Ca Peachio's butter flavored crackers? No, but I can order them. The shelter girls developing a gourmet taste?"

"Looks that way. How long will it take to get them?"

"Give me two or three days, and I'll have them for you. Going to cost you though, since I have to order such a small amount, and I don't aim to get stuck with them. There's not much demand for fish eggs and fancy crackers in these parts."

Katie swallowed and placed the order. She was a pushover and she knew it, but an idea had occurred to her. If Clara won reelection, she might be influenced by her brief stay at Candlelight. Katie didn't know what she had to offer a woman like Clara Townsend. But maybe if she upped the ante, provided a few luxuries, when it came time to vote on the Horse Slaughter Act, Katie could remind Clara ever so gently that her vote was crucial to pass the bill.

Payola. She believed that was the correct term.

Longer life, a horse would say.

Two days later the phone rang and Katie answered. Jack was on the line. "I got the items you wanted, Katie. When do you plan to come get them?"

"Today, I guess. Why?'

"Caviar is a perishable item. It won't keep forever. As much as you're paying for it, you don't want it to go out of date."

No, she certainly didn't want that. "I'll be there within the hour."

Funny, she hadn't seen Clara this morning. She wasn't at breakfast, and her bed was made up. Maybe she would be more responsive now that her order for caviar and crackers was about to be realized.

When Katie reached the grocery store, Jack held up a finger cautioning her to wait. He went to the back and returned with a tin of caviar and a box of crackers. "This what you wanted?"

"To tell you the truth, I don't know much about caviar. My income puts a damper on luxuries." Though she doubted she'd eat fish eggs if someone gave her a batch.

Jack grinned. "Mine, either. I've tasted it though, and I'm not all that high on it." He figured up the bill and gave Katie the amount.

"How much?"

He repeated the total. "I told you it would cost."

"I know. I guess I hadn't realized how much." Enough to pay the phone bill. That's how much. Was she out of her cotton-pickin' mind? Warren would have a cow. "Fifty dollars an ounce for caviar?"

"That's right. Of course you could have ordered Iranian royal beluga at a hundred seventy an ounce."

"No, that's all right. This will do."

"Had to order a case of crackers. They come to thirty dollars, plus ten for shipping."

Katie mentally gulped and whipped out her checkbook, praying the check wouldn't bounce. Maybe she could talk the phone company into giving her an extension. When she walked into the kitchen and took the items out of the sack, Tottie shook her head when she read the can. "There's a new one born every day."

"Meaning me?"

"You know what I mean. Why did you do this? We can't afford to feed ourselves, let alone buy things like this."

"I have a plan."

"And I don't want to hear about it. I've got dinner to fix."

Clara wandered into the kitchen.

Katie motioned toward the table. "I've got a surprise for you." Instead of the gratitude she expected, Clara barely glanced at the high-priced goodies.

"I don't feel well. My stomach is upset, and I think I'm running a fever."

Katie smile fell. She was sick? Was it contagious?

Clara sat down at the table and opened the container of caviar. Using a spoon, she dipped out a generous helping and spread it on a cracker. One bite and she was on her feet, disappearing into the bathroom. Katie stared at Tottie. "Does she have a stomach virus?"

Tottie nodded. "All morning."

"Great. Let's hope the others don't catch it."

Meg entered the kitchen and noticed the open container. "What's that?"

"Caviar." Katie figured they might as well eat it. Now that it had been opened, it wouldn't keep long.

Meg spread some on a cracker and stuffed it in her mouth. "What is it?"

Ruth had entered the kitchen behind her. She picked up the container, and read the ingredients. "It's fish eggs."

Meg's mouth dropped open. "Yuck!"

"Fish eggs. That's what it says here."

"Cooked?"

"Doesn't say. I'd guess not." She took a sniff and jumped back.

Meg looked a little green around the gills. "Why would people eat something like that?"

Janet had joined them, and she and Ruth sampled the delicacy. Both wrinkled their noses, and Janet spat hers out into a napkin. Katie decided that was good. She wanted to sample it herself. If she liked it, she and Tottie could finish it off.

She turned around to find Cleo, Tottie's cat, in the middle of the table polishing off the open jar.

After dinner, Katie ventured to the barn to check on the horses. The lot gate was standing open and Sweet Tea was gone. The gate to the pasture was closed. Katie ran for the jeep. If Sweet Tea was out in the road, she could be hit by a car. Katie drove a couple of miles each way, but saw nothing. She was about to give up in despair when her cell phone rang.

"Hey, Katie! This is Doug Harper. Your Appaloosa missing?"

"She sure is. I'm driving the back roads looking for her right now."

"Well, she's at my place. I've got her shut up in the barn."

"Is she all right?"

"Fine as frog hairs. I'll keep her safe until you get here."

"I'm on my way, and Doug, thanks."

"No sweat, Katie. You'd do the same for me."

Yes, she would. So would the rest of their neighbors. She was blessed to have friends who would help anytime help was needed. Only one thing puzzled her. How could Sweet Tea get all the way over to Doug's? It was a good five miles to his ranch. Why would the horse drift that far from the ranch?

Doug offered to haul the horse home for her, and as soon as Sweet Tea was safe in the lot again, Katie brought out a chain, wound it around the gatepost, and fastened it with a lock. Once the lock was secure, she leaned on the fence railing to study the Appaloosa.

Sweet Tea didn't open that gate by herself.

Returning to the house, Katie picked up the land line and called Ben. "Hey."

"Hey yourself. Anyone been following you lately?"

She'd reported the strange incident of being followed—or thinking she was being followed, and Ben had taken the report seriously. He'd promised to double up on the shelter's security, but because she hadn't taken down the sedan's license plate number, there was nothing more he could do at this point to enhance the women's safety. Katie kicked herself a hundred times for not noting the plate, but hindsight was always better than foresight.

"What's happening? Blue moon?" asked Ben.

"You can't claim that I don't call you often enough," she accused. "Seems like I'm reporting trouble every day or two."

"Trouble, yes. I'm thinking one of these days you might call and say, 'Hey, Ben. I'm hungry for one of those chicken fried steaks the café is noted for.'"

"Yeah, well, I suppose it could happen. But not today."

"No problem."

"Listen." Katie briefly explained Sweet Tea's adventure and the sense that someone was watching her.

Ben's tone sobered. "You think you're being stalked?"

"No, not that. Just ... watched."

"You're sure one of the women didn't accidentally leave the barn door unlocked?"

"Positive. That's the last thing I check at night."

"I'll drive out and take a look around. I need to talk to you anyway."

"About what?"

"Seems the owner of those horses is getting antsy. She wants to reclaim the animals the moment they can be safely transported."

Katie's heart sank. "Why? I'm taking good care of them."

"Don't know. I just got a call earlier today that said she'll be moving the horses as soon as they can be moved."

"I don't get it, Ben. Why would the woman suddenly change her mind? If she cares about the horses, she won't risk moving them for weeks."

"I'm not a mind reader, Katie. I just do my job, and my job is to inform you that the horses are going to California as soon as they're healthy enough to make the trip."

Katie hung up more puzzled than ever. Why would the owner change her mind and so quickly?

Eleven

The illuminated bedside clock read four-thirty. Katie was awake, ears tuned for some sound to indicate that one of the women was stirring, maybe in the bathroom. But all was silent. Apparently she was the only one awake. She had a vague recollection that she had been dreaming about something, but after trying to remember what, she gave up and threw back the light blanket. Enough.

She got out of bed and went into the bathroom, thankful to find it unoccupied. Maybe no one else would catch the stomach bug, or so she hoped. She paused at the top of the landing, listening. Silence. The women were sleeping. She was just jittery over the day's illnesses and Sweet Tea wandering loose.

Back in her room, Katie stepped to the window to look out. Moonlight shone brightly, although the large pine tree on this side of the house threw the yard into shadow. The stars were out, glowing pinpricks of light against the black curtain of the night sky. A flicker of movement caught her attention, something out of the corner of her eye. She pivoted to stare at the patch of moonlight on her right. Had she really seen a moving figure, or had she just imagined it? Nothing there now, but she returned to the door, stepping out in the hall to pause and listen. Moving quietly, she checked the women's rooms and found that they were all accounted for, sleeping soundly. She didn't think the other three women would go outside at night. But Clara might decide she needed a smoke, and a little thing like rules wouldn't stand in her way. But Clara didn't feel well, and she was tucked snugly in her bed.

Although Katie wanted to slink into her bedroom and lock the door, she took a deep breath, every nerve end prickling, and crept downstairs to check the doors. Front door, side doors, back door, all were locked. She moved quietly through the house on slippered feet, peering out of the windows. Moonlight and shadows lent an artificial quality to familiar objects, but nothing was out of order. She finally went upstairs to her room, but it was a long time before she could go to sleep.

Morning came and the women congregated at the breakfast table.

Appetites were missing. Tottie made waffles, and there was cereal. Lots of cereal. Enough to last until the Rapture, according to Tottie. Clara didn't come to the table. As soon as Katie finished her waffle, she went upstairs to tap on the door of the politician's bedroom.

"Come in," a weak voice called.

Katie opened the door to find Clara lying in bed, face pale, eyes closed. "How are you feeling?"

"Terrible. I'm sorry about the caviar. I know it's expensive, but my stomach just can't handle it right now. I know the request was extravagant. I'll have my people send you a check."

"That would be deeply appreciated." Ordinarily, Katie wouldn't accept the offer, but this wasn't a normal purchase.

"You and the others can eat it."

"Actually, they tried it and didn't like it, and before I could get to it, Cleo helped herself."

Clara opened her eyes. "The cat?"

"The cat." *That was fifty dollars down the drain. Or down the cat.*

"I hope she enjoyed it." Katie could swear that she saw Clara's lips twitch.

"Seemed to." Katie cleared her throat. She hated to suggest this, because it would mean a trip to town with Clara. Their celebrity politician needed to stay out of sight, but if she was ill, she needed to see a physician. "Would you like for me to take you to a doctor? Little Bush has a clinic."

Clara shook her head. "Tottie was just in here with a handful of zinc and vitamin C." She indicated an empty mug. "She brought some kind of tea. I don't know what it was, but it tasted good. She said it would help the nausea."

"Ah. Well, Tottie knows her teas." She had a great store of herbal lore passed down from mother to daughter, generation to generation, part of her Cherokee heritage. "If you change your mind, let me know."

"I'll be all right. It's just a bug. In time it will run its course."

"Get some rest then, and I'll check on you later." She turned toward the door, but Clara's voice stopped her.

"Katie?"

"Yes?"

"Thanks for buying the caviar. It was nice of you."

"No problem." She didn't think the utility company would be as sympathetic, but she'd face that later. "You concentrate on getting well."

Katie left the room thinking this was the nicest Clara had been since she arrived at Candlelight. Too bad she had to be ill in order to behave herself. Katie passed the bathroom and heard someone being sick. *Oh, please God, don't let anyone else come down with this, whatever it is*. A moment later the door opened and Janet tottered out.

"I don't feel well, Katie. Do you think what Clara has is contagious?"

"It's possible. Why don't you lie down, and I'll have Tottie brew you a cup of peppermint tea to settle your stomach."

"I don't think anything can settle my stomach. It feels like I've got a volcano rumbling around in there, and it just erupted."

Katie grinned at Janet's sense of humor, and then realized she was serious. "That sounds terrible."

"It is. Just pray you don't get it."

Janet staggered back to bed, and as Katie went to the kitchen, she hoped neither she nor Tottie got sick. Who would keep things running if they were down? Tottie glanced up when Katie entered the kitchen. "Meg is sick too."

"Oh, dear. Janet is too."

"I can treat the others, but Meg should see a doctor. She's looking pretty bad."

"I'll take her to the clinic. Is she awake?"

"No. She finally got to sleep around five." Tottie rinsed a plate and placed it in the rack. "It can wait until she wakes."

Katie put a cup of water in the microwave, waited until the machine dinged, and dunked a peppermint tea bag in the cup. At Tottie's questioning gaze, she shrugged. "There's nothing wrong with me. I just like the taste of it. I told Janet that I'd bring her a cup."

"You sit down and drink your tea," Tottie ordered. "I'll fix a cup for Janet, and then I want to talk to you."

Katie sipped her tea, thinking it would be easier to simply buy a bottle of Pepto-Bismol, but Tottie's tea worked, and using the remedy kept the housekeeper happy. In the spring, summer, and fall, she kept the shed in back of the house filled with the fragrance of drying herbs as she replaced her supply of medicines.

The shelter was quiet, and Katie sat half dozing over her tea until Tottie returned. She stretched and yawned. Not enough sleep last night. Too much time spent lying awake worrying, with nothing to show for it.

Tottie knelt beside her, her expression serious. "There's something I want you to see."

The gravity of her tone alerted Katie that something was wrong. "What now?"

She shook her head. "This isn't something I can tell you about. You have to see it for yourself."

Rising, she moved to the back door, and a puzzled Katie followed. Suddenly fear jolted her as she remembered last night and her near certainty that someone was prowling around the house.

Tottie swung the door open and pointed to fresh scratches in the wood around the lock. "Someone tried to break into the house last night."

The scratches stood out conspicuously against the painted wood. Obviously someone had tried to jimmy the lock. The hair on Katie's arms furred. So there really had been someone prowling around last night. She hadn't imagined it.

Tottie must have realized something was wrong. "What is it? Tell me."

"I woke up last night and looked out the window. I thought I saw someone, but when I came downstairs and looked around, I didn't find anything."

Tottie's expression turned forbidding. "Did you go outside?"

"Do I look like a fool? I went back to bed convinced it was my imagination. But there are too many things happening for these things to be 'my imagination.' Who could be doing this?"

"I guess Ed could be out of prison by now. He was mighty peeved at you a few years back."

"It wasn't Ed Mathis. The authorities would have notified us when he was released. Then again, who knows? Maybe we're on edge and making a big deal out of everything, but sure as I'm standing here, somebody tried to jimmy this lock. Either last night or maybe weeks ago, and we're just now noticing."

"We'd have noticed anything that apparent."

Tottie's brow settled into a concerned frown. "Listen to me, now. Never go out of this house at night by yourself. You come and get me, and I'll go with you."

Katie started to protest, but there was no disputing the wisdom of Tottie's warning. "That holds for you too. No going outside on your own. We go together. We're a team."

Tottie returned to the sink followed by Katie, who drank the last of her tea.

"I've got typing to do. Let me know when Meg wakes up, please." Katie walked through the living room to find Ruth sitting alone, crocheting. "Oh, good. At least you're not sick."

"Wrong. I'm sitting here so I'll be close to the bathroom. It's become my home away from home. Lucky it's such a comfortable one."

Katie shook her head and laughed. "At least you've retained your sense of humor."

"Not for long. I heard you talking to Tottie. Are you going to take Meg to the doctor?"

"That's right. Do you need to come along?"

"No, but I think it's a good idea for her to go. You don't want to take a chance on inducing an early labor." Ruth hastily put her crocheting aside. "Excuse me. I have to run."

Ruth made a dash for the bathroom. Katie hoped Ruth had not been in the living room when she and Tottie were discussing their nocturnal visitor. Katie didn't want to upset the guests. The women had more than one reason to fear midnight intruders.

Meg woke up, and Katie drove her into Little Bush to see the doctor in spite of her protests that she didn't have the money to pay. His verdict was intestinal flu; baby was fine. He prescribed bed rest and plenty of liquids. The mother-to-be slept on the way home, her youthful features pale from the draining episode. The silence gave Katie plenty of time to think. Who was the prowler? And to what extent would he go to reach his intended victim? And why didn't the dogs bark? Did they recognize the intruder, or had he managed to slip past without alerting them?

By noon Katie's stomach was roiling. She couldn't get sick—she didn't have time. She entered the kitchen to find Tottie dragging around. "Oh no, you too?"

The housekeeper sank weakly into a chair. "I'm okay. Not as bad as the others, anyway."

"What's wrong with us? Why are we all sick?" She was beginning to think the illness was part of an evil plot.

Tottie got up, filled two cups with a light tan liquid, and carried them to the table. "I've brewed up a pot of tea. Sweeten it with honey. It should help."

"The doctor says that Meg has an intestinal virus, but is it possible that we could have eaten something bad?"

"The caviar?"

Katie shook her head. "I didn't eat any." She took a cautious sip of tea. She'd been drinking this woman's potions all of her life, and she had learned that some tasted better than others. "What is this?"

Tottie stirred a teaspoonful of honey into her mug. "It's a mixture of ginger root, orange peel, dried lemongrass, peppermint leaves, and yarrow flower, all good for you."

The hot tea opened Katie's sinuses and eased her unsettled stomach.

They drank tea in companionable silence. Katie sighed. "Have you noticed that the problems we're having started when Clara came? If I had any sense, I'd send her to the Sundance shelter. Maybe whoever is sneaking around here would leave."

"You won't do that." Tottie sipped from her cup. "You wouldn't send a woman away once she's taken shelter with you."

"No, I can't, but it would be nice if I could. The election will be over soon, and she'll leave. But it's hard to understand why God would throw such a tempest in our nice, neat teapot."

"Ah, the mysterious workings of God. The women did get along better before she came. I don't think she means to be so disrupting. She just doesn't know how to get along with people like us."

"What's wrong with people like us?" Tottie's words put Katie immediately on the defensive.

"Nothing. I meant she's used to a different sort. She spends her time in Washington, and you know it's nothing like Devils Tower, Wyoming."

Katie wrapped her hands around her cup. "You know what I think? I know any one of these women could have been in touch with the men they're running from. And maybe one of them could be harassing us, but I really believe Neil Townsend is behind it."

Tottie shook her head. "You can't seriously believe that man would be skulking around this shelter. He's got too much to lose. He's as recognizable in the public eye as she is."

"You've seen him on TV: head shaved, mouth running at full volume, harsh, angry, and practically snarling. He's the slash-and-burn type, leave no witnesses. I wouldn't trust him as far as I could throw him, and no, I don't think he's here in person. But he could have hired someone to do it."

"But why, Katie? If he's her husband, a husband with a temper, why would he want to frighten her? I'd think he'd want her to win."

"Maybe he does and maybe he doesn't. I don't know. But I do know something is going on around here, and I'm going to find what and who's doing it." Katie sat lost in thought. Then she said, "I overheard Clara talking to one of the horses recently. Seems Neil wasn't always abusive—in fact, if I heard right, this was the only incident, set off by something that Clara told him."

Tottie leaned back in her chair, her face drained of color. Katie suddenly realized how sick she looked. "You need to be in bed. I don't know how you've managed to keep everyone supplied with juice and tea and take care of yourself too. You get some rest, and I'll fix dinner."

"I've got a chicken stewing. Some homemade chicken soup will be good for the women and light on the stomach. I'm all right, Katie. Don't worry. We'll get through this."

Katie sighed. "Isn't that what we always say every time we're faced with a challenge? I'm not sure we can keep on getting through things. This whole week has been one depressing event after another. First the budget, now this stomach thing, and someone harassing us. I don't know, Tottie. I've never felt like quitting before, but now I wonder if it wouldn't be best." Tired and lonely, and wanting someone to take care of her, Katie said, "It does seem like life is working against us."

"Seems that way."

"What do we do now?" Katie meant the question rhetorically, but Tottie seized the moment.

"I have no answers, Katie. Perhaps it's time to close the shelter, tighten our belts even more, and save what we can of the farm."

Even the suggestion sickened Katie. They'd both worked so hard to keep the shelter open, not to mention the years of backbreaking work Grandpops and Grandmoms had put into the farm. When they'd lost all of their savings to the stock market, they'd been crushed, but they never would have dreamed that Katie would let the farm fall victim to bad management.

"I hate to let the shelter go."

"So do I, but better lose the shelter than lose everything. You're too stressed, and these incidents can mean big trouble. They must be connected to Candlelight in some way. If we close, whoever is harassing us will stop."

"I know you're right. Common sense says you're right. It's my heart that I can't convince." Katie had been having the same thoughts and conclusions. She couldn't lose everything. Grandpops would roll over in his grave, and Tottie's Social Security American Indian Heritage check was all she had. Katie couldn't bring herself to quit now. Not yet. She hadn't given the budget enough time to produce results. A few more weeks, and the financial picture would brighten. "I guess I'll just have to pray harder for God to provide a way."

"We'll both pray, but we must be open to God's leading. If the answer we get isn't what we want to hear, we have to be willing to submit to what we believe he's telling us."

Katie nodded, but her soul didn't agree. God couldn't want her to close this shelter that had offered refuge to so many battered women. She couldn't make a hasty decision based on a monetary crisis, not yet. But she didn't see how they could continue much longer. Warren's budget had better work. It was their last hope.

A few days later, Warren phoned. "Thought I'd come out today and see how you're doing with the budget. Is that all right with you?"

"Sure." She didn't want to sound disinterested, but she wasn't ready for another financial discussion that left her feeling that she'd never get the hang of saving money. There was no reason not to let him come, though. The women were feeling better now, almost back to normal. The sun was shining. Nothing unusual had happened lately, and Katie had begun to relax. Maybe the strange incidents of late were caused by kids playing pranks. At least the harassment had ceased for the time being.

Warren sat across the desk, thinking Katie looked a little pale. "Are you all right?"

"I'm fine, no new problems, other than we've all had a stomach bug."

"Oh yeah? Everyone doing okay now?"

"Sure. We're over it." She handed him the latest figures on the week's expenditures, and he zeroed in on one glaring amount.

"You paid how much for what?"

"Ninety-five dollars for caviar and a case of gourmet crackers." The tilt of her chin told him she wouldn't take kindly to criticism. "Eighty dollars plus shipping and handling."

"You're nuts."

"Maybe so, but a guest felt that she needed it."

He leaned back, shaking his head. "I thought you were smarter than this."

If he hinted one more time that she was an imbecile, she was going to lose her temper. "I know it's extravagant." Even more so since Clara hadn't eaten a bite of the caviar. But there were still a few crackers around.

He took a stab at guessing the reason. "Clara missing her little treats?"

For a moment Katie wasn't going to answer, and then she nodded. "She says she'll have her people send me a check, but I won't do that again."

"If I were you, Katie, I'd send Clara packing. She's a politician. She craves the spotlight, and she'll eventually give her location away. You know that, don't you?"

"I can't ask her to leave. We promised her a safe haven till after the election."

Warren's next words shocked Katie. "She lived with him while he was abusive. What makes you think she'll be any different once the elections are over? Is she going to change, fight back, and have the louse thrown in jail? What?"

She didn't care for his barely civil tone. "I don't know, Warren. That's up to her. But while she's here, Candlelight will provide her shelter." She saw no point in telling him her suspicions that this was a onetime incident. Not that it mattered. Once was enough.

"Katie my friend, you're in a dangerous business. You need to watch your back."

"I understand your concern, Warren, but you don't understand mine. These women, including Clara, have a mortal fear of their abusers, and they won't do anything foolish. They're here because they need help. I strongly believe God gives grace and shelter when we ask for it. He'll take care of the shelter and the women, and he'll take care of me."

When Warren left, Katie was glad to see him go.

Twelve

Janet usually wanted to get the mail, but today she was help-ing Tottie in the kitchen. So after lunch Katie walked to the rural box, opened the lid, and peered inside. A wad of some-thing floral met her eyes. On closer inspection, she found a bouquet of roses, crumpled roses. She stared at the crumpled arrangement. Who?

These had to be for one of the women, but who would send such an insulting arrangement in such a discourteous manner?

A man who wanted to show his scorn for the recipient.

A name rose unbidden to her lips. Neil Townsend. The election was growing near, and Neil had to have sent these to torment Clara. Katie looked at the crumpled bouquet and fumed. The image of the smooth-talking abuser chatting ami-cably with Hannity and Colmes infuriated her. If the public only knew. But the flowers answered her question. Neil knew where to find Clara. The floral offering was a sick reminder from an even sicker man.

She fished her cell phone out of her pocket and punched in the sheriff's number. He answered on the second ring.

"Ben?"

"Katie? What's up?"

"I need to talk to you."

"About what?"

She told him about the crumpled flowers. "I'm sure Neil Townsend has discovered Clara's location. I want a restraining order."

"Why don't I lasso you the moon instead?"

"I don't need the moon. I need a restraining order."

He whistled under his breath. "That won't be easy. Clara needs to get the order, and if her husband is bothering her, a restraining order won't stop him. It's only good when it's enforced.

"Tell Clara to call her lawyer. Some men will pay attention to an order and some won't, and I'm betting Townsend won't. He's not doing it anyway—he's having someone else do his dirty work. Dollars to donuts, Townsend's sitting up in Washington innocent as a newborn babe. Besides, you don't know the flowers were meant for Clara. Maybe they were meant for you. You're a beautiful woman. A lot of men might be moved to send you flowers."

"Dead flowers?"

"I might. Considering that I can't get your attention any other way."

She fell silent. The only man she knew gutsy enough to cram dead flowers in her mailbox was ... Ben.

He wouldn't dare.

"I'm not trying to, Katie." His tone dropped. "But I can. We had fun at the ballgame the other night. I was thinking, how about dinner and a movie Saturday night?"

Katie felt a flicker of irritation. This was no time to get personal. She needed help. "I'm sorry, Ben. I've got too much going on right now. Everyone at the shelter's been down with a bug, and in spite of what you think, something weird is going on here."

His tone sobered. "More weird than usual?"

She went over the events of the week—the door jamb, unexplained noises at night—and her general sense of unease.

"Relax. The flu bug has you antsy. Let me take you out Saturday, and you'll relax."

Katie tapped her finger on the mailbox and did not answer.

"Let me guess. You have to wash your hair."

"No."

"Paint your nails."

"No." She rolled her eyes.

"Shave your legs."

"Wrong."

"Okay, I'm down to your last excuse. You're going to have to help me. You have the mumps. Hives. Headache. Iron poor, tired blood. You have to give blood, have a blood transfusion, drive a Blood Mobile?"

"No. No. And no."

She heard a sigh. He said, "Last one. 'Another time, Ben.'"

She grinned. "That'll do for now."

"Ten-four." His professionalism returned. "Ma'am, I advise you not to worry about the weird happenings. I will personally come by and check all the doors, windows, and outbuildings, and the tire tracks around the mailbox."

"When?"

"The moment I hang up." He sounded preoccupied then. She could hear the click of computer keys. So he was taking her serious, taking notes. Good. He needed to take her seriously.

She ended the call, wishing she could get more excited about the man. He wasn't a slug. He was cute, actually, but the spark wasn't there. But Warren, as frustrating and moody as he could be sometimes, still had the power to send her pulse racing. Katie hoped Warren would eventually come around. His emotional scars were still fresh. But she couldn't shake the growing sense that maybe, just maybe this was the one, the man she could eventually love with all her heart and soul. The one God had been holding back until she was sure of what she wanted.

And if her feelings proved right, she wanted Warren Tate.

Katie carried the bundle of wilted flowers back to the house, debating whether to tell Clara about them or not. Not. What good would it do to tell her and upset her unnecessarily? After all, they weren't addressed to any one specifically. For all Katie knew, Ben *could* have sent them to her.

Oh, he wouldn't. He wouldn't dare.

She searched for any sort of note, but there was none. Where the flowers came from was anybody's guess. On closer inspection, she decided they came from a local grocery store. But were they from a frantic spouse or suitor, desperate to make amends, or a threatening husband sending a voiceless warning?

Or someone just desperate?

Thirteen

Katie dialed Warren's number and waited while it rang three times. He picked up on the fourth. "Hello?"

She must have caught him at a bad time, because irritation tinged his voice, and she immediately thought about hanging up and calling at a more convenient time. "Are you busy? I can call back later."

"What do you need?"

"I wanted to talk to you about this budget. I've got a couple of unexpected typing jobs lined up, which will give me a little more money to play with."

"You don't have any money to play with. What part of *broke* don't you understand? You have to stick with the original budget. If you don't, then you're going to go under."

"I can stay with it. It will be hard, but not impossible. I just thought the extra typing money would help."

"You're blessed with additional income. Thank your lucky stars, and stick it away for necessities."

"Okay."

Warren laughed, his tone softening. "I'll bet you'll do just that. How many lattes have you had this week?"

"Only a couple. I'm getting better."

"If you say so."

All right, this was not her imagination. There was a definite hint of sarcasm in his words. "I'm sure I can, with your help."

Silence fell between them. Then his voice came over the line, holding a tone of finality. "No, Katie. I'm not going to be your conscience. I've given you a budget, but you have to follow it on your own. I'm backing off, as of now. It's up to you to prove you want to keep that shelter going."

"Of course I'm going to keep the shelter open. I'm committed to these women. There is no way I'm going to close it."

"Have you considered that you're being selfish? Is it fair of you to run through Tottie's money? She's getting older. What will happen to her if you aren't able to support her? Cross the wrong abuser, and you'll be a statistic in the morning newspaper. Have you considered that?"

Warren's years of management seeped through. He was a tough boss, but Katie didn't take offense. He was accustomed to having his orders met, and she was responsible for following his advice regarding the budget. But she refused to consider closing the shelter. Not yet.

"What about the women?" she demanded.

"They'll manage. Most of us do one way or another."

Katie sighed. Poor Warren. His lack of faith sagged to a new low, and she wasn't exactly a shining beacon of hope. "They don't 'manage' very well, but I respect your advice. It is my responsibility to follow the budget, and I will. You'll be proud of me."

"I'd be more proud if you'd stop trying to save the world. I don't want you hurt."

"I'll be all right. God's done a good job so far."

"Yeah, right. We have to take care of ourselves in this world."

He hung up, and Tottie breezed into the room. "Are you going to town today?"

"I can. What do you need?"

She held out a list. "Not a lot, but we're out of a few things, if you don't mind driving in and getting them."

Katie took the paper. "I might as well run a few errands while I'm at it. Keep me from having to go back tomorrow."

When she reached Little Bush, Katie automatically turned onto the street where she usually drank her lattes. Change was hard. Sticking to a budget was worse, especially for a woman who craved caffeine. Her problems were larger than lattes, but the steaming cup of fragrant, ground, Costa Rican beans, blended and roasted to create a tangy, full-bodied beverage ...

Stop it! Get a grip! Your problems are bigger than a cup of coffee. Yet as Katie got out of the jeep and slammed the door, her imaginary sense tasted the heavenly brew. She should have parked a mile away from this place and not tortured herself with the smells coming from the local hangout, but she didn't. Head down, she set her mind on her reason for being here. Business.

Mary Hoskins' big, black Lincoln Navigator pulled into an empty spot. Mary. Katie and Mary used to sit in a back booth and drink lattes on a weekly basis BTB (Before The Budget).

Ah, the good old days.

Katie quickened her stride. Utilities bills were due today. As loathsome as the budget was, and getting more so every day, this would be the first time a bill was paid on the due date regardless of the caviar and peachy crackers. Warren's plan worked—even indulging Clara's whim (which the cat enjoyed), with the extra typing making up the deficit. Lattes aside, Katie felt good about the small achievement. She'd prove to Warren that she could stick to a strict regime.

"Katie!"

She froze, recognizing Mary's voice and her intent. She would insist they have a latte and catch up. Katie was already one latte in the red.

She turned with a quick smile. "Mary!" How was she going to explain that she had two lattes yesterday, so today she couldn't have any in order to make up for her reckless spending. It was bad enough that Warren knew her financial muddle; she didn't want the whole town aware of her peccadilloes.

Mary crossed the nearly empty street and approached. "It's been ages. Where have you been keeping yourself lately?"

"Oh, busy. How about you?"

"Always." Her gaze swept the coffee shop. "Latte? I'm buying."

She had just said the enchanting words.

"Sure, love one."

They backtracked the short distance to the shop and within minutes settled into a back booth, lattes ordered.

Mary unwound an expensive looking scarf and laid it on her leather jacket. The scent of imported perfume mingled with the bouquet of roasted coffee beans. Some envied Mary and the perks that marriage to a high-profile attorney brought, but Katie only felt sorry for her. Mary led a lonely life, and her marriage was a highly profitable sham with infidelity only one transgression on her husband's long list of mistakes. As far as Katie knew, Mary wasn't physically abused and from all appearances had grown comfortable with the lifestyle and the material rewards her husband's sins provided.

Coffee arrived. Katie took a sip then leaned back and savored the full-bodied, rich warmth trickling down her throat, glad she didn't have to worry about cheating husbands. But cheating or not, it would be nice to have someone to care for her. *Didn't all women seek that goal?*

Sure, but Katie was smarter. She was an eyewitness to the atrocities and pain resulting from the wrong choice. She knew men, and the reason why she remained single was the fact that she had yet to find a man who would be equally yoked. Grandmoms said, "Marry a man of strong faith, and your troubles will be less." Not trouble free, but less. The older Katie got, the more she understood that, religious fanaticism aside, when God made laws, he didn't speak to hear his head rattle. Warren flashed through Katie's mind. Granted he had an abrupt manner, and at times he didn't appear to share her faith and that concerned her. But they'd barely been reunited. Important stuff like faith and future goals would come up eventually. She would never marry a man who didn't share her faith, but Warren had as a child. The more she was around him, the more she understood that like Grandpops, Warren's bark was worse than his bite.

Mary arranged her cup. "So how're things at the shelter?"

"Good, but busy. Seems like there's never enough time to do it all. I keep hoping someday I'll catch up, but I suppose I'd be bored if that ever happened."

They chatted about this and that. Cups drained. Mary signaled for two more.

My lucky day!

"What's this I hear about Warren Tate hanging around your place lately?"

Warmth flooded Katie's cheeks, and it wasn't the result of the hot coffee. "Who told you that?"

"Never mind who told me, is it true?" Mary leaned forward, eyes bright with curiosity. "What I want to know is how did that man go from a nerd to a Harrison Ford in the years he's been gone?"

Katie shrugged. "He's smart, Mary. Really brilliant in business affairs. He was a Wall Street genius, you knew that?"

"I heard — but then he's always been a brainiac, just not exciting. Somewhere between here and New York something changed." She leaned forward. "I hear he's quite a financial catch."

"Really?" Katie had not considered his financial worth. She'd been poor for so long, she saw money as merely a requirement to live. She attached no particular sentiment to a person's bank account. She never had much of one.

Something had changed about Warren. Maybe it did concern money. Somewhere between here and the Big Apple, Warren had developed an aversion to trust. And maybe even to God.

Fresh lattes arrived.

"Did I tell you I've been asked to be a part of Devils Tower festival next year?" Mary tapped a pink package of artificial sweetener into her cup.

"How nice — are you going to accept?"

"I don't know—thinking about it. Working on this year's centennial was fun. Maybe." She lifted the cup to her glossy lips and drank. Katie's gaze focused on the long, manicured acrylic nails.

"Love your nail polish. What's the color?"

Mary lowered the cup. "I'm-Not-Really-a-Waitress Red."

"Beg pardon?"

"That's the name of it!" She lowered her hand to study the striking red on each of her nails. "I'm-Not-Really-a-Waitress Red."

"Nice."

Minutes flew by as Katie savored the last of her cup. Mary's pink Razr phone rang a funky version of an Aretha Franklin tune. She unsnapped her purse and punched on. "Yes?"

Katie folded a napkin. Should she mention how the shelter was in dire need of donations? Mary had occasionally donated, but Katie hated to put friends on the spot. It didn't seem fair, yet she knew if she mentioned the need, Mary would whip out her checkbook ...

"No kidding."

Katie drained the last of her caffeine, pretending oblivion to the personal conversation.

"He did, did he?"

She reached in her purse for lipstick. The colder weather was murder on lips.

"No. No—I said no! I'll be there in a few minutes." She hit disconnect. "Jerk." She reached in her purse, took out a pair of designer sunglasses, and slipped them on. "Sorry, Katie. I have to run. We must do this more often."

"Sure." Katie half-rose, expecting to follow her to the register. Instead, Mary picked up her oversized handbag and hightailed it out the front door.

When the bell over the door jingled, Katie's gaze froze on the bill lying coiled on the table like a prairie rattler.

Hey Katie! How about a latte? I'm buying!

Resigned, Katie took a deep breath and picked up the check for four house lattes. Some days it didn't pay to get out of bed.

As soon as she stepped out on the sidewalk, she spotted Ben headed her direction, his ruddy completion whipped pink by the wind. "My doting fan."

"Sheriff." She ignored his tease.

"Buy you a latte?"

The mere thought sickened her. "Thanks, I've had my fill."

Ben fell into step with her. "Any more strange, bump-in-the-night incidents?"

"Not today." She hadn't forgiven him for teasing about the flowers. Even if nothing more had happened, she wouldn't tell him. Well, maybe she would, but not now.

He pushed back his ball cap and grinned. She silently read the writing on his sweatshirt: *Bad Cop, No Donut.*

"Sorry if I didn't appear to take you seriously the other day. I do. I just can't connect Neil Townsend and roses wadded in a mail box. He might be a jerk, but he's got class. Have you seen the guy on TV?"

She nodded. "I've seen him, and I don't see class. I see an abuser who would wad grenades in a mailbox to disconcert his wife."

"You cannot wad a grenade."

"Point taken."

"You said the flowers didn't have a name on them."

"They didn't have to, but I'd bet lunch that they were meant for her."

"Really? Okay, lunch it is."

"Don't be so smug, O'Keefe. We'll never know who sent those flowers."

"Oh, we'll know," he promised as he kept step with her. "I'll make sure that I find the culprit. Hamburgers or meatloaf?"

"Lobster, if I must."

"For lunch?" He shook his head. "You drive a hard bargain, lady."

She switched subjects.

"Did I tell you Sweet Tea got out? I think someone left the gate open."

"One of the women could have forgotten to lock it."

"They say not." She shrugged. "Who knows?"

Ben's expression sobered. "Tell you what. I need to bring Fritz some of those fresh bones that he likes. I'll take another look around. I could have missed something earlier, and I can always look into Meg's boyfriend and the other abusers' present situations to see what they've been up to."

"You're spoiling that dog."

"He's a good ole mutt."

Katie spotted Warren's pickup driving past. He didn't look their way. Was he still upset with her over the budget, or did he fail to notice her? She turned back to find Ben watching her.

"There's a guy who's changed since high school."

Katie agreed. "He's a lot more sophisticated, more outgoing. Being out in the world has definitely added some polish."

Ben was silent for a minute. "Maybe, but there's nothing wrong with Little Bush. It's always been good enough for me."

"Me too. At least, I've never left." Sometimes she wondered what her life would have been like if she had moved away from her roots, taken a different direction. Would Warren be willing to settle for a down-home girl when he'd met women who were glamorous and confident? He seemed content to be back in town. She sighed. She'd always been too comfortable with her life, never feeling that she needed a man to make her happy.

Now, she wasn't so sure. Maybe a good, strong, protective male was exactly what she needed.

That night during Bible study, Katie decided to tell the women about her situation. If the shelter went under, it would affect them too. She gazed around the small circle, commanding their attention. Clara was missing. She'd attended one Bible study and announced that was enough. She had enough religion to last for a while.

Ruth gave her a shrewd glance. "What's wrong, Katie? You've looked worried lately."

Had she been that obvious? She didn't want to tell them about the strange things that kept happening, not yet. But they had to know the financial scare. She took a deep breath. "It's about the shelter."

"What about it?" Meg sat up straighter. "Something's wrong, isn't it—I knew it. Everywhere I go something bad happens—"

"Nothing's wrong. It's just that money is a little tight. Sometimes there isn't enough to go around. I've asked Warren to help, and he's worked out a budget. I'm trying to stay on it, but it's hard. I seem to be bookkeeping-challenged."

Janet frowned. "Are you broke?"

"No, at the moment we're hanging on, but it's getting tougher all the time. I've got a little work coming in, enough to keep us afloat for a while. But I feel it's only fair to tell you I might have to close."

"Are we going to have to leave? I know I'll be an even bigger expense when the baby comes, but I can get a job. Help out. Grandma said she could spare a little out of her savings," Meg said.

The sudden apprehension in her eyes broke Katie's heart. Where would Meg go? On her own she might make it, but there was the baby. Closing the shelter would be a disaster for this young mother. "No. I'll work something out. It's not that desperate yet. I just wanted you to be aware of the financial situation. Right now the feed bill is high with the additional horses, but they'll be leaving once they can travel. That should help."

Tottie, who had been quiet, spoke up. "It might help if we keep the thermostat set lower, maybe on sixty. We can dress warmer."

"Yes, and use more blankets on the beds," Janet added. "Now that we know the problem, we can economize. Why, I'm fairly good with figures. We could get one of those money programs, and I can keep the books. I got A's in high school math."

"We have wood to burn," Ruth said. "The fireplace will heat the living area and we can spend most of our time in there. We can work it out, Katie. Don't worry. We won't let you go under."

Meg's eyes roamed the circle. "I know I'm not as religious as the rest of you, but it seems in a time like this we should pray."

"Of course." Still, Katie was surprised. Why hadn't she thought to mention prayer? She tried every day to bring the spiritual into conversations, hoping to win these women over. Apparently Meg had been paying attention.

They joined hands and prayed around the circle. Even Meg offered a few simple words, though Katie kept the petitions voluntary. Not everyone was comfortable praying out loud, and Katie respected their wishes. It touched her that they cared so much about her shelter. They were good women. Life had been painful for them, so they needed a place like Candlelight. God would make a way, but she knew she was asking for a miracle.

Katie gazed around the circle at their flushed, earnest faces, feeling a bond she had come to expect. There was always a tie between her and the women she sheltered. Many stayed in touch, even the ones who went back to their old lives. She wanted to protect them. If she told them about the odd occurrences that had been happening, they would be frightened. But even worse, it could damage the progress they were making in reclaiming their lives. No, she couldn't tell them, but there was something she could do.

"Let's talk about something more enjoyable. Why don't we all bring out family and 'significant others' pictures and share them."

Tottie shot her a curious look, but Katie ignored her. She would explain later, but right now, she wanted to see pictures of the women's abusers to see if she could spot a familiar face, someone she might have seen around town, and try to put a face to a stalker.

Meg shook her head. "I don't have many. All I could think of was getting away. There wasn't time to take much. I do have one in my wallet."

Janet got to her feet. "Like Meg, I don't have many, but I think it's a good idea to share. I'll get what I have."

When Ruth left the room, Tottie frowned at Katie. "You're up to something."

Katie shook her head. The others soon returned with a pitiful number of pictures, all they'd been able to bring with them. But they shared them, talking about the people there, people they loved but who hadn't been able to help them escape from their tortured situations. Katie listened to the stories and looked at the pictures, but it was just an exercise in futility. She'd never seen any of these people.

The women retired to their rooms for the night, and Warren called. Katie was surprised at how glad she was to hear from him. She had been afraid he would stop calling and coming around, especially since he'd ignored her this afternoon. They chatted for a while about nothing in particular, just friendly conversation.

"I saw you with Ben in town today." So he had seen her.

"I was telling him about a strange incident. Someone put some flowers in my mailbox. The bouquet was crumpled and disgusting."

"Did the gift have an enclosed card?"

"I don't think anyone in their right mind would leave a card."

"Maybe you're not a good judge of flowers."

She laughed. "Guilty. I haven't been the recipient of many in my lifetime, but these concern me."

"Tell you what. Don't bother Ben the next time something happens. He's got a lot of territory to cover. Call me, and I'll take a look around. That's a promise. You have my cell phone number, and I always have it with me."

Katie grinned. Well okay. *Progress—something that seemed long in coming.* She couldn't resist a little teasing. "Clara has been asking about you."

The warmth in his voice faded. "What's that broad want?"

She flinched. The term *broad* set her teeth on edge.

"Don't call her a broad. It's disrespectful."

"I meant it to be." He chuckled, and she realized he was teasing. "She's not my type."

Katie wanted to ask him what kind of woman he considered to be his type, but resisted. "She's all right once you get acquainted."

"I know all about women like her, and the less a man has to do with them, the better off he is."

This man was really jaded when it came to pushy women. Katie kept her tone light. "Well, God loves her."

"I'm no expert on what God does, but when it comes to women like Clara, I'd say he has his work cut out for him."

Katie was no expert on God either, but she figured he had his hands full with Warren's cynicism.

Fourteen

A noise woke Katie.

She lay still, eyes adjusting to the darkness.

It was a muted *whump*!

She froze, listening.

Whump.

Someone was breaking into the house.

Shelter safely 101: never dismiss a sense of danger or overplay it. Most of the abusers' victims had a restraining order, for all the good that accomplished. A piece of paper wouldn't stop a determined man. That's why Tottie had an ear tuned to anything strange. She was armed with baseball bats, a shotgun, and if the attacker was still on his feet, the dreaded mace.

Adequate, but not impenetrable.

Whump.

Reaching for her robe, Katie slid out of bed, her feet softly touching the floor. Indian summer was over and falling temperatures had turned the house into a dank tomb. Shivering, she tied the sash around her middle and felt around with her toe for her slippers.

Flashlight.

She automatically reached for the twin beam, keeping an ear tuned to the sound.

Maybe a shutter was banging in the wind?

She moved down the dark hallway, creeping past the rooms of sleeping women.

Whump. The sound came from downstairs, maybe in the kitchen or service pantry?

Her hand tightened around the flashlight, and she switched on the beam. Wouldn't a shutter make a *whump, whump* sound instead of one brief *whump*?

She paused, shining the beam around the hardwood floor. Light searched out each corner, each closed door. A board creaked as Katie moved through the dark living room into the kitchen. She flashed the beam on the wall clock. 1:45. The wind had come up, rattling bare oak branches outside.

God, I hope you're watching.

Her gaze focused on the cellar door. Closed.

Was someone hiding in there?

Cold penetrated her robe and she shivered. A gust of wind rocked the house. She waited, listening. Nothing.

A broken shutter didn't repair itself.

Whirling, she focused the beam in the living area then moved it slowly to the cellar. She sensed someone was behind that door. Her hair prickled.

Call for Tottie! Clammy palms tightened their grip around the flashlight.

But if she called Tottie, she would scare off the intruder, and what if she woke everyone only to determine she'd made a mistake?

A numbness that didn't have anything to do with the cold house washed over her. The only way to know what lay behind that door was to open it.

Fear gathered in cotton wads that blocked her airway. She'd barely escaped harm once from an abuser. When she'd come out of that scary episode alive, she'd promised herself and Tottie that she would never risk her life again for the shelter. She'd promised Warren. And Ben.

The closed door screamed silence.

She switched off the beam. Darkness swallowed her, and she realized that the outside security light was out. Why hadn't she noticed? Had someone cut the power source?

She stepped back, wiping sweaty palms on the sides of her housecoat.

Okay. Open the door.

Her hand slowly closed around the icy knob and inched it open. Then she jerked.

Something lunged toward her. Katie fell backwards, her petrified screams shattering the night air. Her head slammed against the floor. She had an impression of something hurtling past, and then pain and darkness overcame her.

❦

Katie woke to a blaze of light and Tottie bending close. She blinked at the sudden brightness. Her head hurt. Her shoulder throbbed. "What happened?"

"You tell me." Tottie's voice was acid-sharp, her eyes pinpoints of slanted light. "We heard you scream and rushed downstairs and that thing was batting around the room."

Katie tried to sit up, but the room whirled and she sank back down. Something large and moving fast flew overhead. Tottie ducked. The sound of breaking glass shattered the room. Clara, prominent politician Clara, dashed past holding a large towel, arms outstretched. Katie shut her eyes and then opened them again. Clara was attacking people? Had she been hiding in the cellar?

Katie pushed up to one elbow in time to see Meg run toward the living room, screaming, "Catch him!"

"Him?" Katie glanced at Tottie. "Who?"

"Not who, what. A barn owl. Apparently he was in the cellar."

"That's what hit me? An owl?"

"I think you fell and hit your head."

Katie ducked as the owl flew past, the women in hot pursuit. Janet knocked over a chair, staggered, and fell against the table. Ruth swatted the air with a broom, sending the owl in headlong flight toward the kitchen window.

Janet opened the door, propping the screen back with a stick of wood. "Head him this way. Maybe he'll fly out."

"We're trying," Clara panted. "But he's not cooperating. Reminds me of some senators I've known."

"Wait," Meg shouted. "We're just scaring it more. Give it time to calm down."

All activity ceased as the women stood silent, waiting. The owl swooped overhead, and came to rest on the floor. Clara inched forward, towel outstretched.

"Watch that thing," Tottie said. "It has strong talons and a beak that can rip your arm."

Clara paused, turning to look at them, mouth open, eyes wide. Then she swallowed and took a slow step toward the owl. Meg, brandishing a dishtowel, moved in from the opposite direction.

In one swift movement, Clara lunged at the large bird, covering it with the towel. "I've got it!"

Apparently the smothering cloth cowed the owl into inactivity. Clara lifted it, grunting with the effort. Meg ran to open the kitchen door, and together the two women stepped outside and released the feathered intruder.

Meg grinned. "We make a good team."

"None better." Clara shook out the towel and glanced around the room. "He sure made a mess."

Katie, still on the floor, looked around at the shambles the owl had made of Tottie's kitchen. She thought Tottie would have a fit.

But the housekeeper remained silent, eyes searching the cellar door. Then she glanced back at Katie. "What I want to know is who put that bird in the cellar? It didn't get in there by itself."

The women suddenly fell quiet as her words echoed in the room. Fear, like a smothering blanket, kept them frozen in place. Katie took a deep breath. Tottie was right. There was no way that owl could have gotten into the cellar on its own. Someone had put it there, the same someone who was behind all the other things that had been happening?

Tottie shoved herself to her feet and reached down to help Katie get up. "Let's get a cold compress on that head."

"I've got a headache." Probably had a lump the size of Mount Everest rising too.

The housekeeper nodded. "I'll make a pot of coffee. No one can sleep now anyway. Sit here. We need to talk."

Katie agreed, though she knew she would hate the subject. It didn't take a mystic to see Tottie had had her fill of scares.

Meg dropped into a chair opposite her. "Why would anyone put an owl in the cellar?"

Katie spread her hands in a shrug. "I don't have a clue. A prank, I guess." Tottie measured coffee while Janet brought a broom and dustpan to clean up the glass shards from a shattered vase.

Katie's eyes roamed the kitchen, realizing anyone standing outside could see in. Tottie was waiting for an explanation, so she collected her thoughts. She didn't want to frighten the women until she knew what had really happened.

"We're just guessing someone put the owl in the cellar. In the morning we can find out more about it. And while the excitement was exhilarating, no lasting damage was done. So let's not jump to conclusions."

Ruth returned from checking the doors. "Everything's locked up tight. No one has been in the house."

"So let's have a cup of coffee and a sweet roll and then go back to bed." Katie spoke with a brightness she didn't feel. She had a hunch Tottie was right.

Someone had put that owl in the cellar.

Early the next morning, Katie walked around the house looking for signs of how the bird had gotten in last night. A broken cellar window at the back of the house seemed to be the point of entry. A loose feather caught in the branches of the forsythia bush fluttered in the wind. The ground was too hard to hold a footprint, but why would a barn owl be on the ground at the back of the house? It would have had to fly into the low window hard enough to break it, and she couldn't see how that could have happened. No, Tottie was right. That owl had help getting inside.

After breakfast, Katie took the list Tottie handed her. Clara downed her coffee and pushed back from the table. "Mind if I ride along?"

It was the first simple request Clara had made. It wasn't a good idea, but Katie relented. "If you remain in the car unseen."

"Fine. Anything to get out of here for awhile."

Katie drove into Little Bush with Clara in the passenger seat. Regardless of what the budget said, she needed a latte. Needed it bad. She parked outside the grocery mart and warned Clara to stay put.

"Pick me up a package of Salems, will you? I'll have my people reimburse you."

Katie nodded, but she was tempted to remind her that she was still waiting for the check on the caviar.

"Want a latte?"

"No, just the smokes."

Katie met Ben on the sidewalk outside of the coffee shop.

"Hey, girl-of-my-dreams-who-won't-give-me-the-time-of-day." His eyes sparked with devilment. "Let me buy you a cup of coffee—better yet, marry me and I'll buy you a latte machine."

"Make that a Starbucks and you're on."

He held the door to the café open for her and followed as she walked inside. They settled in a booth and gave their orders, and Ben looked at her speculatively. "You look peaked. Bad night?"

"No, not really, why?"

He leaned back and twirled a coffee spoon. "Oh, I don't know. You look scared, tired, and you've got an egg-sized lump on your head."

"Tottie called you."

"Yeah. That too."

She explained what happened the night before, trying to make light of it, but Ben didn't laugh.

"That owl more than likely didn't get into that cellar by itself."

Katie sighed. "I know, but I don't want the women upset over an owl."

"Forewarned is forearmed. They'll be safer if they're on guard."

"Or maybe they'll leave and put themselves in harm's way. What would anyone have to gain by putting an owl in the cellar? It seems so pointless."

"You make any enemies other than me lately?"

"You're enough," she teased. "But every man whose woman takes shelter with me is my enemy." She told him about the incident two years ago with Ed and how it had unnerved her.

Ben shook his head. "You may have stirred up a hornet's nest this time. Someone is trying to cause trouble."

"Nothing threatening happened until after Clara came."

He tossed the spoon on the table. "Neil Townsend isn't skulking around your house playing pranks, Katie. He's too high profile for that. Someone would spot him in a minute. More likely, it's Meg's boyfriend. Or Janet's husband. Could even be Ruth's husband. Why focus on Townsend?"

"Neil has friends I'd bet who wouldn't mind terrorizing a bunch of women."

Ben nodded. "You could be right—not likely. My checks haven't turned up anything suspicious."

"Warren is working on it too."

"Goody for Warren. He's really, *really* swell."

"Give me a break. Why don't you like Warren?"

"Do I need a reason?"

She glanced at her watch. "I have to go. Tottie needs those groceries for lunch, and Clara's waiting for me in the car."

"What's she doing here in town?"

"She was going stir-crazy in the house. I thought it wouldn't hurt if she rode along."

"I'd advise you not to allow that in the future."

"I know."

Ben paid the bill and they parted on the sidewalk. "Look. Watch your back. I think these incidents have you spooked, but I'm on it. Call me anytime — day or night. Understand?"

"Understood."

She had turned to leave when he said the oddest thing. "One of these days, Katie Addison, I'm going to give up on you and marry the first woman who will have me."

This time his voice didn't have a hint of humor. In lieu of the serious tone, Katie spouted, "Grow a couple of inches, and we'll talk."

"No." He stood his ground. "You shrink a couple of inches."

Ben bumped into Clara, strolling along window shopping, on the way back to his office. Holy—

She turned to acknowledge him. "Sheriff. Cold today, isn't it?"

"Aren't you supposed to be in the jeep?"

Clara returned to window shopping. "Whatever do you mean?"

"Didn't Katie tell you to stay in the car?"

Clara's chin lifted. "I'm not fifty feet away from the vehicle."

"Mrs. Townsend, you're not only inviting trouble for yourself, but you're putting the other women in jeopardy. Go back to the jeep and stay there."

Her eyes turned as cold as the whipping wind. "What I do is none of your business, and don't speak to me in that tone again." She turned and sauntered further down the street.

Ben counted to ten and walked on. *Katie Addison, I hope you know the trouble you have on your hands with this one.*

Owls. Snotty women. It was enough to try Job's patience.

Over dinner the discussion turned to the upcoming holidays looming on the horizon. Katie's thoughts turned from owls to a live nativity at the women's shelter. Janet thought up the idea.

"Let's have a live drama — a nativity scene. By Christmas Meg's baby boo will be here, and she can play Baby Jesus."

Tottie frowned. "You shouldn't refer to Meg's baby as baby boo. It's not fitting."

Meg helped herself to the stroganoff. "Why not? That's my pet name for her."

Katie interrupted. "Are you serious? A drama might be fun." Something to take the women's minds off the recent trouble.

"I'm serious. What about you guys?"

Everyone agreed.

"Anyone invited other than the women?" Ruth asked.

"Just the women," Katie confirmed.

The change of pace would be nice. The women could practice their drama as the election approached. Thanksgiving would come and then Christmas. That's what they needed. This sleuth stuff was taxing.

Fifteen

November ushered in cold winds and the reminder that winter, if not by calendar date but by nippy winds, had come.

Katie shivered on the way to the barn as the cold north wind sliced through her heavy jacket. She'd have to depend on typing work from now until spring. Winter and its additional fuel bills grabbed her concentration. Propane had nearly doubled in price this year. However, wood was plentiful. Downed trees alone would heat the downstairs, but someone had to cut it.

Katie missed Warren. He hadn't been around much lately. If she could get him to open up to her, to tell her what rattled him so much about women, then maybe, just maybe, things between them would be different. Or was that only wishful thinking?

The latter, Katie thought. But it hurt to think he'd walked away from her and her problems when she desperately needed him.

You're content with God's timing. You don't need a man to make you happy.

She was content, and now wasn't the time to doubt God's wisdom, and yet lately she'd began to wonder why Warren fascinated her. Certainly it wasn't his sunny disposition, because he didn't have one. Good looks could only take a man so far. The excuse that he'd been wounded by another woman was getting a little thin, even with her. At times she wanted to take him by the shoulders and shake him and say, "Grow up!" Anyone who lived long enough would encounter disappointments and betrayal. Katie had come to realize these things *were* life, and you had to get a grip and pray for sunnier days.

Then other days her thoughts would soften and think that Warren's reticence was her fault. If she wasn't so stupid, if she knew how to stick to a simple budget, he wouldn't be so cranky.

You're not ignorant.

Then what made him so distant? What made Warren drop her like a hot iron when the relationship was going well? Tentative, but well.

A truck pulled into the drive, breaking Katie's concentration. The vet got out, her hair blowing in the light breeze. "Hello there!"

Katie fell into step, and the two women chatted on the way to the barn.

"How're the horses today?"

"Well on their way to good health." Katie hated to admit it, because admitting it would mean losing the animals, and she and the women had fallen in love with the horses. The injured souls had provided therapy that Katie couldn't buy.

"That's good to hear."

The horses looked up when the women entered the barn. Sweet Tea snuffed, bobbing her head. Katie stepped over to greet her while the vet began work.

"The wounds are healing nicely," she called. "Looks like you've been doing your job."

Katie ruffled Sweet Tea's mane. "The women have done more than me. They've been a real help."

It had taken willpower to stay clear of the horses as often as she could, and Katie rarely found the barn empty. Meg had practically moved in, overseeing the horses' water and feed. It was as if by nurturing the horses she was healing her wounds.

A half hour later, Katie accompanied the vet to her car. "I can't thank you enough for your generosity. I don't know how I would afford a vet bill."

"My pleasure." She paused and removed her gloves. "I've loved horses all my life. They nourish my soul. I can't say that about all animals, though ironically, I love all animals." She sighed as if she didn't understand the statement herself. "Another week and they'll be ready to travel."

Katie ignored the painful twinge. "One week?"

"Maybe two or three. It all depends on what develops the next few days." They walked on. "I could stretch it a little, but I know the feed bills are eating you alive."

"They are," Katie admitted. For once she was going to use common sense. The horses had to go sometime. "Just let me keep them as long as possible," she conceded. "I understand that the owner has been in contact with you?"

The vet chuckled. "Daily. But you don't need to worry. The lady loves the animals. She's just not in the position to care for them, so she's arranged for a longtime friend to keep them until nature takes its course."

Overhead a helicopter came into view, the whip-whop of blades interrupting the conversation.

"Thanks again." Katie held the truck door open as the vet climbed inside, waved, and drove off. The whip-whop grew louder as Katie started back to the house.

The helicopter suddenly dipped lower, zeroing in on the house. Panic seized Katie. *Clara. The press found her.*

Breaking into a run, she raced to the house and burst into the kitchen.

"Where's Clara?"

Tottie came out of the laundry room. "She was in her room last I knew."

Meg appeared in the doorway. "What's happening?"

"It's the press. They've discovered Clara's whereabouts."

One by one the women came to investigate, faces taut with the developing situation.

"It's okay." Katie went to the living area and jerked back the curtains. "They're after Clara, not you. Stay hidden."

Ruth wrung her hands. "My husband can't know that I'm here—he'll come after me. We were supposed to be safe. Katie, you promised."

"No one is going to know you're here." Katie drew the tremulous woman close to her side. "I'll take care of this—and you." After giving Ruth an assuring hug, she turned to the others. "Go to your rooms and stay there until it's safe to come out."

The room emptied, and Katie turned back to Tottie. "What do we do?"

"We stay put and let the sheriff and state police handle it."

"I'll call Ben." She wanted to call Warren so desperately, but she wouldn't.

Tottie stepped to the window, her eyes scanning the quiet yard. "I don't think Ben needs to be told that something big is up."

How had the media found out? On second thought, Clara hadn't been all that careful. But Katie couldn't believe anyone in Little Bush would alert the media about Candlelight's high-profile guest.

"I'll get Clara." Katie headed for the politician's room and found it empty. She located Clara on the small side porch, smoking a cigarette.

"What are you doing out here? Get inside." Didn't the woman have the sense God gave a goose?

Clara ground out the cigarette underfoot. "Is all this fuss over me?"

"That would be my guess." Katie eyed her stringently. "Does that concern you?"

Clara brushed past Katie and entered her ground floor bedroom. "What do we do now?" Fear tinged her voice. Katie wished she knew. In the years the shelter had been in operation, other than the one incident involving her and Ed Mathis, nothing like this had happened. She'd never had a victim with Clara's high profile, but she should have known it was only a matter of time before someone learned the politician's location. Days before a midterm election, the news of Clara's tragic personal life would be a late November surprise that opponents longed for, and it had just been laid in their lap.

"For now, you stay put. I mean it. Don't leave this room until I tell you it's safe to come out."

The phone rang. Tottie answered and called for Katie. "It's Ben. He wants to talk to you."

Katie picked up the extension. "Ben? We have a problem."

"You've got a very big problem. Do you have your television on?"

"No, why?"

"Every station is carrying a breaking news release of Clara's whereabouts. I'd say you have maybe fifteen minutes or less to get her out of there."

"Where do I take her?"

"Just get her out of there. Now! There's a bunch of news vans here in Little Bush asking directions to Candlelight. The town's turning into a circus. You're going to be under siege shortly."

"Can't you prevent them from hounding us?"

"I would if I could, but as long as they aren't on your property or blocking a public road, there's not much I can do."

Katie hung up, her thoughts racing in a hundred directions. Where could she hide Clara? The answer was evident. *Warren. He lived a few miles away, and they could take the back road to his place. Where was he? He would help.* She reached for her cell and punched in his number, wanting to leave the landline open in case Ben tried to call back.

She listened to Warren's cell phone ringing. His voice came on the line and she blurted, "What do I do? I think they discovered Clara."

"You think?"

His sarcasm was hard to overlook, but she figured she had it coming. He'd warned her that this would happen.

Humility tasted very bitter right now. She swallowed. "What should I do?"

"I don't know that you can do anything. The press know where she is."

"Or they think they do."

"What?"

"They think they do — they can't be certain until they have her in sight."

"How do you know they don't?"

"They haven't seen her yet. She's in her room right now. I've told her not to leave until I tell her it's safe."

"And you think she'll listen."

"I think she's smart enough to do what she's told when the election is days away."

Tottie called from the kitchen. "Katie! The town mayor's on the phone. He's in an uproar — wants to know what's going on!"

"Hold on a minute, Warren." Katie covered the cell phone mouthpiece. "Tell him the circumstances — that we have a high-profile guest, and we believe the press has discovered her location. Give our apologies to the town. This will be over quickly."

She had no idea what she was saying. She didn't have a clue how soon it would be over or, for that matter, what would happen next. She returned to Warren and repeated, "What shall I do?"

"I'll be over in a minute." The line went dead.

"What a mess." Tottie came into the room, shaking her head. "The whole town's in upheaval over the commotion. What are we going to do, Katie?"

"Warren's on his way over."

Tottie turned stoic features her way. "And he's going to save us?"

Katie didn't like her stinging tone. "He'll think of something."

The landline rang and Katie picked up. Ben's calm voice said. "I'm sending two cars out."

"Okay." She needed help; she wasn't a total fool. "Hurry."

Now the important question. Could he or Warren do anything to stop the impending disaster?

A few minutes later two sheriffs' cars pulled into the farm lot, with Warren right behind them. Ben got out of the first car, and the three police officers and Warren talked for a few minutes before coming to the house. Katie met them at the door, taking note of their serious expressions.

"What are we going to do?" she asked.

Ben met her anxious eyes. "Exactly what I told you to do. We're going to get Clara out of here before the press descends on you. Get her down here."

Tottie hurried to Clara's room and returned in a few minutes with the politician in tow. "Now what?"

Clara didn't look so smug now. "This is a disaster. How could they have found me, and days before the election?"

Warren snapped. "How could they not have found you? You've taken pointless chances. Someone tipped them off."

Tottie threw down a dish towel. "Let's not haggle! We don't have much time."

Ben glanced at Warren. "No one would look for her at your ranch. Take her with you."

"Are you serious? What would I do with her?"

"Nothing, I can assure you," Clara said. "I'll not be passed around like an unwanted piece of baggage."

"You don't have a choice, Mrs. Townsend." Ben shifted stance. "Come on, Warren. We have to get her out of here so Katie can truthfully tell the media that she isn't here. Take the back road — chances are the press doesn't know about it."

Katie wasn't very proud of her man. The unmitigated arrogance in Warren's eyes bothered her. No one was happy about the situation.

"Why me?" he insisted. "You can drive that road as easily as I can."

Ben crossed broad arms. "In a marked vehicle? She can be gone before we're surrounded by press cars. We don't have time to haggle. Just take her and go."

Tottie spoke up. "Surely you can manage for twenty-four hours, Warren."

"Please, Warren. You're our only hope." Katie realized she was pleading. Overhead a copter whirled.

"All right," Warren relented. "I'll take her, but I don't want a bunch of newshounds on my tail."

Clara for once was quiet. She didn't complain when Tottie volunteered to go along. Dressed in jeans and a T-shirt and wearing the black wig she had arrived in, Clara bore little resemblance to the woman whose features were plastered on their TV screen. Tottie, Clara, and Warren piled in the pickup and sped away from Candlelight.

Sixteen

Janet turned to face Ben. "What do we do? I don't want my face on the evening news."

"You stay in the house." Ben said. "Stay away from the windows. Pull the curtains. A telescopic lens can pick up a fly on a steer's rump."

Meg stood flattened against the living room wall. "They're here."

"Ben—I have to look. Just one quick peek," Katie promised.

"Just one quick peek," Ben mimicked. "You women *won't* let me do my job."

Four vans pulled up behind the two sheriff's cars blocking the private drive. Katie was thankful for the long driveway. At least the press couldn't get on the property. But her relief was short lived as one van broke away from the others and zoomed up the drive to brake in the front yard. The others followed. Soon the grass was trampled by people holding cameras and microphones, milling around and getting in each other's way. Ben would have to move them back to the road.

Meg had left the wall to turn on the television set. "Look, there we are."

A picture of the ranch flashed on the screen. An earnest-looking woman whose name Katie couldn't remember stared into the camera. "A private source says that Clara Townsend, Senate candidate, has been hiding from her husband in a remote corner of Wyoming. Mrs. Townsend allegedly has been the object of domestic abuse and has taken refuge in a private shelter for battered women. The question is what impact will this have on the election, only days away? Both parties are in turmoil over this revelation. We go now to Maggie Whitecliff, with our onsite crew. Maggie, are you there?"

The view switched to a dark-haired woman dressed in a red jacket and black pants, makeup professionally done, smiling into the camera. Katie recognized her as a member of the media who was standing outside her front door.

"Thank you, Kari. We're here at Candlelight, the shelter where Clara Townsend has allegedly taken refuge. No one has seen Mrs. Townsend, but we have it from a reliable source that she is inside."

Meg switched channels where another anchorwoman repeated the same story. Katie sighed. "I guess we're in lockdown mode. I'll have to talk to them eventually, but I'll put it off as long as possible."

Ben scribbled on a legal pad. "We need to get our story straight." He rubbed a hand over his chin. "You got any coffee?"

"I'll get it," Janet volunteered. "You and Katie can plan strategy."

We should be so lucky, Katie thought. Maybe Ben knew what to do.

She was fresh out of ideas.

At the Tates, Tottie stood at the kitchen window, eyes taking in the neat corrals and the well-kept house and yard. It was a man's home, with none of the fancy touches a woman would have added. Warren wasn't a happy host. So far he'd allowed Clara to retire to the comfort of the guest room, where Tottie figured the politician was on the phone plotting with her campaign staff about how to handle the unexpected crisis.

Warren slumped in a leather recliner, brooding. Tottie left the window and sat down on the sofa. "Why are you so upset about this? I'd think you'd want to help Katie out of a bad situation."

"Katie shouldn't have gotten herself into this situation. I could have told her that woman was trouble. Her kind always is."

"What do you know about her kind?"

"All I need to know. She doesn't have a thought beyond herself."

The housekeeper frowned. "This isn't about Clara. It's about the shelter. The other women are in danger too, and they don't have Clara's resources. They can't afford to be found."

"Maybe it would be best if they were discovered. They could go home to their husbands, and Katie could focus on taking care of herself."

Tottie fixed him with chilly stare. "You don't mean that. And if you do, shame on you. Katie is doing her best to help these women. You could be more supportive."

Warren sat up straighter. "And you need to mind your own business."

"Katie *is* my business."

He fell silent, then nodded. "You're right. I was out of line. I'm sorry, but you know I've tried to help Katie. She's too much like her grandfather. Bullheaded. If these emotionally crippled women didn't occupy her time, Katie would be able to spend more effort on us — me and her, and a future together."

"Warren, consider all the good things she's done for the shelter and for the community. People here respect Katie, and she's earned that respect. Her goodness will only enhance a future with you. Why do you stand in her way?"

"A person can only be 'savior to all' when he or she has the money to indulge. Katie doesn't have it. That shelter is on its last legs financially, and when it goes down, Katie will lose her shirt. Why can't you see that I'm thinking of Katie's welfare, and possibly you're not?"

Tottie slapped both hands on the side of the chair. "You arrogant, mule-headed heathen. God helped Katie open Candlelight, and if he wants it to succeed, he'll see that it does. And Katie is a praying woman. God takes care of her, and there's no one, Warren, *no one* on this earth who cares for that woman more than I do. So *shove* your pity, mister, and listen to common sense. Katie won't ever give up on that shelter, so if you want a future with her, you best stick that in your craw and chew on it."

His mirthless laugh was anything but agreeable. "If that pack of reporters spots her, the shelter will be a thing of the past. She'll get so much bad press out of this situation, she'll be forced to shut down."

With a disgruntled snort, Tottie shoved out of the chair and left the room.

⚜

Katie woke the next morning to sounds of copters, satellite trucks, and complete chaos at the end of the drive. Ben had quickly dispersed the news hounds to public property. She'd spent the night in her chair, Ben on the sofa. They had talked into the wee hours, but came up with no clear-cut plan on how to handle the media. Last night the story had dominated the news. CNN and Fox were putting a new slant on the special reports. Talking heads were now portraying Clara as a helpless victim.

Katie went into the kitchen to start coffee. She flicked on the small TV on the kitchen counter and found *Good Morning America*'s Diane Sawyer talking about Neil Townsend, pinpointing his life and the abuse he had heaped on Clara. Ben joined Katie, taking the cream out of the refrigerator. Katie yawned. Staying up all night had taken a toll on her. Meg had crept into the living room to join them around midnight, listening as they tried to form a plan. Katie had finally sent her back to bed around four a.m.

Ben indicated the television. "You got to hand it to Clara. Her campaign managers have done a heck of a job on damage control. She'll wind up with the sympathy vote and win by a landside."

Katie took bacon and eggs from the refrigerator. "Is that possible?"

"Anything is possible in politics. Remember a few years back when Missouri elected a dead man to the Senate? Mel Carnahan was killed in a plane crash, and with the media's help, he won the race. His widow served in his stead."

"So you think something similar will happen in Clara's case?"

"It's possible. After breakfast we'd better meet with the reporters and give them a story. They're going to stay until we give them a reason to leave."

Wincing, Katie shook her head. "I'm not looking forward to that." She turned the sizzling slices of bacon.

The women gathered, and when they finished eating, Ben and Katie stepped outside to face a solid wall of men and women with cameras and microphones. A good number held notepads. Katie took a deep breath, grateful for Ben's steady support.

A reporter thrust a microphone at Katie. "I understand Clara Townsend is here. Would you like to comment on that?"

Katie shook her head. "Your information is wrong. Mrs. Townsend is not here."

"Then where is she?"

"All I can say is that she isn't here."

"You run a women's shelter. Is that correct?"

Ben had told her to answer without lying, and she was doing her best. "That's correct, a shelter for women and horses. We have four horses recovering from the semi accident a few weeks ago. They've coming along nicely, and their plight would make a wonderful human interest story."

"Horses?" The woman frowned. "What about Clara Townsend?"

Ben spoke up. "Miss Addison has told you the truth. Clara Townsend is not on the premises; however, you people are trespassing. You need to move off the property before I arrest you. You'll have to look for Mrs. Townsend elsewhere. Your information isn't correct."

Grumbling broke out, but the press began to pack up and move out. Katie watched from the window as the final van pulled away. Behind her the television rehashed the story, repeating the same skimpy details over and over.

She reached for Ben's hand. "Thanks. You handled that well."

He smiled, a tired effort, and squeezed her hand. "You need to get some rest."

"Not until you do."

"That may be awhile."

"I'm in no hurry." The sudden warmth she felt for this man overpowered her. Maybe it was lack of sleep, or the rush of adrenalin, or whatever, but Warren paled when she compared the two men's compassion.

"Look, there's Clara's husband on TV," Ruth exclaimed. "What did she ever see in him?"

Katie turned in time to see Neil Townsend walking out of his Washington office, holding a newspaper to conceal his face. One persistent reporter must have gotten under his skin, because he turned and snarled, "I'll tell *you* things about Clara Townsend you don't know."

The camera switched back to the regular newscast.

Bitter, the talking heads said. Vindictive.

The phone rang and Katie went to answer. Tottie's voice came over the line. "Is it safe to come home? I'm tired of listening to Warren and Clara carp at each other."

"All clear. Do you want me to come get you?"

"No, let Warren bring me. Maybe a ride in fresh air would do him some good. Sweeten his disposition."

"He needs one of your cherry pies to sweeten him up."

"He'll not likely get one of my pies anytime soon."

"Come on, Tottie. He's just grumpy because he moved back here for peace and quiet and has very little. Can you blame him for being testy? And you know Clara gets under his skin. He's really a nice guy."

"I suppose I can't blame him, but I wish the man would get over whatever's eating him."

Katie hung up, grinning at the thought of Warren and Clara cooped up together for twenty-four hours. Ben got up and reached for his hat. "I have to get back to the office. I've done all I can here. If the press return, call and let me know."

"I will—and thanks for the help."

"No problem." He settled the hat on his head. "It may be the one and only time I'll ever spend the night with you."

"Yeah?" She waved a piece of crisp bacon under his nose and jumped when he snapped it up.

He'd been a blessing last night. There was a lot of *nice* about him, characteristics she hadn't noticed. Like the way he grinned when something wasn't meant to be funny or the way his expression would turn dead serious when she'd attempted to wow him with her sparkling, spontaneous sense of humor, which he apparently didn't conceive to be spontaneous or humorous.

She had a hunch they could have been a great pair in their earlier years.

Seventeen

Warren phoned later, and Katie listened to his list of Clara grievances. "You've got to get rid of her, Katie. I can't stay outside day and night—though that's preferable to being with her."

"What's she done now?"

"What hasn't she done? Taken over my house, dominates the conversation, and we don't have the same political views. I make her smoke outside in the metal shed, and she's highly ticked."

"So don't talk politics. Change the subject and ask her to smoke in the well house. She wouldn't like that either, but it is a concrete building, and she wouldn't be visible."

"The woman is obsessed with government. She lives, eats, and breathes it. She comes across as concerned, but let me tell you, that broad is hard as nails. She'd sell Neil Townsend down the river to save her own neck and never shed a tear."

"Please don't call her a broad."

"She is a broad."

His gruff, blustery tone disturbed Katie. The whole situation had been hard on him, and she regretted that she was the primary cause of his distress. But *broad* was a disrespectful term in her opinion. The whole cauldron was her fault. If she had been able to keep Clara in line, the press might not have found her so easily.

Maybe in the end, it would all work out for the good. Clara, though probably as guilty as Neil, could now finish her campaign and go home and the shelter could return to normal. The holidays were fast approaching and Katie, for one, would be glad when this whole mess was over. Everyone would be glad. Only one good thing could be said of the invasion. Clara had certainly livened up Little Bush. This was the most excitement they'd had since the high school basketball team won the state playoffs.

Needless to say, Warren was eager for his guest to check out. "It amazes me how the press plays Neil Townsend as a crooked scoundrel and Clara as Mother Teresa."

Katie couldn't quite picture Clara in the simple white sari Mother Teresa had adopted to identify herself with the poor. The true extent of the woman's involvement in her husband's activities might never be known, but Katie wouldn't be surprised to learn in later years that she had known and probably orchestrated much of Neil's criminal activity.

"Well, you know the media," she said. "Anything to boost ratings."

"You're lucky to have kept her hidden this long. It was only a matter of time before they found her."

"Right. Look, Warren, I know she can be a headache, but can you keep her a little longer, at least until we can arrange a way to get her away from Little Bush?"

"Katie, I'll do it for you, but you do something for me. You think about closing that shelter. Everyone thinks I'm the bad guy, that I'm should be looking after your interests. The truth is I am looking after your interests. I care for you, Katie, and I care if you're in danger. Your friends can accuse me of being thoughtless and heartless, but to tell you the truth, you're all I care about. You. Not those other women. Is that a crime?"

"Of course not, and I'm flattered by your concern."

Maybe everyone had been coming down too hard on him. He was gruff, but he was sincere in his feelings for her. He was worried about her. In spite of all his complaining, he was an old softie.

"Clara's in touch with her people. When it's safe to go, she'll be gone."

"Can't be too soon to suit me."

Katie grinned. With the aggravation removed, Warren would be more likely to resume what had been a tenuous but growing attraction between them.

Please, Lord. I've waited patiently for the right man, the man you wanted me to have, and I sense Warren is that man. Help me to help heal his hurts, and to show him that not all women are devil spawns.

Though Clara Townsend must surely have reinforced his misgivings, given a chance Katie would show him how wrong he could be.

After Warren hung up, Katie checked the locks and switched off the living room lights. She'd go to bed early for a change. The past few days had sapped her energy. She looked forward to a sound night's sleep without keeping an ear tuned for intruders.

She climbed between flannel sheets, wiggling her toes in search of warmth from the hot water bottle. Peace felt so heavenly. The women had all gone to bed early, drained by the day's activity.

Thank you, God, that through your grace I was able to protect them. Not one name had escaped from the shelter to the press. The women were safe. She, Katie, was safe. But Warren's plea dwelled in her mind. How soon would another, then another incident come along that would frighten her and threaten the women's safety?

Close the shelter, Katie.

How can I walk away from women in need, Lord? I promised you that I would always help whomever and whenever I could.

Close the shelter, Katie.

Is that you, Lord, or Satan speaking? Sometimes when she wanted something and felt agreement, it was hard to tell who was doing the talking.

She was too tired to argue. If Warren refused to help her, refused to work with her until she could pull out of the crisis, she would be forced to close.

Her eyes drifted shut. Tomorrow she would appeal to his compassionate side again, convince him that she could adapt, she could operate efficiently. Given enough time.

That was the key to her problem. Time.

Eighteen

During the night, Katie heard someone stirring in the house and got up to investigate. Ruth sat at the kitchen table nursing a mug of tea. She looked up when Katie approached, eyes reddened and tears dampening her cheeks. Katie took a mug from the cabinet, heated water in the microwave, and then dropped a tea bag of Sleepy Time into the cup, figuring it might help. Only when she was seated across the table from Ruth did she speak.

"Bad night?"

Ruth swiped at tears. "It's this media circus. It has me on edge."

Katie took a sip of tea. "It will be over soon. The election is in a couple of days, and Clara will leave. You don't have to be afraid."

Ruth wordlessly shook her head. "I'm just so apprehensive. My husband can't know where I am. He just can't."

"And he won't." They sat for a minute in silence. Then Ruth glanced at Katie. "Pictures of the shelter are all over the news. It's not a secret anymore. I'm afraid ..."

"That your husband will see them and come investigate?"

Ruth nodded. "I can't go back to him, Katie. I can't."

"You don't have to."

"I left my daughter behind because I knew if I didn't, he'd come after me and possibly harm me and take my baby somewhere I could never find her. Right now I know where she is. As soon as I can afford a top-notch lawyer, I'll fight to get her back. But for now I can't let him know where I am. I know he would never hurt the baby, but he's vindictive, and he knows that baby is my life. He'll make sure I never see her again, and if he finds me ..." She visibly shuddered.

"That's not necessarily true. We do have courts, and no judge in his right mind would choose Bill over you to have custody of that child. And you're forgetting about God and trusting that he has you in his sight."

Ruth's eyes brimmed with bright tears. "What if Bill takes her and leaves the country? It happens. You know it does."

Katie had thought of that, and she couldn't argue. It did happen — all too often, and the media wasn't helping the odds.

"I can't guarantee anything, you know that, but the shelter has never had such an occasion."

Ruth wiped her eyes. "But there's always a first time."

"It's in God's hands, Ruth, and he knows what's best. Trust him." When it came down to it, what choice did they have? Believe the worst or pray for the best.

"I do trust, Katie. I know he led me here. But now all of this has come up, and it's just not fair that we should be put in jeopardy because of Clara. She'll be reelected and leave without a backward glance, not caring if she's turned our lives upside down. The shelter is already in financial trouble, and I have nowhere else to go."

Katie reached out and touched Ruth's hand. "This isn't a state-run shelter. It's private, and if anything happens to Candlelight, your judge will see that you're placed somewhere safe. I know Clara seems hard, but God can use anyone, even someone like Clara. We don't know how this will play out. She hasn't won the election yet, and I suspect that she's been sent here for a reason. I can't know that for certain, but I have a sense about this." She couldn't believe that God sent trouble just to make trouble.

"You know what? This is hateful of me, but I'm not sure I want her to win." Ruth offered a wavering smile. "We were getting along so well before she came."

Katie grinned. "Well, she's not here now, so let's enjoy the peace and quiet."

Ruth laughed, then sobered. "Katie? I know I said I wouldn't go back to Bill, but if it was the only way to save my daughter, I would. You know that."

"I know. Ultimately, that's your decision, but you know what will happen. You're a smart woman."

"I'm a woman who loves her child." She drained her cup and got up from table. "I'd better go back to bed. Tomorrow is another day in the Candlelight soap opera. Wonder what it will bring."

"Nothing, I pray. Just good ole peace and quiet. "

Ruth rinsed her cup and left the room. The helicopter had gone away for the night, and a blessed silence wrapped the house. The news crews were still camped across the road, and she felt under siege. But it *would* soon be over, one way or another.

Tottie came into the kitchen, yawning. "You still up?"

"I thought I heard something and came downstairs. Ruth was having a cup of tea, so I joined her."

She nodded. "Think I'll have one too. I'm having trouble going to sleep."

"You'd think we'd be exhausted after the long day."

"Running on nerves. We're too keyed up to sleep." The microwave dinged, and Tottie removed her cup of hot water. "We'll all be glad when this is over."

"Did you clean Warren's house today?"

"Clara isn't the neatest woman in the world, I can tell you that. Drops things all over the house, eats and leaves a mess. She's about to drive Warren up a wall."

"She's used to having people wait on her. Probably has servants and aides and all of that."

Tottie removed the tea bag from her cup and sat down at the table. "You know, sometimes she isn't all that bad. In fact, get her off to herself without Warren around, and she's nice enough. She's had a hard time. I know she's spoiled, used to having her own way, but she was raised poor. Clara has had to work her way up the chain, and it hasn't always been easy."

"And then she was unfortunate enough to marry an abuser."

"She's not the first woman to make that mistake." Tottie took a sip of tea, her manner preoccupied. "You know there's more than one kind of abuse. There's physical, but there's mental and emotional abuse too. I think Clara has been emotionally abused as well as physically."

"Sometimes that leaves the deepest scars."

"It's true."

Tottie was silent for a minute, and from her expression Katie could tell she was in serious thought. Finally she looked up. "You think we can hold on to the shelter?"

"I don't know. Warren wants me to close it. He thinks keeping it open is dangerous."

"It can be, but nowhere is safe these days. People get killed working in a post office or convenience store. I don't suppose it's any more dangerous than anywhere else, if you really think about it."

"I told him I'd consider closing, but I can't bring myself to seriously think about it. It's so much a part of my life."

Tottie nodded. "Guess when all is said and done, you owe it to your grandparents' memory to save it if you can."

Yes, of course, and without Tottie's help, physically and financially, she could have never opened the establishment. She had been left the ranch in an agreement of trust. Her grandparents had worked hard to build up this property. She couldn't betray their confidence. Somehow she had to find a way to keep it and the shelter too.

Tottie moved the mug, creating wet circles on the table-top. "What if Neil Townsend isn't behind the harassment? What if it's someone you've never considered?"

"I guess we'll soon know," Katie admitted. "If Clara leaves and the harassment stops, then it was Neil."

"And if it resumes, it wasn't Neil."

Katie glanced up. "You don't think it's over?"

"I didn't say that, but we can't know for sure. Anything is possible. You're trusting, Katie. You may have an enemy you don't know about. A deadly enemy."

Coldness washed over Katie. A killing frost. "It has to be Neil Townsend. Who else can it be?"

Tottie shook her head. "I have no idea, and maybe you're right and it is Townsend. I'm just saying we can't drop our guard until we know for certain." She got up and carried her cup to the sink. "I'm going back to bed. Tomorrow's another day. If I'd known I was going to be a TV star, I'd have lost a few pounds before the cameras arrived."

Nineteen

The phone shrilled before daybreak. Startled from a sound sleep, Katie fumbled for the receiver. Sleep tinted her voice. "Yes?"

Ben's friendly timbre greeted her. "Sorry to call so early, but we need to move quickly on this. I've arranged for Clara to move to Whispering Springs—"

"In Cope?" Cope was bigger than Little Bush by a few hundred people, but it was a safe distance away.

"They can accommodate her, and the place is so remote, it's unlikely the press will find her before the election."

Katie sat up clearing her throat. "How will we move her without the reporters spotting her?"

"Here's the plan: dress her like Bobbi Weller."

Jodi Weller's sixteen-year-old? It could work. Bobbi's "Britney Spears" obsession was about to ruin her. Any tasteless bit of fashion to hit the streets drew her like a magnet.

"Bobbi runs errands for you, doesn't she?"

"Occasionally." Before Warren put a stop to the unnecessary expense.

"Then it shouldn't raise suspicion if Tottie left and came back with Bobbi, then half hour later came out of the house with Clara dressed in Bobbi's clothes, would it."

"No — it could work. Clara is small like Bobbi. And Bobbi has black hair, and Clara has a black wig."

"She has a wig? Great. Can you get Bobbi?"

Katie glanced at the darkened window. "It isn't daylight, Ben." Good grief. Without telling the Wellers the whole messy story, she couldn't show up on their doorstep at this ungodly hour requesting that their daughter run an errand for her on a school day.

"Get around as early as you can. We have to shake the press. The town is getting antsy with the disturbance. My phone's been ringing off the hook."

"I understand."

Ben clicked off without saying good-bye. Katie fumbled the receiver back on the cradle, then groaned and yanked the sheets over her head.

Katie waited until six o'clock to call the Wellers. Jodi, Bobbi's mother, answered the phone. "Katie? You're up early. What's wrong?"

"Nothing. I need Bobbi to do something for me. I'll pick her up, and then when she's through, I'll take her to school."

Jodi's tone had a frown. "What do you need Bobbi for this early in the morning? Can't it wait until after school?"

"No, actually, it can't." Katie searched for a plausible reason why Jodi Weller should allow her to pick up Bobbi at six-thirty in the morning. She didn't blame the woman's reservation.

"Look, Jodi. You know the situation we have out here."

"How could I not know? It dominates every television channel day and night."

"Well, I need Bobbi for something involved with that. I'll take care of her, I promise."

Silence.

"Jodi?"

"I'm thinking. Katie, I really don't want Bobbi's picture all over the television screen. It's not safe."

"I agree, and she won't be, I promise." That word again. Hopefully she could deliver. She didn't want to expose Bobbi to the pitiless eye of the camera either.

Jodi sighed. "All right, Katie. I trust you. I guess it will be all right."

"I appreciate it. I really do. Tell Bobbi I'll be there in a few minutes."

Bobbi downed the last of her cereal when Katie arrived. She calmly buttered a piece of toast and swigged milk. "I'll be ready in a sec."

Katie glanced at her watch. "I don't have a sec. We need to leave right now."

Bobbi's expression turned rebellious, but Katie gave her a stern glance. The teenager rolled her eyes and then drew a deep breath. "Fine." She shrugged into her coat, pulled on her backpack, and grabbed her toast. "Let's go."

Once in the car, Bobbi munched her toast, not speaking, which was fine with Katie. At this point, she didn't have anything to say.

Bobbi finished her meal, took a tube of something shimmery out of her pea-sized purse, and swiped it across her lips. Her dark hair was longer than Clara's, but hopefully no sharp-eyed reporter would catch the minor detail.

"I'll miss cheerleading clinic."

"I promise to have you in class no later than ten."

"Too late." She sat back and stuck a piece of sugarless gum into her mouth. "Practice is over at 8:30."

Katie stepped on the gas, her thoughts focused on Ben's earlier summons. Even with Clara dressed like Bobbi, how did the sheriff intend to divert the reporters' attention? At this point, they were suspicious of anything. Bobbi perked up when they passed the reporters who were on the job, cups of steaming brew in their hands. The coffee shop was experiencing a financial boom from the hullabaloo.

"Am I going to be on television?"

"I hope not. I promised your mother you wouldn't."

The teenager's expression fell. "But it would be awesome. Everyone would be so jealous."

"Sorry, won't happen." Katie hit the gas and zipped up the drive to park in front of the house. A stock trailer was backed up to the barn, and Ben's deputies were in the process of loading the injured horses. The barn lot was a beehive of activity.

Katie exited the jeep, pulling the hood of her coat up closer. A sharp wind cut through her. Ben approached, removing his leather gloves. He was dressed in a khaki uniform and a black ball cap with the letters SHERIFF emblazoned across the top. His cheeks and ear tips glowed with winter's bite.

Katie huddled against the blowing wind. "What's going on? Why are you loading the horses?"

"Need to borrow them for a day or two."

"Why?"

He paused, smiling. "We need a distraction in order to move Clara." His gaze located the jeep. "I see you have Bobbi."

"I promised I'd have her in school by ten."

"No problem. Clara arrived here a few minutes ago."

"How? Without being seen?"

"Arrived in a U-Haul truck. The shelter just received a new mattress donation."

"Really!" They could *use* a new mattress!

"Not really. Warren purchased one recently and still had the box in the garage."

"Rats."

"Take Bobbi into the house, then have her switch clothing with Clara. Come out again in fifteen or twenty minutes with Clara dressed as Bobbi. Get in the car and drive away. Take the main highway to the school allowing the reporters to keep you in sight. Let Clara out at the school and tell her to walk through the main hallway and meet you at the back exit. I've already spoken with the principal, so they know what's going on. Pick Clara up at the back exit and take her to the Conoco station. I'll arrange for one of my men to transport her to Whispering Springs."

"Who'll take Bobbi to school?"

"Tottie will, once we pull this off."

"What if she doesn't have a change of clothing in her backpack?"

"She'll have something."

Right. The girl was a hound for fashion and changed clothes as often as a woman changed her mind. "Where's the press while all this is taking place?"

"Keeping an eye on the horses. Janet will come out dressed in Clara's clothing and get in the back of the trailer with them."

A giggle escaped Katie at the image of Janet hunched on hay bales surrounded by horse poop, all for Clara's sake. "Then what?"

"I've arranged for a friend to take the horses for a couple of days. He'll take good care of them, Katie. He's a vet. Janet will ride back with me, and I'll deliver her to the shelter late tonight."

"What does Warren think of the plan?" He'd have to love it. He'd be rid of Clara and the confusion.

"Haven't talked to Romeo. I'll let you handle that." Ben turned and headed toward the activity.

"You don't believe he'll want to help her leave. He can't wait until she leaves!" Katie accused.

His reply was a barely perceptible lift of shoulders.

She reached for her cell and hit speed dial. Warren answered on the first ring.

"Hi."

"Is she leaving?" He didn't have to mention names. Katie knew he was referring to Clara—and they weren't talking about garbage. They were talking about a woman in trouble.

"She's being moved practically as we speak." She filled him in on the plan and how Ben thought it would work.

Silence. Then, "She's not coming back here, Katie."

"Warren—"

"I mean it. I wash my hands of the whole mess."

Katie closed her eyes. *God, tenderize his heart. Not all women are bad. Not all women are Clara or the woman who hurt him. Grant me the ability to show him the difference.*

"I know she's been a pain, and I'm deeply indebted to you for giving her shelter. After today, she won't be a problem."

"I wash my hands of it, Katie. I left New York because of the hassle, and I don't want it brought here. That's what the shelter does—you do know that? This was a quiet town until you brought those women here."

"I know. I'm sorry and I understand." Though she didn't. Not one shred of this attitude. Warren assumed that all women were bad, that all women were out to hurt and fleece a man. Granted, Clara wasn't the warmest guest or as pure as the driven snow in deed and thought, but Katie encountered moments when she saw through the thick protective veneer to the real woman. Clara was just a woman who wanted what most women want. Love. Acceptance. Security and respect.

Katie glanced at Bobbi, who was clearly restless. "I have to go — would you like to come by the shelter tonight for dinner?" She owed him a good meal if nothing else. Maybe something homemade would soothe his frayed hackles. "We're having meatloaf."

"Not tonight. I'm going to bed early."

"We're having mashed potatoes too."

His tone softened. "One night next week, I promise. And I promise to be in a better mood. I know I've been a jerk, Katie, but I can't stomach Clara or her kind. The incident has disturbed the whole town, and I'm sick of it."

That he'd made evident.

"Sure, one night next week." She hung up thinking she'd take what she could get so she could soften the man's irrational dislike of women.

God, you've sent me a work in progress, but that's okay. I'm content with your choice and I thank you.

Warren wouldn't shed his baggage easily. His wounds were still too fresh, too new, but eventually he would come around. Katie had thrown him into the lion's den with her financial problems, the shelter, and Clara. No wonder he was so antsy. All she had to do was think of his smile, his smarts, and the way he had been willing to help her at first. She knew that waiting for the right man—the man God created for her, wasn't a burden but a blessing, a show of faith.

The old gypsy woman surfaced to mind, and she quickly dismissed her. Katie did not believe her circumstances had *anything* to do with the present situation—but the prediction was eerily close . . .

Bunk. All she had to do was convince Warren that he had chosen his first love unwisely. Then they could form a deep and lasting relationship—or try.

She circled the jeep to the passenger seat and opened the door. Bobbi blew a bubble. "What's the hangup? What did you want me to do?"

"Come with me." She could just imagine Bobbi's reaction when she was asked to hand over her clothing to Clara Townsend.

But the plan went without a hitch.

Bobbi had a pair of gym shorts in her backpack, and when she put on her long coat, the inappropriate dress wasn't noticeable. Katie was forced to explain what was happening, and Bobbi quickly jumped aboard the ruse.

"I'll call Mom and tell her to bring me an extra set of clothes to school. She won't mind."

Clara was less cooperative. When she put on Bobbi's miniskirt and slashed-neckline blouse, she shook her head, uttering disgust. The black wig she'd worn on arrival went back on. Black boots and voila! She could pass for a teenager—from the air or at the end of the barn lot where the reporters waited.

Fifteen minutes later, Katie and Clara, dressed as Bobbi, walked out of the house and got into the jeep. A helicopter hovered overhead, but Katie started the engine, adjusted the rearview mirror, and a minute later drove off. The helicopter

turned and followed while Ben and his deputies finished loading horses into the stock trailer. Camera lenses moved from
Katie and the teenage girl back to the horse activity.

As they reached the group of reporters clustered at the end
of the drive, Clara leaned forward, fiddling with the radio
dials; the long black hair of her wig swung across her cheeks
like a curtain. The helicopter circled over the horse trailer,
claiming the reporter's attention. They let the jeep through
without a second glance.

Following orders, Katie pulled up in front of the high
school shortly before ten o'clock. Clara bounded out, slamming the door. Looping her arms through Bobbi's backpack,
she blew a bubble and popped it. Then she turned and sidled
up the walk. Katie drove off.

Katie circled the building, and the jeep sat idling as Clara
emerged from the other side. She got in the back seat and lay
down, pulling a blanket over herself.

Back on the highway, Katie pulled into the Conoco station and waited until two large semis tunneled the pumps.
She squeezed the jeep between the two trucks and got out.

"Can you get any *closer*, lady?"

Her cheeks colored, but she ignored the trucker's remark.
She zipped her credit card through, selected the gas grade, and
then began to pump.

Clara cracked the door open, looked around, and then
shimmied into a waiting car at the opposite pump. The car
drove off with Ben's plainclothes deputy at the wheel and
pulled onto the highway.

As easily as that, Clara Townsend was on her way to a
new shelter.

Around three o'clock, Katie flipped on CNN. The breaking news banner scrolled across the bottom, and a news commentator broke into the programming. Katie backed into a chair to listen.

"Breaking news regarding Neil Townsend, former presidential campaign manager. NBC has learned that Townsend was taken into custody one half hour ago. Viewers will recall the recent national search for Townsend's wife, senatorial candidate Clara Townsend, who's in a fight for a second term seat and was located in a battered women's shelter. It appears Senator Townsend has been hiding from her abuser, Neil Townsend. Information has been obtained concerning Neil Townsend's activity in illegal campaign contributions. Townsend is accused of helping to divert nearly two million dollars of state funds into his party's election campaign."

Shaking her head, Katie switched off the television. Relief filled her. It was over. Clara could leave the shelter and resume her campaign with a day left to bask in the unexpected turn of events. She was glad for the woman, but sad that one guilty party went free and pulled the wool over the voters' eyes, because Katie had serious doubts that Clara was unaware of her husband's illegal activities. It was possible that the knowledge was the central cause of the abuse, but then she would never know.

If only Katie's financial woes could be solved as satisfactorily as Clara's public problems, the shelter could grow, and she could get back to two lattes a day, a harmless pleasure to blunt the larger issues.

Twenty

At last, calm reigned. The press and whumping helicopters disappeared like snow on an April day. Katie breathed a sigh of relief, and then set about making the women feel comfortable, assuring them that the ugly event was behind them. Best of all, the horses were back.

Normalcy returned, and Katie had had enough excitement to last her a good long while.

She closed the door to her office and lifted the receiver. Warren had turned down her earlier dinner invitation, but he should be happy now. The crisis was over. Clara had left Cope, and today the voters would make their political choices at the polls. Katie wanted to resume the congenial footing she had with Warren BC (before Clara). She dialed his number and waited. He picked up on the third ring.

"I hope I didn't catch you at a bad time?"

"Not at all. What's up?"

"Nothing. I called to invite you to dinner tonight. Tottie is cooking a pot roast, and there's chocolate pie with whipped cream for dessert. We eat at six, which should give you plenty of time to get your work done."

"Can't, Katie. I'm not feeling that great. Think I'm coming down with a virus."

"You're sick?" How many excuses could a man come up with? But then again, a flu bug was still going around.

"I'm just lying here, don't feel like working, and I'd hate to make anyone else sick."

"Yeah, especially Meg. She just had a bout with a bug recently, and she's only weeks away from delivery."

"Then it's settled. I shouldn't be around her."

He sounded grumpy. Poor guy. He couldn't catch a break. Well, if Mohammed wouldn't come to the mountain, she'd come to him. Not that she could cure him, but Tottie's herb-laced chicken soup had speeded recovery for the other women. "Take care of yourself."

"Will do. Thanks for the invitation." The line went dead, and Katie shook her head. What man would take care of himself the way a woman would? She'd take him some soup and make sure that he was taking plenty of vitamins, maybe do a few of his outside chores.

Tottie was at the stove when Katie entered. "Do we have any chicken thawed out? I want to make a pot of soup to take to Warren. He's coming down with a bug."

"Land, tell him to stay far away from here." The housekeeper turned, holding a knife and a carrot. "He seemed fine yesterday."

"Well, he's sick today." Katie dug out the stainless steel soup pot and held it up for inspection. "Is this pot okay?"

"That'll work." If Tottie disapproved of Katie's act of kindness, Katie was thankful she kept it to herself. "There's a stewing hen in the freezer."

"Great. I'm going to vote before I take the soup to Warren."

Tottie nodded. "Did that early this morning."

"Think Clara will win?"

The housekeeper shrugged. "I voted for her."

A couple of hours later Katie backed out of the drive with a steaming pot of chicken soup sending fragrant vapors throughout the jeep. Warren would be feeling better in no time. The absence of the press was salve to her frayed nerves.

Katie pulled out to pass a tractor. She really needed to talk to Warren. The last few days had been amazing, and she wanted to sit down with him and rehash every aspect. The news media were making Clara out to be a heroine, and her reelection should be a breeze. Who would have thought it would turn out like this?

Katie voted at the Veteran's Hall then got back in the jeep and headed to the Tate place. Hammering caught her attention as she got out, balancing the pot of soup. Warren wouldn't be in the barn, feeling as badly as he did. Curious, Katie set the soup back on the floorboard of the jeep and followed the sound. When she stepped into the barn, she spotted Warren swinging a hammer, nailing a board onto a stall.

He stopped and straightened, then caught sight of her. For a split second he registered surprise, then irritation. "Well, look who's here."

"Hey. I brought you some soup." He didn't look flushed or indicate any kind of illness. His color was good.

He reached for another nail and hammered it home. "Be with you in a minute. The horses damaged the stall, and I want to get it fixed. Everything back to normal?"

"Pretty much so." No mention of the supposed illness. No embarrassing stammers that he'd been caught in a lie. "Neil Townsend has been arrested, and Clara is predicted to win her reelection bid. Everything has turned out okay. I'm relieved."

Warren nodded. "You were lucky this time." He whacked a nail. "Women like Clara can go to other shelters. Let someone else worry about them."

"Well, let's agree not to agree about that."

"Still gullible, I see. Women like that will never have a home. Women like that will always be attracted to losers." He whacked another nail. "Women like that are plain stupid."

Stupid? Her chin rose a notch, then two. "I'm a woman. Do you think that I'm stupid?"

He turned to look at her, heightened color creeping over his features. "No, of course not." He stepped closer, pulling her into his arms. "I don't think *you're* stupid. That's not what I meant."

"I'm a woman."

He grinned. "I noticed — and a darn fine one. Look, I know I'm hard-nosed about the subject, and I'm working on my attitude. Okay? I know I've got issues, and I need to let go of them. Tell you what, let's go to the house, and you can fix me a bowl of that soup. What'd you bring me?'

"Chicken noodle."

"My favorite."

He walked her to the jeep and carried the kettle of soup inside where she set the pot on the stove and reheated the soup. They sat at the table, talking as he ate. "This is great. Did you make it?"

"It's Tottie's recipe. I just followed it."

"Seasoned just the way I like it. Lots of black pepper."

"Warren." He'd kept silent about the lie, but she couldn't. "I thought you were ill."

"Yeah — craziest thing. An hour ago I felt like I was coming down with a bad case of something. But I took a hot shower, and I suddenly felt better."

"Really."

He glanced up. "Honest, Katie. I know I refused dinner at your house, but at the time I felt bad. Really bad."

She could heighten the situation and argue that he felt good enough to work on the barn, but she didn't. Sometimes a hot shower did do wonders.

They chatted about community affairs, not touching on the shelter or his averted illness again. Later curled in his arms before a roaring fire, Katie sighed with contentment. "I'm so glad that the harassment is over. I'm sure all the strange incidents were just Townsend trying to get back at Clara. There's no reason for his cronies to bother me any longer."

"I hope you're right."

There was a moment of silence, and Katie and Warren both realized what the other was thinking. Lips parted. He tasted of warm coffee and cream. She snuggled closer, and his mouth settled more firmly over hers. Odd that exploding rockets and blaring bands weren't spinning in her head. His kiss was expert; practiced and certainly without fault. Just odd that she didn't melt and run into her stockings, the way she expected she would feel when he finally got down to the business of romance, of kissing her with a purpose instead of a benign peck, or worse, an obligatory gesture that hinted of real interest. Popping fire, cozy room. Everything needed for a romantic evening between a man and a woman. Did it matter that John Philip Sousa and his marching band failed to materialize for her? He deepened the kiss, and she settled into his embrace. Relationships took time, and theirs was still in its infancy. *Time, Katie.* Relationships took time to build and grow and flourish. Just because she had high hopes for the bond didn't mean that Warren reciprocated.

After the kiss, their conversation resumed as if it had never been interrupted.

"Of course I'm right, but I still wonder why a man as prominent and wealthy as Neil Townsend would want to jeopardize his career by pestering me."

"Katie." He playfully bonked her on the head. "Open your eyes. You were a threat to him. You had his wife, and he wanted her."

"I suppose that's the reason."

"I'm not saying it's right to hit a woman, but Clara might have had it coming."

She sat straight up. "You're not serious."

"Settle down, I didn't mean that in a threatening way, but some women can get real aggravating, Katie. You have to know that."

"And a man can't? I don't care how aggravating a woman — or a man becomes, no one has the right to use physical force. When you say things like that, Warren, I have to wonder where your mind is. I know you've been hurt by a woman. But you can't judge all women by your bad experience, and I really would appreciate it if you would stop making these kinds of remarks."

He chuckled, reaching out to soothe her. "That shelter is really a hot button with you, isn't it?"

"Violence, any violence against another person, is a hot button with me." Sometimes she plain didn't understand this man, and she was starting to wonder if she even cared to.

"You don't know the women's personal lives. You're meddling. If you stayed out of it, women like Clara would have to stay home and change their ways. They'd be forced to make their relationships work. Isn't that what God wants? A woman to stay with her man?"

Katie fumbled for her shoes, the fun evening suddenly not so fun. Warren caught her hand and stopped her. "Close the shelter. I have a bad feeling about that place, Katie. Please listen to me. Right or wrong, you can't change the way people think. Close the shelter before someone closes it for you. If not Neil Townsend, then someone else will come after you. Get out while you can."

A ripple of fear snaked up her spine, and for once she was tempted to consider his dire warning. Perhaps he did care, and in some strange way he sensed danger where she didn't. The thought scared her even more than the gravity of his tone.

Twenty-One

Late that night, the women gathered around the television set focused on the talking heads predicting a landslide victory for Clara. From the way they gloated, you'd have thought the woman walked on water. The scene shifted to an earlier time, showing a group of steel workers. Meg jabbed a finger toward the set. "There's Clara."

"Where?" Janet leaned closer. "Oh, I see. Looks nice, doesn't she?"

She did indeed. Every hair coiffed, makeup perfect, poised and confident. She looked nothing like the woman who had caused so much upheaval. A reporter shoved a microphone close to her mouth. "Mrs. Townsend, if you're reelected will you see this as vindication of the accusations made against you?"

Clara smiled, Reese's-Pieces sweet. "I believe the American people know that I knew nothing about my husband's behavior. I'm deeply ashamed of what he has done and pray he will learn from his mistakes. You know, I can only say that if I had known, I'd have been the first to do something about it. If the people vote to send me back to the Senate, I'll represent them the best I know how."

"Smooth as butter, isn't she?" Tottie said with a tinge of admiration coloring her voice. "Never would have thought she could pull it off, but I think the polls are correct. She's going to be reelected. Philpot doesn't stand a chance."

Katie watched as Clara used all her charm to convince the reporters, and by extension, the voters, of her complete innocence. Charm oozed from every pore. Well, it was over, and Clara wouldn't dominate every newscast. Katie expected to be relieved, but to her surprise, she was too numb to feel anything. It had been so long since she felt safe. The feeling would take some getting used to.

Clara disappeared from the screen to be replaced by a blonde with long, straight hair whipping in the breeze. "As the polls begin to close, Neil Townsend is out on bail, but he will be facing numerous charges ..."

"Big deal," Meg chortled. "He'll buy his way out."

Katie shook her head. "I don't think so, Meg. Not this time."

Ruth agreed. "But you know what, I hope Clara wins."

Meg shrugged. "I know she was hard to get along with, but she was sorta cool in her own way."

"She put up a big front," Janet said.

Katie passed a bowl of popcorn. "Why do you think that?"

"Because she spent a lot of time on the side porch, and she wasn't always smoking. Sometimes she just sat and looked out over the landscape. She enjoyed the quiet."

Tottie shoved out of her chair. "She's better off in Washington. Maybe we can get back to normal now, whatever normal is."

Katie tuned out her surroundings. She hadn't heard from Ben today, and she wondered why. Now that the crisis had passed, had he decided to take her at her word and leave her alone? That's what she wanted, wasn't it?

That's what she'd wanted earlier. Now she wasn't so certain. Warren was getting to be more sarcastic than fun—

Katie! You're losing it. Concentrate on Warren's attributes.

❧

Meg switched on the television before the women sat down to breakfast the next morning. Tottie looked up from the stove and frowned. "I'll be glad when this election thing dies down. That's all those newspeople can talk about. Surely there's more than that going on in the world. Looks like the weather is going to turn bad again. Why don't they tell us more about that?"

"They will." Katie stuck a piece of whole wheat in the toaster. "Who runs our government is important—oh, by the way, Clara won."

Tottie sniffed. "Could have told you that."

For the life of Katie, she didn't know what Tottie had seen in Clara Townsend. She was usually a better judge of character. But then Tottie admired strong women.

"Hey, look at this," Meg called and Katie and Tottie left the kitchen to join the others. There was Clara, shaking hands with factory workers and handing out coffee and doughnuts.

"Making like a real politician, isn't she?" Meg rubbed her protruding stomach. "Got to hand it to her, she knows how to make an impression."

Katie eyed the televised image, wondering how Clara managed to look so perfectly put together at that hour of the morning. She was accepting her victory like a seasoned trooper. "I'm going into town this morning. Need anything, Tottie?"

Tottie returned to the kitchen and tore a sheet of paper off her scratch pad. "Here's my list. Don't buy anything that isn't on the list, and for the love of mercy, don't go near Warehouse Blowout."

Katie folded the list and tucked it into her jean pocket.

"Look, there's Clara again," Janet said. "I'll say one thing for her; she sure knows how to get around."

This clip showed Clara in front of a battered women's shelter. She peered into the camera, projecting an image of sincerity. "Believe me, I know what these women are dealing with. I've been there, and I promise them and you that I will do all I can to initiate stronger and more forcible legislation against wife batterers."

"You go, girl," Meg said.

Katie had another take on it. She resented what Clara was doing. It was one thing to try to win an election but something else entirely to use women who had been abused to elicit future votes.

"They shouldn't have shown that," Ruth said. "That's two shelters that have been revealed because of politics. Don't they care about the women who are there?"

"Probably not," Janet said. "We're not important. Just flotsam washed up on the shore."

She sounded bitter, and Katie knew she was thinking of her husband and the way he fooled people into thinking he was kind and compassionate. Now he was living a normal life and Janet was in hiding, trying to put her life back together. And she was right. It wasn't fair, but then life seldom was.

Later Katie braked in front of the grocery store. She stuck to the list and finished in less than fifteen minutes. She carried her purchases out to the jeep, which she locked from force of habit. A cold wind blew in heavy sleet then snow. By the time she left the market, the streets glistened with the wintry mix.

Katie spotted Jodi Weller, Bobbi's mom, parallel parking. They stopped to talk under the shelter of a shop's awning. "I was going to vote one way," Jodi said. "But after listening to Philpot, I changed my mind and voted for Clara."

Clara might have made a bad impression on the shelter women, but the sentiment hadn't carried over to others, Katie realized.

"You know her, Katie. Don't you think she's been badly mistreated?"

Katie was spared answering by Warren, who stepped over the curb to join them. "Nasty weather, isn't it? How are you ladies this morning?"

Jodi grinned. "Good, thank you. I trust the election results went your way?"

Warren's face turned expressionless. "Never talk politics or religion, ladies." Jodi left and Warren fell into step with Katie.

"Sometimes I think we made a mistake when we gave women the vote."

"I'm going to pretend you didn't say that."

He grinned, reaching over to tug her nose. "Touchy, are we? Your candidate won."

Katie shook her head and smiled. She didn't tell him she'd voted against Clara. She had great empathy for the woman's plight, but her compassion didn't bleed over into politics.

Warren continued to the barbershop, and Katie stopped at the cleaners, gave a covetous glance at the coffee shop, and then started back to the ranch.

A heavy wind rocked the jeep. The wipers could barely keep up with the mixture of wintry precipitation falling from the sullen sky. Katie checked the mailbox, shifted to four-wheel drive, and barely made it up the incline leading to the farmhouse. A light glowed in the kitchen window. She smiled, recalling the reason why she'd named the shelter Candlelight. The old house gave off an ambience, a gentle refuge from life's furious storms. This afternoon the sight welcomed her, and she knew how the women must have felt the day they arrived. All except Clara. What *had* Clara felt or thought? Had she grieved over a husband who beat her, or was she indifferent to pain? She had never shed a tear or uttered a single sympathetic comment to others unfortunate enough to walk her path. *Don't judge.* Sometimes it was a tough command.

The milk of human kindness had dried up in Clara Townsend. She wet nursed no one.

Katie sniffed the air as she got out of the jeep. *Roast.* Tottie was cooking dinner—new potatoes, carrots, and cheesecake for dessert. The women took turns picking dessert. Tonight Meg had the honors, and for sure there would be a cherry cheesecake with nine hundred calories in a slice languishing in the refrigerator.

How did the Golden Girls on the television sitcom eat *so* much cheesecake and not gain an ounce?

Lugging heavy grocery sacks up the slippery walk, Katie decided she should have pulled the jeep closer. Tire tracks wouldn't gouge the grass this time of year, and it would've made her job a lot easier. She was glad the horses were safely back home and in their warm stalls. Even Sweet Tea was inside the barn out of the driving wind.

After dinner, the storm raged around the eaves while the women washed and dried dishes. Katie suggested a game of dominos afterwards. A shutter banged against the siding on the back of the house, grating on her nerves. So many needed repairs and so few funds to make them.

Janet raised her head from contemplating a play. "Good thing the reporters aren't out in this. I didn't like having them here, but I wouldn't wish them any harm."

Katie reflected on just how downright nice these three women were. Warren was wrong. Maybe some women gave as well as they got, but others were pure victims. Meg shifted in a hard-backed chair, touching her rounded belly.

"Dominos giving you a pain?" Katie teased.

"No." She winced. "Just can't find a comfortable position."

Janet was down to her last domino. "Want me to rub your back?"

Meg smiled but declined. "I'm fine. I think I'll take a hot bath and go to bed early."

Ruth pushed back. "I'm with you. I couldn't get a good hand if I bought one." She paused, cocking an ear, listening. "Does anyone hear that?"

Katie looked up. "Hear what?" *Calm down. The threat is over. If there is a sound, it's wind- or storm-related.*

We're all safe now.

"That soft … creak. Like someone coming up the basement stairs."

Eyes pivoted to the closed basement door. Katie thought of the owl incident and grimaced.

Ruth pursed her lips. "I've heard it twice now. Hasn't anyone else heard it?"

"Loose shutters," Tottie admonished. "They've been banging all over the place. Have you just noticed?"

Meg pushed her empty chair up to the table. "I guess we can relax now."

"We can. The threat is over," Katie promised.

Janet shook her head. "No … not shutters. I heard that—the other sound."

Eyes swept the room double-checking locked windows before returning to Ruth. Katie spoke first. "I haven't noticed anything. What's it sound like exactly?"

Meg's facial features suddenly twisted, and she sucked in a quick breath. "Wow. I'm not sure, but that might have been a labor pain."

"Too soon!" Ruth blurted.

Tottie held up a calming hand. "Lightening—that's what they call it. It's the baby slipping into the birth canal. The birth is still weeks away."

Meg visibly relaxed, rubbing her belly. "Hurts."

The observation induced nervous laughter.

"Let's all get some rest." Tottie gathered up dirty glasses and set them in the sink. "If you have any trouble during the night, call me, Meg. I'm just two doors away."

Katie agreed. "The same goes for me. Call me if you need me."

"Thanks—I will." She winced and blew out short puffs. "Hurts, hurts, hurts!"

Katie turned out the living room lights, sparing a moment to peek out. The world was ice coated. Beautiful, but so treacherous. A horrible night to rush someone to the hospital to give birth. She dismissed the unthinkable. If anyone knew pregnancy, it was Tottie, and if she said the baby was slipping into the birth canal, Katie wasn't going to argue. She didn't know where babies went prior to birth.

The house quieted quickly. Katie crawled between floral-smelling flannel sheets and stretched for the hot-water bottle. She liked to tease that it was a true lesson in faith when people reached out and their needs were met. Tottie had found a good ministry—hot water. Katie closed her eyes, luxuriating in the moist warmth.

A shutter banged and her eyes flew open. *Ruth.* What had she been saying about a second noise? They hadn't explored the issue because of Meg's sudden discomfort. Had she heard something other than the loose shutter?

Get a grip. The threat is over. All is well. Normalcy at Candlelight Shelter had been restored. The noise was probably just ice-coated tree limbs creaking from the weight.

But Katie still strained every fiber, alert to imagined or real jeopardy. Wind howled through brittle branches. Sleet slapped windowpanes.

All is well. Go to sleep.

It was after one when she finally dropped into a fitful doze and dreamed of a faceless, shadowed figure who meant to harm her in some way. She struggled through snowdrifts, buffeted by the wind, and always followed by that macabre shadow ...

An icy hand touched her shoulder, and she bolted upright, screaming.

A tremulous voice jerked her fully awake. "Don't, Katie. It's me."

Katie fumbled for the bedside lamp, her heart pounding against her chest wall. The sudden glare of light revealed Meg standing beside the bed, her face as white as her robe. Outside, the storm growled, though surely with a decreased intensity.

Katie reached out to the trembling woman. "What is it, Meg? The baby?"

Meg shook her head, appearing to be on the verge of tears. "It's my room. Oh, Katie ..."

"Your room?" What was in her room that would upset her this way? Katie swung her legs over the edge of the bed, groping for her slippers. She reached for her robe, pulling it close around her shoulders. The blowing wind funneled through every tiny crack in the old farmhouse.

Katie put her arm around Meg. "Don't worry. Whatever it is, we'll fix it."

"I'm not sure you can."

Katie didn't pursue the topic. Obviously Meg was having a fitful night. An icy wind whistled around her bare legs. Where was a draft this strong coming from? As soon as she reached Meg's room, she had the answer. Wind and snow poured through a hole in the roof. Pieces of shingles and other debris lay on the floor. Katie put out one hand to touch the doorframe for support. The roof had collapsed. Was the weight of ice and snow that heavy? If so, was the rest of the house in danger?

Janet, Ruth, and Tottie bolted into the room, drawn by the freezing cold and the lash of wind. "Oh my." Janet clutched her robe to her neck. "How did this happen?"

Tottie swung into action. "Get towels and blankets. We'll sop up the worse of it. I'll get the broom and the kitchen trashcan and start cleaning up the mess. Watch out for nails and splinters. We don't want anyone getting hurt."

"I'm going to put on something warmer, and then I'll be back," Ruth said. "No point in all of us getting sick."

Katie nodded. "Good idea. Let's all put on warm clothing and shoes. This mess isn't going anywhere. It will be here when we get back."

It wasn't like anyone was going to sleep after this.

Katie hurried to her room to pull on jeans and a warm sweatshirt. While she was tying her shoes, she heard the furnace kick on. Well, of course. With the storm turning Meg's bedroom into a winter wonderland, the mechanical device would kick in. She added the cost of propane to roof repairs.

And where was she supposed to come up with all the money? Warren's budget didn't grant any leeway for a collapsed roof and a drained propane tank.

When Katie reached Meg's room, the others were already busy. Tottie was down on her hands and knees mopping icy water. "I turned the thermostat down as much as I could, and if we close the door and put a blanket across the bottom, maybe we can keep most of the cold in this room."

Katie nodded. "I'll get a blanket."

Tottie and Ruth picked up pieces of shingles and dumped them in the large kitchen trashcan. Janet stripped the sodden linens from the bed and bundled them in a soggy lump to take to the utility room. Katie sighed. Add the cost of a new mattress to the list, and she'd probably have to replace the carpet.

The storm seemed to have abated, or at least the wind was dying down. Katie paused to listen. It had shifted directions. Maybe the front had blown itself out. The horses. Had the barn withstood the brunt of the storm? The roof was high pitched. Had ice accumulated there the way it must have on the house roof? She needed to check.

Ruth brought the wastebasket from Meg's bathroom, dumping the litter into the larger trashcan. She and Janet wrung out soggy towels, using the wastebasket to catch the water. Katie swept up a dustpan full of snow, praying the worst was over.

Her gaze zeroed in on Meg, standing hunched over, holding her stomach. "You okay?"

The young woman shook her head. "No. Something's wrong."

"What do you mean *something's* wrong?" *Everything* was wrong! "What is it, Meg? You look like you're about to faint."

Meg's body arched, her jaws clenched, and it was obvious she was fighting pain. "Oh, Katie, I'm sorry to be so much trouble, but so help me, I think the baby's coming."

❧

"Ben? Katie. I need your help." Funny how this time there'd been no choice on who she called. Logically, she should have called Warren to assist them into town. He was closer, and right now time mattered. But after their evening alone, she wasn't sure she wanted him in a crisis. Especially a woman's crisis. He wouldn't be happy being called out of a warm bed in the midst of a blizzard to transport an unwed mother in premature labor to the hospital.

"I'm on my way."

Katie hung up, trying to wiggle feeling back into her feet.

Tottie had put Meg on the sofa, and she was timing her contractions. They stalled at seven minutes apart.

Meg latched onto Katie's hand. "I'm scared. Will the baby be okay ... it's way too early, right?"

Yes, way too early. That much Katie knew. But if they could get Meg to the hospital, the doctor might be able stop the labor and give the baby a few more weeks to develop.

"You'll be fine, Meg. God's on the job."

"He won't worry about me." She grasped her stomach and moaned. "I've never done anything but rebel against him."

"Well, now that's the nice thing about God. When he sent his only Son to die on the cross for my sins — and your sins, he didn't exclude anyone from his grace. Whosoever will come." Katie brushed hair away from the frightened girl's forehead. "If God carried a grudge, or put limitations on what he'd done on the cross, we'd all be in trouble."

Meg's hand tightened in hers. "Come with me to the hospital? I don't think I can do this alone."

"Of course. I'll be with you every step of the way."

Groaning, Meg rolled to her side, and Katie got up to look out of the window. Snow flew in furious bursts. She could barely see the outline of the barn roof. She couldn't check for ice, but Tottie would when Meg was on her way to the hospital.

Ben. How would he get here? The squad cars were big and heavy, but nothing much moved in this sort of weather.

Half an hour past. Forty-five minutes. Meg's contractions dropped to five minutes apart. This baby wanted to be born, though Katie couldn't imagine the world she'd be thrust into. Her father was a batterer who beat the child's mother senseless. Her mother was a young girl barely old enough to comprehend the facts of life, now in charge of another innocent life. What chance did this child have to survive all that the world could throw his way? What chance without the knowledge that God had a plan for his life and that he was a living, breathing, worthy soul sent for a purpose?

But for what purpose?

And who would be there to guide, teach, and love this baby as she grew into adulthood?

Could Meg, a child herself, begin to fill that role, or would circumstances and a string of bad choices defeat her before the process even began?

Please, God, help Ben get here.

Katie could picture him racing through the night, slipping, sliding, and risking his life on icy rural roads to meet a need. Her need.

A thought hit her. He hadn't even *asked* why she needed him.

He was accustomed to being at the public's beck and call.

That was it. He was accustomed to being awakened from a sound sleep by hysterical women.

The small hand on the clock edged closer to two a.m. Still no headlights appeared in the drive. Meg's pains were closer, three and half minutes apart. The young girl lay for awhile, and then got up to pace. The house was cold and miserable. Ruth, Tottie, and Janet, wrapped in wool blankets, took turns looking out the window.

Twenty-Two

Finally car lights flashed at the end of the drive. Katie grabbed her coat and raced to the back door. The sleet had frozen the screen shut. She banged her way free and braved the howling wind.

Her feet slipped and she went down. Grunting, she grabbed hold of a nearby stump and pulled up, losing her footing a second time and slicing her hand in the process. Fresh blood mingled with newly fallen snow.

She found a tissue in her pocket and wrapped it around the cut, then ran on.

When she reached the hill, Ben was at the bottom, kneeling at the back bumper.

"Where's the sedan?"

"It wouldn't make it on these roads. I borrowed Bill's pickup."

"Can you make it up the hill?" she shouted over the relentless storm.

"Can't — barely made it this far. The back wheels are stuck."

He slid back behind the wheel and revved the engine as he rocked the vehicle back and forth. On the third attempt, the wheels released from the heavy ice pack. Ben waved. "What's going on?"

"Meg's in premature labor! Can you get her to the hospital?"

He shook his head, then after a moment said, "It's rough going, but if I stick to the main road, I can get her there."

The main road would be the long way, but Katie didn't want to deliver the child here. "I'll get her!" She whirled and made her way back up the incline, slipping and sliding.

How will I get Meg down the hill without her falling? Dear God, I need mercy! If you'll help me and Ben get her to the hospital safely, I'll never think a bad thought about Ben ever again.

Tottie and Janet had the waiting Meg ready. She was bundled and padded so tightly that if she did fall she'd just roll without injury. Ruth, dressed in coat and boots, was ready to help. Katie took Meg's hand. "Ready?"

"As ready as I'll ever be." Her voice trembled like a leaf in a hurricane.

"Hang in there." A burst of snow blinded them when they maneuvered her out the back door. No one could hear above the shrieking wind. Katie took Meg's left side and Ruth her right side. The women started inching the mother-to-be down the incline. The whole world had turned into an ice skating rink. Boots slipped. Heavy tread shoes couldn't find traction. Ben climbed to meet them. Meg almost went down. Pausing, the sheriff scooped the bundled woman up in his arms and carried her the remaining distance.

Warm air rushed from the heater as Katie climbed into the front seat of the big GMC. Ben grabbed a blanket and wrapped it around Meg, taking a moment to say something to her. Katie couldn't hear the comment, but whatever he'd said seemed to calm her.

He slid behind the wheel and turned around in the middle of the drive. Then the three were off. Meg lay across Katie's lap, moaning. The pains were close now, dangerously close. Katie, pressed to Ben's side, whispered, "Do you know how to deliver a baby?"

Meg moaned.

"I've delivered my share."

"Thank goodness." She leaned back, breathing easier. Meg would be safe, barring complications.

The truck took a mean slide, but Ben managed the wheel and brought it around without incident. There were two hospitals in the area, Campbell County Memorial in Gillette or one in Sundance with a sixteen-bed unit. At this rate, they'd never make it to either one.

Little Bush's city limits came into sight, and Ben announced, "I'm calling Doctor Meadows."

Katie nodded. Doctor Meadows ran the local clinic and gave Meg her monthly checkups. The facility wouldn't have the needed equipment to treat a preemie, but the infant could be transported by air when the storm abated. Ben got on the CB and barked orders to a dispatcher to have the doctor at the clinic when they arrived at, he estimated, 2:45 a.m.

When the truck pulled in front of the clinic and braked, Ben was out in a flash to gather Meg in his arms. He was halfway into the lighted clinic by the time Katie caught up.

Twenty-Three

Doctor Meadows took one look at the situation and motioned for Ben to carry the patient to the examining room. Katie collapsed in a nearby chair, exhausted.

And worried.

And cold. Her feet felt like two snow cones. She wasn't sure she wanted to be a mother. It sounded terribly painful.

Ben emerged and took the chair beside her. Removing his hat, he ran his fingers through his hair. Katie noticed his hairline was receding, which was normal for a man his age, but he had nice hair. Thick. The color of red clay. "What does the doctor think?"

"He's given her a shot of ritodine to stop labor. She's got what? Four, five more weeks before her due date?"

Katie rested her head against the paneled wall. "Something like that. Poor kid. Trouble won't let her alone."

"Yeah, I feel sorry for her. She's scared."

Katie remembered she'd promised to stay with her. She got up, but Ben blocked her efforts. "Doc said he'd let us know when anyone could stay with her."

Katie sank back in the chair. "I need to call Tottie. They'll be wondering if we got here safely." But when she opened her cell, she saw there was no signal.

"Darn storm. The phone lines are down too." She pocketed the phone. Silence fell. They sat side by side waiting for news.

Ben fiddled with his watch. "Meadows alerted Sundance. They're prepared to receive the baby if it comes now. They'll send a copter when the storm lets up."

"Good." Meg had caught a break. "But he's trying to prevent the birth, right."

"Right."

More silence. Katie felt she should make conversation, but she had ignored Ben for so long, she didn't know what to talk about. Yet she desperately needed to thank him. She couldn't fathom what would have happened if he had not come to the rescue.

"Ben."

"Yeah."

"Thank you. I didn't explain why I needed you to come on such short notice and with the storm — well, you came anyway."

"That's my job."

Maybe, but Katie thought it went deeper than that. She wasn't a fool. Ben had been around since their kindergarten days. He was always the one in the trouble chair, and until he was in the second grade, he'd never enjoyed a full recess. He sat on the concentration cushion half of his third grade year. By fourth grade he'd figured out his mistakes, and other than recesses, he'd behaved himself. He never, except on rare occasions, corrected the teacher. And to prove his repentance, he declared that he never, personally, shot out another school window.

But there was the one peculiar incident when he and another kid were accused of putting an illegal cherry bomb in a hall locker and blowing it to smithereens. However, nobody could ever prove it, and the incident was never repeated.

Locals ceased to wonder if Ben would ever change. In an overwhelming vote, they harnessed his energy and made him county sheriff—the best Crook County had ever elected.

A picture of Meg with Ben flashed in Katie's mind. Meg and Ben. Now wouldn't that be something . . . Both free-spirited, both adventurous.

Both in need of love. Doctor Meadows emerged a short time later. "I don't know—the medication has slowed her contractions. Let's give it a while before I transport her to Crook Memorial."

Katie nodded. "Can I sit with her?"

"You can, but she's exhausted right now. Why don't you wait awhile longer?"

"Of course."

The doctor left, and Katie reached for a magazine and prepared for the long night that by now was half over.

Twenty-Four

Ben stretched. "You want some coffee?"

"I'd love some." She eyed the empty clinic pot that looked as though it had boiled dry. "Want me to make a fresh pot?"

"I'll get some." He stood up, slipped on his hat, and left the clinic. Katie thumbed through outdated issues of *Prevention* and *Junior Scholastic. Like Ben was going to find fresh coffee in Little Bush at this hour.* Twenty minutes passed before he returned balancing two large foam cups. Handing one to her, he set his down and slipped out of his jacket.

"Are you staying?"

"Might as well keep you company. I'm on duty in a couple of hours."

She grinned. "Thank you. I could use the company." She took a sip of coffee, and her taste buds exploded. Latte.

Latte.

She sipped and sipped again, closed her eyes, sipped again. "Where did you get a latte this hour of the night and in Little Bush?"

"I have a key to the coffee shop."

She turned to gape. "You have a *key* to the coffee shop?"

"Yeah, I might need to get in there some night. Rita gave me the key and told me to help myself."

Ben didn't know it, but he might as well have said that he was heir to Bill Gate's empire, and she was the last woman on earth. The impact generated the same reaction. Unlimited lattes. *Free* lattes.

"I love lattes."

"I know."

"How do you know?"

"Half the town knows."

"I can't have them anymore—well, one a day, but that only makes me want more. So I've decided to give them up completely, but then I know I won't." She took another leisurely swallow.

"Why can't you have them anymore? Too much sugar?"

"No. They cost too much."

How did he know that lattes were her weakness? She took another sip. Had he been following her? Wait. Was *he* the one who'd been stalking her? Not Neil Townsend and not one of the other abusers. Ben?

She stole a sidewise look at him. Possible. He had every opportunity—nah. Not Ben. He wouldn't bother stalking her. He'd rather pester her. He wouldn't hurt a flea unless the flea broke the law. Then he'd hurt him. In school he was ornery and couldn't focus, but he was never mean or spiteful. She'd seen him deal with hard-core criminals with more compassion than she would have felt. Tough. Yes. But fairminded.

Get real. Ben would not try to scare you. He isn't so gung ho to date you that he'd resort to criminal intent. Lack of female companionship didn't affect the sheriff. The number of single, available women in Little Bush was limited, but not nonexistent. How many times had she heard Judy Lewis confess she'd marry the sheriff in a New York minute?

Katie warmed her hands on the cup. Lattes taste better when shared. Everything in her life was serious talk — counseling the women on problems that had temporary answers at best, fighting with the budget, wondering where she'd get money for a new roof. Her homeowners' insurance probably didn't cover ice since it was an act of nature. She took another sip. "I pray Doctor Meadows can get Meg's labor stopped."

Ben nodded. "That's my prayer, but if it's time for the child to be born, then it's time."

Katie smiled. "If Mary and Joseph would have had a car, do you suppose they would have slipped and slid to the manger?"

Ben picked up the game. "Would Joseph wade snow and ice three feet deep to carry Mary down a hill?"

The game, born of worry and boredom, ceased when they ran out of similarities. Katie glanced at her watch. "It's been two hours since the doctor talked to us."

"He'll be out if Meg's condition changes."

"Yeah." She shifted, seeking a more comfortable position. Babies took their time deciding when they wanted to be born. "I need to count blessings instead of troubles."

Ben looked up from a *Junior Scholastic.* "More troubles?"

"Part of the roof caved in tonight. All the excitement threw Meg into labor."

He shook his head. "You do have your share of problems."

"Yeah." She put her hands in her pockets and stared at the ceiling. "I have no idea where I'll get the money to repair it.

Tottie says our insurance probably doesn't cover acts of nature, but she'll check in the morning. I'm hoping the barn roof holds. Clara has returned to politics, and so I no longer have to fear someone is harassing me."

He turned a page without looking up. "You still think Neil Townsend did the harassing?"

"Not Neil himself, one of his cronies. Someone he hired." She lowered the magazine she'd picked up. "Don't you?"

He shrugged.

"You don't."

"I didn't say that, but I'm not convinced Neil was the one causing the trouble. There's no other likely suspect at this time, though."

"What about Meg's boyfriend? Or Ruth's and Janet's husbands?"

"Meg's boyfriend is doing twenty to thirty years in Folsom prison. When I checked on his status, he was in solitary confinement for attacking a guard. Ruth's husband has the kid and hasn't missed a day's work in the past six months."

"Janet's husband?"

"The professor. He's clean. He's back in church Sunday mornings and wants to stay that way, my sources tell me. When I checked with Chicago police, they told me he's behaving himself."

Katie sank back. "Then it had to be Neil."

Ben shrugged again. "Possibly, but not likely. The man had too much to lose. You witnessed the results when someone leaked the story to the press. He would have been a fool to harass you or anyone connected to his wife. You don't take foolish risks when you're a Neil Townsend."

"Then who?" And even more disturbing, if Townsend wasn't involved that meant the danger wasn't over. Perhaps it had only started.

Ben put the magazine aside, his features sobering. "Just watch your back, Katie. Don't take unnecessary chances until we can find who's trying to cause trouble, and for what reason."

"Ben?"

"What?"

"Why have you been checking on these men? Janet's and Ruth's husbands, Meg's boyfriend?"

"It's my job to know what miscreant is in my district. You're in my county, so I check on those most likely to cause you trouble."

She eased to the edge of her seat. "Then you do think someone is deliberately causing trouble. It isn't my imagination." According to Warren, she was paranoid. A ditz with a credibility problem.

"From what you've told me, yes I do, but there's no concrete evidence. You've had a sense someone was following you. Who hasn't had that sensation? Unexplainable noises during the night. No go. Owl in the cellar? Scary, but not threatening."

"What about the flowers in the mailbox?"

He fell silent.

"Ben?"

"Yes."

"The flowers. How do you explain that?"

"I can." He shifted. "I just don't want to."

"Don't want to? What kind of answer is that?"

"A stupid one. Almost as stupid as the fact that *I* could easily have put those flowers in your mailbox, but I didn't."

"Then who did?"

"I don't know. My point is that this could be a comedy of errors. Let's say someone has a crush on you, Katie Addison, someone who has a poor way of delivering flowers. But does that make this person a stalker? Someone intent on doing you or the shelter bodily harm? Not in my book." He rubbed his hands over his eyes. "On the other hand, there could be someone out there wanting to shake you up, drive you nuts trying to figure out who and why the flowers were delivered—and to whom they were intended."

Katie's jaw dropped, her mind still trying to digest his earlier admission that he could have sent the rumpled bouquet. "*You* could have sent them?"

"Hey. A county sheriff isn't exactly Bill Gates, but I make enough to buy roses at the Grocery Mart."

She couldn't take her eyes off him.

"Okay, I'm weird, but hey, I've tried to get a date with you since I was in kindergarten. The flowers could have been a sick way to get your attention."

Katie released a pent-up sigh.

Ben reached for another magazine. "You wouldn't be so bent out of shape if they'd come from the nerd."

"The nerd. I suppose you're referring to Warren?"

"The nerd."

Drawing a deep breath, Katie sat up straighter. "He is no longer a nerd, Ben. He's a smart, no, brilliant man without whom I don't know what I would do." If there was even a fraction of a chance to keep the shelter open, Warren was the key. If he could help her pull through this financial crisis, she could put up with his eccentricities provided he let up on women in general.

Ben turned a page. "He's a nerd. Why do women fall for a pretty face with no substance?"

"How can you say he has no substance? He was a Wall Street genius."

"And that makes him a good man?"

"You're jealous."

"Maybe. Why wouldn't I be? What's wrong with me? Why do you go all goggle-eyed over Warren, and you refuse to date me?"

Katie focused on an ad. "I tried to date you once."

"For someone who says she doesn't hold a grudge, you sure manage to bring up the prom on every viable occasion."

Katie closed the magazine. "I bought a new dress, had my hair and nails done, and waited until ten o'clock that night for you to come." She snapped the magazine open. "You didn't come, Ben. I missed my high school prom."

"I know, and how many times have I apologized? Blame my dad. He's the one who had a gallbladder attack. Or my mom who insisted I get him to Sundance and the hospital. Or blame Grandma who said he wasn't going anywhere without her."

"You could have phoned."

"Katie, in those days I didn't know how to use a pay phone, and cell phones were not an option. I'm sorry. If you would let me make it up to you, I would."

Katie closed the magazine and pitched it on the table. "I forgive you."

"Yeah, with about as much sincerity as Goliath when he kissed David, shook hands, and apologized for being a bully."

"Goliath didn't do that."

"I know."

Nor had she forgiven him. Not completely.

"Good news." Doctor Meadows appeared, face haggard but confident. "Meg's labor has stopped. She hasn't had a pain in over an hour. Why don't you two go home, and I'll call if her labor starts again. I want to keep her into late afternoon."

Katie closed her eyes with relief. "Of course, doctor. Can I see her a moment?"

"Yes, but only for a moment."

Katie sidestepped the two men. "Excuse me."

"You're excused," Ben said. "And I forgive you."

She was about to leave when it suddenly seemed imperative that she reciprocate. She turned.

"Hey Ben?"

"Yeah?"

"I forgive you too." There. She'd said it, years overdue. What's a prom compared to a good, no, a great friendship?

Saluting her with his index finger, Ben graciously accepted though there was no missing the cocky grin on his face.

Twenty-Five

During the ride home, Katie kept to Ben's far right, crowding the door handle. Was he the one responsible for the mysterious incidences? Somehow her mind wouldn't fathom the thought. Ben was her friend. He wouldn't harm her.

The rain and snow had stopped. The sky was gray and heavy when they pulled into the farm lot. It was barely six o'clock, but a light burned in the window. Refuge. Shelter from the storm.

Katie got out, yawning. "Thanks, Ben." She paused. "It seems like I'm saying that a lot lately."

He grinned. "Do you want me to bring Meg home later?"

"That would be very kind of you. Thanks." She had this unreasonable urge to hug him, but she refrained. She trudged to the back door where a light burned.

What now, Lord? I'm in a deep hole and it's getting deeper every day with a damaged roof and the shelter in imminent risk of closing. Granted the missed prom was still in the back of her mind, but she didn't carry grudges. Even when she learned the circumstances of Ben's father's illness, she had sent a note with her sympathies. Ben had been a steady influence to the community.

Suddenly the endangered, fragile friendship they'd held on to all these years seemed close to strengthening. Ben was a decent man, in church every Sunday and first in line to lend help where help was needed. Fun. Likeable. Handsome.

Warren had attended church twice since he'd been home and sat on the back pew.

Katie's jumbled thoughts were not sortable this morning. Sighing, she decided to leave the matter alone. Ben was just Ben. So he'd carried a thing for her all these years. She'd known it and refused to acknowledge it. Maybe it was time to take a closer look.

Only one thing bothered her. Where was Warren when she needed him?

In bed, sound asleep while she'd spent a most hellish night. She hadn't called him. Why?

Over breakfast, Katie pondered her situation. Two men. Two diverse personalities.

One person determined to do what? The notion that either man was stalking her was preposterous. She needed sleep.

"Janet and Ruth asleep?"

Tottie scoured a skillet. "Yes. It was after five before they went to bed."

The house was chilled. The furnace and fireplace couldn't keep up with the cold air streaming through the hole in the roof. What was Katie going to do about that?

Climb on the roof with nails and a heavy tarp and cover it?

Not with three inches of ice coating it.

Tottie sat down at the table, her features lined with lack of sleep. She was getting too old for all this hassle. Keeping the shelter open wasn't fair to her. She was donating her only source of income to a sinking ship. The thought nagged Katie's conscience. How much longer could she hold on? *Could* they hold on? Warren was right. She should close the shelter, reorganize and live a more simple life. She owed Tottie a stable home in her declining years. She wasn't *old* in Katie's eyes; she was a surrogate mother who didn't age. But the calendar didn't lie. In March Tottie would turn seventy, and she wasn't getting any younger.

"We need to do something about the roof." Tottie read her mind, nothing new.

"I was thinking about it. I can't climb up and cover the hole until the ice is melted."

"That could take days."

Katie was sure there was a more palatable solution, but she didn't have it.

"I could call Warren and ask him what to do."

Tottie stirred sugar into her black coffee. "You could."

There it was again. The censuring tone, the unspoken current that puzzled Katie. "What do you have against Warren?"

"Me?"

"Yes, you. Every time his name is mentioned you get this attitude in your voice."

"Do I?" She raised her cup. "I didn't realize I did that."

Katie's eyes skimmed the news column. "Don't you like him?"

"He's okay, a little grumpy at times, but I guess I am too."

"You've known him since he was a child, knew his parents even longer."

Tottie fell silent.

Katie glanced up. "Well?"

"Well what?"

"Do you like Warren?" What if she didn't? What if she had strong reservations about the man? What then? It was important that Tottie loved the man Katie might choose to spend her life with because someday she would be living with them, if God willed and their relationship grew, which wasn't likely to be anytime soon. Warren had issues, issues that wouldn't be solved overnight. But Katie had waited this long for him to come along. She could wait a while longer for him to realize the value in her work.

"I suppose the man has some merit."

The answer was an odd one, even from Tottie. The two women sat drinking coffee, trying to wake up. An hour passed before the housekeeper scooted back from the table and went to the window. "Do you hear that?"

"What?"

"Cars in our driveway. Looks like a couple of police cars. Reckon the sheriff called them?"

"Why would Ben be back?" Katie moved to join her. "Do you suppose he needs something?" Two squad cars tried to conquer the slick incline.

"Don't know, but he's got someone with him."

Tires spun. Engines revved. The cars were heavy sedans with snow chains, but the ice and snow resisted all efforts.

Tottie focused on the activity.

Three uniformed men got out of their sedans, and moments later they scaled the incline with great effort, carrying heavy tarps and toolboxes.

Katie pressed closer to the frosted pane. "What are they doing?"

"I'd say they're about to cover the hole in the roof."

"How?" If ice hindered her from getting on the roof, it would stop them too.

The first deputy approached the back step. Tottie dropped the curtain and moved to the back door, Katie trailing her.

When the door opened, a deputy touched the brim of his hat briefly. "Good morning."

Tottie nodded. "Can we help you?"

"No, ma'am, we're here to help you. We're going to cover that hole for you."

Katie stepped around the older woman. "How? The roof has layers of ice. I can't get up there."

"No, ma'am, and you shouldn't." He smiled and lifted a foot to reveal steel-studded cleats. "I used to work for the power company. I can climb like a monkey."

Katie broke into a grin. "Then by all means, climb. The house is freezing cold."

He touched the brim of his hat again, turned, and cleated off. Katie's eyes searched for Ben, and she noticed that he was staying well in the background.

Her cheeks burned when she recalled her earlier suspicions that in some way he might be responsible for the earlier harassment. Now he was here to fix her roof.

Closing the kitchen door, Katie rubbed warmth into her forearms. Warren. She suddenly needed to talk to him. He would want to help. A glance at the clock verified that it was still very early. Better to wait until later when he'd had his coffee. Tottie's attitude toward Warren bothered Katie more than she wanted to admit. What was bothering Tottie about the man other than the obvious? He wasn't a people person, but he had his kind moments. She and Tottie had been a team for so long that Katie was lost without Tottie's wisdom. Maybe Tottie was worried that Warren might come between them. Katie would have to reassure her that nothing could ever damage their friendship.

Certainly not Warren.

Twenty-Six

Thanksgiving Day was right around the corner, and the women were excited. They'd been dreading the thought of spending the holiday without family. But since the ice storm, a bond had grown among them until, as Meg said, they were family. Katie was at her desk staring at her budget figures and trying to wring out a few extra dollars to buy the groceries needed for their feast when the doorbell rang.

Warren!

She hurried to answer, swinging the door open to find Mary Hoskins, her latte-drinking buddy. Her heart dropped. She had been so sure it would be Warren. He hadn't come to help with the roof; in fact, she had barely spoken to him recently. He was always busy, busy avoiding her. "Oh, hi." Katie knew her greeting sounded flat, but it was such a letdown.

"Nice to see you too." Mary grinned. "Want to help me unload?"

"Unload what?" Katie was still having a hard time adjusting to the disappointment.

Mary motioned to the black Lincoln Navigator. "A turkey and all the trimmings, what else!"

Katie gaped. "You're kidding?"

Mary shook her head. "Nope. My gifts to you in appreciation of all you do here. You do a wonderful job, Katie, and I'm so proud of you."

Katie trailed Mary out to the car. "Oh, Mary, I was just trying to figure out how I could provide a decent Thanksgiving meal. This is so thoughtful of you."

"Hey. I'm a sweet person. Have you just now noticed that?" Mary handed Katie a frozen twenty-pound turkey and grabbed six plastic grocery bags, three in each hand. "Lead the way. I'm right behind you."

When they reached the kitchen, Meg watched wide-eyed as Tottie unpacked the grocery sacks. "That's a lot of food."

Tottie placed the turkey in the refrigerator to thaw. "God bless you, Mary. I hope your Thanksgiving is as good as you've made ours."

Mary hugged her. "It will be, Tottie, and God bless you too. You take care now."

Katie walked Mary to the door and watched her drive away. God was good to them. She had no doubt he'd nudged Mary to buy what they needed and deliver it. She'd call Warren and invite him to dinner Thanksgiving Day to prove that the shelter women weren't like Clara.

He answered on the first ring. "Hey, Katie. I've been meaning to call, but I've had a lot to do, with the bad weather and all."

"I understand." She drew a long breath and sent up a silent prayer. "Are you free for Thanksgiving dinner?"

Silence.

Come on, Warren, say yes. Bend a little.

"Sure!" His agreeable voice came over the line, and her knees went weak with relief. *He was coming; thank you, Lord.*

"What time?"

"We'll eat at noon. Is that too early? If it is, we can serve later."

"Noon's great. I'll be there."

Katie hung up, briefly closing her eyes. *Lord, open his eyes and let him see the strength and just plain goodness of these women.* She sailed into the kitchen to tell Tottie they were having a guest and found the older woman seated at the table, peeling potatoes.

"Warren? He's actually coming?"

"He said he would. Isn't that wonderful?"

"Peachy."

Katie frowned. Did Tottie think that she was starting to be as gullible—or tolerant?—as the shelter women? Warren wasn't taking advantage of her. She chose to pursue the relationship, though the start had proven precarious. Maybe she was a romantic at heart and didn't know it. Never would she allow Warren to mistreat her. Other than some unwarranted sharpness, he had been polite, even helpful. She'd lived long enough to know that the perfect man didn't exist; they all had their bad days.

Katie stared at the older woman, perplexed. "I thought you'd be glad. I'm interested in him—really interested."

"What about Ben?"

"Ben? What does he have to do with anything?"

"He's a good friend, Katie. Always been there when you needed him."

"I know that, Tottie, but he's not Warren."

Tottie pitched a potato in the pot. "Warren's changed so much, maybe I just need more time to get to know him."

Katie walked away with her feelings ruffled. It wasn't like Tottie to be so openly partial. Just because they'd both known Ben forever didn't mean Katie couldn't look at another man. And they'd known Warren almost as long.

Thanksgiving Day dawned sunny and cold. Random patches of ice lurked in shaded spots, but the roads were clear. Wonderful smells drifted from the kitchen. Tottie was making Crock-Pot dressing. No boxed stuffing for her. Ruth had made her special orange cranberry sauce. Janet was in charge of the sweet potatoes, and Meg had whipped up a fabulous dessert made of almonds, chocolate pudding, and a cookie-like crust.

A little before twelve o'clock the phone rang, and it was Warren. "Look, Katie, I'm sorry, but I've got a sick cow. I'm waiting for the vet, but he's going to be delayed. You'd better not count on me."

Katie's lips firmed. The call had taken her by surprise. Dinner was nearly on the table. "I'm sorry. We can wait dinner for an hour or so if that would help."

"No, don't do that. I don't know when I'll be through here. I'll grab a sandwich or bowl of soup."

Soup or sandwich? On Thanksgiving? The trade-off seemed sacrilegious, and this was the second time he'd stood her up. She could not find one reason to believe his story. She hung up the phone discouraged. People who made their living raising livestock weren't always free to do as they pleased, but this smelled to high heaven.

Eyebrows raised, Tottie looked up as Katie entered the kitchen.

"That was Warren. He's tied up with a sick cow. He won't be able to come after all."

"Surprise, surprise." Tottie cut off a lump of butter and dropped it into the potatoes she was mashing.

Katie took plates from the cabinet and started setting the table.

Janet, Meg, and Ruth helped dish up the food, and the women gathered around the table. Without prompting they reached out to hold hands while Tottie said the blessing. Katie listened as she asked God to be with each of the women, praying for them by name. A lump rose in her throat as she thanked God for allowing her one more Thanksgiving at the shelter. The women would soon move on. Ruth was going to her sister's, where she would hire a lawyer to regain custody of her daughter. Janet was looking for work. Eventually she would find a job and embark on a new life.

Meg was a different story. Perhaps she could find employment in or near Little Bush after the baby was born. She could stay at Candlelight until she could afford an apartment and earn enough to pay for childcare. The women who came were welcome to stay until they could get their lives back on track; that was a silent promise.

Twenty-Seven

The long holiday afternoon dragged on. The women slumped on the couch and in chairs, drowsy from the feast.

"That was one fabulous meal, Tottie," Ruth said. "I ate so much I'm miserable."

Tottie sighed and shifted her position. "I need a nap."

Janet opened her eyes. "Do you realize it will soon be Christmas?"

Ruth blinked back sudden tears. "The first Christmas I've been away from my daughter."

Janet shot her a sympathetic glance. "We need to start working on the live drama we talked about earlier. Christmas will be here before we know it."

Meg yawned. "Let's hope the baby comes on time—and not a moment sooner."

Katie grinned. "The baby will be our live Baby Jesus."

Awake now, the women's enthusiasm for the pageant gained momentum.

Tottie squinted, half asleep. "What do you have in mind?"

Janet slid forward in her chair. "Let's reenact the night Christ was born. It'll be fun, and the practices will give us something to do on our long winter evenings."

Meg frowned. "What if I haven't had the baby by Christmas Eve?"

"Oh you will! It's due what, the eighteenth?" Ruth grinned. "You'll be home and ready for a little fun by then."

"Not a bad idea." Tottie's eyes drifted shut. "Get some paper and a pen. We'll write the script."

Katie left the women chattering about the drama. She felt a squiggle of anticipation thinking about a new baby being around for the holiday. The first baby born at Candlelight and born at this special time — it was exciting.

Around four, Katie filled a couple of plates of leftover turkey, mashed potatoes, gravy, and stuffing, and wrapped them tightly in foil. If Warren *couldn't* come to Thanksgiving, she'd take Thanksgiving to him. If she found him anywhere but in the barn with a sick cow, the relationship — such as it was — was over. She interrupted the planning session long enough to tell Tottie where she was going and drove to Warren's farm.

The barn was dark. Anger building, Katie pecked on the side door, and Warren told her to come in. She did, juggling the foil-covered plates. Her eyes locked on his form sprawled in his recliner, watching football.

He grinned when he saw the plates. "What's all that?"

"Since you missed dinner, I brought it to you." Her eyes scanned the empty room. No vet.

"That's great." He lifted the foil and sniffed. "I hadn't got around to fixing anything yet."

"How's the cow?"

"She died. Passed on about half hour ago. Vet can't get here until morning, so I left the carcass in the barn and came into the house and cleaned up. Take off your coat and stay awhile."

Katie took in the warm, inviting room. A fire glowed brightly in the fireplace. Dead. She supposed she'd be totally out of line asking to see the deceased animal, but she didn't intend to stay. The shine had been taken off the holiday. "I'd better get back. Enjoy your food."

"No? Well, another time?"

"Right."

She flinched at the thread of indifference in his voice. *Dreams die hard.*

"Sorry about missing dinner." He smiled. "Though I guess it's no secret that being in a room full of women makes me nervous."

No, no secret.

"Maybe we can try supper again one night this week?"

"Sure."

She left, closing the door behind her.

God, why do things have to be so hard? Why aren't choices more clear-cut? Had Warren lied to her a second time? She made a mental note to ask the vet. Sneaky, perhaps, but Warren's excuses were getting thin.

On the drive home, Katie's decision seemed pretty obvious. Unpleasant, but obvious.

Slipping out of her coat at the back door, she drew Tottie to the table. "I've been thinking, and I've reached a decision. When Janet, Ruth, and Meg leave, we're closing the shelter."

Instead of vehement protest, Tottie nodded, thoughtful. "And then what?"

"I'll take on more typing and open the ranch up for additional riding lessons. With more lessons and extra typing, we can live just fine."

Tottie, still openly undisturbed by the announcement, asked, "Did Warren have anything to do with your decision?"

"No. He's been encouraging me to close; that isn't a secret. I've decided that he's right. I can't afford to keep the shelter open, and it's not fair to you or your money. Besides, I'm tired of living in fear." *I'm sick of it all. Sick of fighting Warren. Sick of defending my choices to Ben. Tired of being broke.* Life held so little reward lately.

"I can't believe that you believe what you're saying," Tottie said, shaking her head. "You love Candlelight. You've poured your life into this ministry, but the decision to close or remain open is yours and yours alone. I only have one suggestion. Keep your decision quiet until after Christmas."

Katie nodded, drained. "I don't want to disrupt the women's celebration, but closing won't affect them for awhile. They can stay here until the courts find good relocation shelters or they move on."

"You pray about your decision, Katie."

"You know I will and I do, but I'm confident that this is the right decision. It's the only answer." She couldn't keep putting them through the angst of never knowing where the next dollar would come from, though God had never failed them. Yet he expected his children to show wisdom and not be complete airheads, expecting the world to meet their needs. Still, if he wanted Candlelight to remain open, there would be no power on earth strong enough to close it.

Katie bypassed the front room where the women were still discussing the pageant and ducked into the small office to call Warren. His voice brightened when he recognized the caller. "Just finished eating. The food was great."

"I'm glad you enjoyed it. I've made a decision, Warren. I won't announce it publicly until after the holidays, but I've decided to close the shelter."

She supposed the ensuing silence meant that he was digesting the news. After a moment, he said quietly, "Finally you're getting some financial savvy. I'm proud of you, Katie. The decision to close took guts, but I knew you would make a wise choice."

She shrugged, defeated. "You're right. I can't afford to keep it."

"You won't regret it, I promise you. Maybe now we can move ahead."

His words hit home at the crux of her heart. Maybe they could move ahead. Wasn't that what she had wanted all along, his undivided attention? "That's my hope too. I wouldn't have had the courage to reach this decision without your help."

He cleared his throat. "I'm really sorry I couldn't make it today. How about the two of us going out to dinner, and maybe a movie, tomorrow night?"

Katie shook her head. Mr. Right had galloped up on a white steed, and all it had taken to get him was her giving up. Maybe this was what he wanted all along and why he hesitated to deepen the relationship. Maybe her pride and her wishes had stood in the way of God's plan for her life. "I'd love that, Warren. What time?"

"Will five-thirty work for you?"

"It works fine."

"And Katie?" His tone lowered to one she had waited to hear. Caring. Not soft, but not hard.

"Yes?"

"You've made the right decision. I know I've been a little hard-nosed on the subject, but in the long run, it's best for you, and that's all I care about — what's best for you."

Twenty-Eight

J anet tapped her pencil on the legal pad, eyeing Ruth. "No, your line is, 'Quick, let's follow the star.'"

"Quick! Let's follow the star!"

"A little less emphasis on the 'star.' 'Quick. Let's follow the star.'"

Katie smiled and closed the double parlor doors. The Christmas drama was foremost in the women's minds these days. They spent hours practicing for an audience of two — three if Warren decided to come. Yet their fervor and dedication to reenact the nativity would have been no less for one than for a hundred. Only one problem remained. Meg had yet to produce the male lead. Her due date had come and gone, and still they waited, listening and watching for any indication that the child was about to enter the world.

Katie found the mother to be sitting in the middle of the kitchen floor painting the wooden cradle the women had built from lumber given to them by Warren. The cradle would belong to the new infant after the pageant.

"Looking good," Katie praised as she opened the refrigerator door and took out a bottle of juice.

"Thanks." Meg shifted, her hand absently going to support her back. "It's shaping up nicely."

"Seen Tottie?"

"She's in the barn feeding the cats, or that's what she said. I think she wants to spend as much time with the horses before they leave as possible."

"Which won't be much longer. The vet thought they would leave weeks ago. If the one stallion hadn't developed that nasty infection, they would be in California now."

"I'm going to miss them," Meg said wistfully. "One or two have become close friends, and I don't have many friends."

"You have us."

The tough Meg surfaced. "I don't need anyone, honest." Then her tone softened. "But I have come to love everyone here." She lifted red eyes. "If it hadn't been for Candlelight, I don't know where I and baby boo would be right now."

Pain twisted Katie's heart. She couldn't break now. She had to remain strong for the women. They couldn't learn of her plans to close the shelter yet. She shut the refrigerator door with her hip. "I'm going into Cope for a few hours."

Meg nodded. "Santa shopping?"

Katie grinned. "You got it." Now that she knew she would close the shelter, money didn't have to be so tight. She could afford to buy Tottie and the women small Christmas gifts. Dewberry's was having a big sale, and she wanted to take advantage of it. Once the shelter closed, she'd arrange for a bank loan and make payments on a new roof. Meanwhile, she planned to celebrate the Savior's birth if not in a grand way at least in a caring way.

These days the relief that filled her made any trip more palatable. There hadn't been one single unnerving accident since before election day.

Ben had backed off to the point that he barely acknowledged her when they passed on the road. She knew the rumor had spread about her and Warren's blooming relationship, yet she missed the friendly banter with the sheriff. Even the silly signs, which she still carried in the jeep. Maybe she'd been too hard on him.

Too hard on Ben? Come on, Katie girl! You got what you wanted. He leaves you alone.

Katie frowned. Totally alone. Starting the jeep, she backed out of the farm lot.

Driving through Little Bush, she spotted the sheriff filling his gasoline tank at the local service station. On a whim, she waved.

She supposed his barely perceptible nod was an acceptable if not warm greeting. His fleeting glance was as warm as one he might give to a suspected sniper.

Well, you've earned his ire. And if it hadn't been for him, you'd have fought some pretty tough battles alone, like getting Meg to the clinic during false labor and covering the gaping hole in the roof, which he did without being asked.

National news came on the radio, and Katie leaned to adjust the volume. She caught the last piece. "Today Senator Clara Townsend announced that one of her first pieces of legislation during her second term will be the American Horse Slaughter Prevention Act."

Stunned, Katie stared at the dashboard. Clara? Fighting to reinstate the Horse Slaughter Prevention Act? A grin touched the corners of her mouth. *Why, Clara Townsend, you faker. You aren't as cold as you wanted us to believe.*

Thank you, God, for sending help by a most unlikely angel.

Katie sobered. *God bless you, Clara.*

Katie leisurely shopped Dewberry's most of the afternoon and bought a fleece robe for Tottie, a new top for Meg, and bath products for Janet and Ruth. She also bought a soft black and white stuffed bear for the baby.

The pregnancy had changed Meg. She was quieter, more serious. On occasion the street-smart girl slipped back into her former behavior, but she appeared to be trying to do what was best for her baby. Motherhood was a big responsibility, and Meg was living up to it.

Katie grinned. With the baby's mother and four other women hovering over him, he would be one spoiled kid. Ruth and Janet had dug into their meager funds to buy diapers and gowns. Ruth had embroidered bibs, and Janet had wrapped them in Christmas paper. Tottie was crocheting a baby afghan of soft yellow and white. A baby was a promise of new life, a beginning. Special.

Winter shadows layered the parking garage when Katie emerged from the mall. Store traffic had been reasonably tolerable today, one week before Christmas. An air of expectation, a barely controlled excitement conquered people who were taking advantage of last-minute gift buying. The mall was ablaze in the glow of Christmas. Decorations filled store windows and hung from the streetlights.

Katie hauled packages to the jeep and stored them, climbed into the cab, and then climbed out again. She rummaged through sacks for the chocolate Godiva bar she'd purchased, then returned to the driver's seat and noted the time. Nearly five o'clock.

On the drive home, a muffled pop grabbed her attention. The jeep veered, and she gripped the wheel and pulled the vehicle back onto the road. Now what? She braked, coming to a halt, and slowly lowered the window on the driver's side, listening. Nothing. Her eyes searched the darkness.

Katie sat frozen in place, staring through the fogged window on the passenger side. The jeep sagged on the left side rear tire. A flat?

A quick check of the spare tire showed that it was flat too. When had she looked at it last? Great. She slumped against the rear fender well and let the tears come. *God, are you mad at me? Can't something work out right for me just once in a while? Don't you care that my life is falling apart?*

Katie fumbled in her coat pocket for a tissue. Of course he cared. She was the careless one. She'd just spent money on Christmas presents when she knew the jeep was running on bald tires. Now she had to buy tires. *Instead of standing here feeling sorry for yourself, why not use the wits the good Lord gave you and do something?* She wiped her eyes and dialed Warren.

"You're where?" he asked.

"On the stretch of road between Little Bush and the shelter. I've had a blowout, and the spare is flat."

He sighed.

She waited.

"Okay, I'll be there. Sit tight."

She clicked off, and then called Tottie to let her know what happened. Warren arrived within minutes. When he stepped out of his pickup and advanced in the glare of headlights, Katie rushed into his arms, and to her chagrin, immediately burst into tears. He held her close, soothing her like he would a child until she calmed down.

"It's okay. I'm here." He turned her in the direction of the pickup, and she stopped. "Wait. My packages."

He waited while she retrieved her purchases, and then helped her carry them to the pickup. "Been shopping?"

"Christmas. I bought a few things for the women at the shelter."

"You have money to spend on things like that?"

"They didn't cost much, and it is Christmas." She heard the defensive note creep into her voice, and she waited for him to reprimand her. But he didn't. Gifts. She hadn't bought anything for him. Would he expect something? Did he have a present for her? She'd find something for him in Little Bush. Something small but significant.

Warren slid behind the wheel and turned the truck around. "I left a roast cooking in the oven. When you called, I dropped everything and came. I'll fix the flat and the spare tomorrow. Have you had dinner?"

"No." She huddled close to the rush of warm air coming from the heater. "Well," she amended, "I had a Godiva bar."

By now they'd reached Warren's house, and she followed him inside. Warmth washed over her as she entered the home. Katie moved to the fireplace, letting the heat eat away the chill that had crept into her bones. Rusty, Warren's Australian shepherd, lay a short distance from the hearth, sleeping. He cracked one eye open when Katie joined him, and then closed it.

Warren was rattling around in the kitchen, and she could hear him opening the oven door. A minute later the tantalizing fragrance of roast beef reminded her that she was hungry. She left the fire and wandered into the kitchen to find him taking plates from the cabinet.

"As long as you're here, why don't we eat before I take you home?"

"Okay. I'll phone Tottie."

"Phone's on the hall table." He took the roast out of the oven and set it on the stove. "After the day you've had, you need to relax and let me wait on you."

Katie sat at Warren's table as he dished up roast, carrots, potatoes, and onions, all swimming in rich brown roast gravy. He added sliced French bread brushed with butter and warmed in the oven. The man was a Wall Street genius and an admirable chef. His home was immaculate. Katie felt like crying. This was what she wanted: a home with someone to love, someone to have babies with and grow old with. She wanted Warren, yet she didn't know why she was so dead set on getting him. Just because some old woman once predicted that she would marry a man who'd been in her life all along didn't mean that God had hand delivered Warren back to Little Bush.

She knew this.

So why did she try so hard to make it come true?

He was smart, bright, and on occasion, fun to be with. But a hundred other men had the same qualifications.

What was it about Warren that filled a deep need inside her?

Was it his compassion? No, though he could be compassionate, like now, pouring her tea and adding dressing to her salad. She shook her head, trying to make sense of her jumbled and somewhat faulty analysis. If she cared about Warren and really wanted to deepen the relationship, why did she have this sudden longing to see Ben?

Warren filled his plate and sat down. "Eat up. You'll feel better with something hot in your stomach."

Accustomed to saying grace before a meal, Katie waited, but when Warren reached for a slice of bread and began eating,

she did the same. She had been so sure she could win Warren over, restore his faith in women and mankind—and given
enough time she might, but not by force. That was the problem. She had to initiate every step, orchestrate every effort to
make her dream come true.

Maybe—just maybe, her dream wasn't Warren's dream
no matter how hard she prayed for his transformation.

After the meal, Warren refused her offer to clean up. "No,
I need to get you home. You've had a rough day, and Tottie is
probably wondering where you are."

"I called her. Meg's due anytime—I try to stay close by."

He gathered up plates and forks. "Maybe I need to get
those tires fixed tonight."

"No, we have the old farm truck for emergencies. I hope
we don't have to use it, but it's there if we need it. Or I can call
someone to help."

He chuckled. "Well, don't call me, at least not for that
kind of trip."

Why didn't his comment surprise her? She wouldn't call
him; she'd call Ben. Her conflicted thoughts only puzzled her.
She stood up, suddenly homesick. "I am a little tired. Would
you care to run me home?"

She stopped by the hall table while he brought their coats.
Neat, like the rest of his life. The only items on the table were
a bronze statue of a rider on a bucking horse and the phone.

Neat and tidy. Just like Warren. Inanimate objects with
no feeling.

Twenty-Nine

Late that night, Katie propped her elbows on a stall and studied the horses. Like the shelter, they'd soon be gone. The animals were healthy enough to be moved now. The infection had cleared up on the stallion. After the holidays, they would be on their way to California. Had it only been a couple months since she acquired the livestock that began a chain of events that Katie couldn't fathom? Warren unexpectedly reentered her life. Clara Townsend, who appeared to be a curse, could possibly turn out to be a blessing in disguise if she got the bill through the Senate.

Tottie's voice interrupted her musings. "It is late. Why are you still up?"

"I couldn't sleep." Katie stared at the horses. "Everyone will miss them. They're good therapy for the women."

"The owner wants them back, and they're an expense we don't need." Tottie huddled deeper into a sheepskin-lined coat. "You have to admit, California would be nice this time of year."

Nice. And expensive. Tottie had a distant cousin in Southern California. She'd visited there once, and Katie still recalled Tottie's wistful tone when she relayed her adventure. Warm winds, white surf.

But instead of California, Tottie had been stuck helping Grandpops and Grandmoms raise Katie. By then she'd fallen in love with Katie and could hardly walk away, especially since Grandpops wasn't in the best of health. She *could* have then and years later. But she'd stayed on, saying that Katie was her family now, Katie, who kept her tied to a battered women's shelter, danger, and failing finances.

The older woman turned from the railing. "Come on, you need your rest, and it's very cold."

"Am I doing the right thing, Tottie?"

"I don't know, Katie. Only God knows the future. We have prayed, and we have our answer."

"I hate the answer."

"No one knows the mind of God. Whatever happens, it will be for your best. You know that. Now come. I'll fix you a mug of warm chocolate to help you sleep better."

Katie absently nodded. "I'll be in shortly."

Tottie walked away. The horses would leave, and then Katie's personal stock would be liquidated. She caught sight of Sweet Tea's ears, visible in her stall. She'd have to keep her. She couldn't give riding lessons without a horse.

Resentment burned like a hot brand in her stomach. The pain had stayed with her since the moment she'd decided to close the shelter. Yes, it was the prudent thing to do, but no, she didn't have to be happy about it.

A remembered passage of Proverbs drifted through her mind, and she spoke it aloud. "In his heart a man plans his course, but the Lord directs his steps."

If that's so, Lord, where did I take the wrong path?

Faith is the substance of . . .

Faith had always been her strong point. So when had she started doubting? Doubting herself, but worse, doubting where God had put her?

It happened about the time Warren reentered her life. Katie turned from the barn lot and walked to the house. She had a stack of work waiting to be typed, but her mind refused to abandon the subject.

Later she sat in front of the computer and stared at the blinking cursor. Finances had always been tough, especially after Grandpops lost his savings. Bills were late but always paid. They ate well. The stock was fed.

Katie focused on the small plaque hanging over the computer: I believe.

I believe. She believed that God knew her circumstances and could change them in an instant, if he wanted. If he didn't want, then it meant for the time being she was where she should be.

So accept, and do what you have to do.

She glanced at the report waiting to be typed, and her fingers automatically set to work. Then she paused.

But if she was exactly where she should be in his plan for her life, then why should she change circumstances? Why should she close the shelter, cave to someone making her choose between her vocation and love? At that instant, sitting in Grandpops's old chair with his personal effects surrounding her — pen, pencils, a glass paperweight — she was never more sure of her purpose to serve others less fortunate. It was hard to imagine anyone with more problems than she faced, but she only had to look as far as the women taking shelter under her roof for comparison.

Having money didn't mean having fewer problems. Ask Janet. Her professor husband provided a good life and had community influence. Having power didn't make for a perfect life. Talk to Clara.

Katie shifted, biting down on the end of a pencil. Brains helped, but they didn't produce a euphoric life. Warren would tell you that.

Love. Maybe Ben would have a thought or two on unrequited love. Goodness knows she'd been rude to him at times, and she regretted her impulses. But nobody ever said you had to love somebody back.

Resentment fanned the coal pit in her stomach. If she were happy with her life, chaotic as it might be, then why change it because of a crisis of faith? Or Warren?

Katie slapped her hand on the desk, bouncing paper clips from their plastic holder. *Why* should she change what she perceived the Lord was telling her to do? If the shelter was God's plan, then he was capable of sustaining it in both good and bad times. How? She had no clue. Her troubles seemed insurmountable, but running away wasn't going to help. She'd pinch a penny harder. She'd scrimp. She'd stretch one cup of soup into two. They'd pile on more sweaters and cut more wood. The spring garden would be bigger, and she'd preserve more produce for next winter. She could and she would take on a second or third job, even work a night shift, wait tables, or clean bathrooms. Others did.

Her fingers flew over the keys. She could type twice the amount of work she now had.

Tottie could ...

She stopped short. *Tottie.* She would have to agree to the plan. Katie couldn't lose her. She was the only family Katie had left.

Katie spit the pencil out of her mouth and went to ask Tottie's blessing immediately. She wouldn't sleep until she knew Tottie supported her decision to stay with the shelter.

Katie might not have answers to all the questions, but she only needed one to set her life back on a path of normalcy.

The right one.

Thirty

Nine a.m. Katie glanced at the bank clock and realized she was the first customer of the day. Tottie had not only supported her decision, she'd sprung out of bed and hugged her. That was verification enough for Katie.

Across from her, a neatly dressed bank officer consulted the loan form. "You would need the loan for thirty-six months?"

"Yes. I can offer my home as collateral." She'd promised Grandpops to never risk the home unless hell froze over. She was pretty sure they were wearing overcoats down there today.

"Well, I don't see any reason why we can't help. When will you need the money?"

"As soon as possible. We have an expectant mother who is due anyday. The house is really cold and drafty for a newborn. We needed a new roof yesterday."

"I understand."

Katie left the bank with the promise of a loan and renewed hope. One thing left to do — no, two things. She had to arrange for a new roof and call Warren and tell him she'd decided to stay. Tough it out.

Bite the bullet.

Grab the bull by the horns, and pray it didn't gore her to the ground.

Do what God had called her to without fear.

Test Warren's true feelings for her.

December wasn't ideal roofing weather, but on the positive side, the roofers weren't busy. Milder weather created puddles of melting slush, but the roof was clear. With a promise to "get right on the job," Katie left the contractor's office feeling pretty good about the whole thing.

On the way home, she phoned Warren. "Hey."

"Hi. What's going on?"

She told him about the loan and imminent roof repairs.

"You added another bill?"

Yes, Katie, that is irritation in his tone. But repairing the roof was hardly a frivolity.

"I have no choice, Warren. The women are cold — I'm cold — and we can't bring a newborn home to a frigid house. Besides, the gas bill is climbing sky high."

"I would have helped nail shingles over the hole."

"When I called to ask, you were too busy."

"I can't help my time schedule." *Oh yes, definite irritation,* but she wasn't backing off of this. The spine that had been missing, hers, had been implanted.

"That's the problem. There have been too many shingles nailed over too many holes over the years. A new roof is the only sensible answer."

"That's why you'll never have one red cent. Why? I don't understand you — do you thrive on trouble? Do you enjoy hardship? Do you have a brain in your head?"

She noted he didn't even bother to say "pretty head." "I do the best I can." That's all God asked of anyone, their best.

In the end he agreed it was her call. Financial suicide, but her call.

She knew that. She'd made her share of bad choices, but like Grandpops would say, in for a penny, in for pound.

Katie was no quitter.

Thirty-One

Katie had planned to spend the time between dinner and bedtime typing. She had put out feelers, trying to drum up more work. The bank had mentioned grants, and she needed to find one. Somewhere there was a source to keep her afloat until donations picked up again. If she could expand her transcript-typing business, maybe branch out into other types of at-home work, she might avoid taking a second job. She needed to be available to the women whatever their needs.

They had just finished clearing the table when someone knocked on the door. Katie opened it to find Warren standing there. He grinned sheepishly. "I was pretty hard on you today. How about going out for a latte?"

She didn't feel the immediate elation she usually felt, but she never passed up a latte. Going out would mean staying up later to finish her work, but the idea was doable. "Let me grab my coat."

She disappeared to her room where she changed to black pants and a sweater, combed her hair, and slapped on lipstick. He was in the living room with the women when she returned. When she appeared he was on his feet and urged her out the door. She barely had time to say good-bye to the others. He was never at ease around the shelter women.

"Are we in a hurry?" she asked as they quickstepped to the truck.

He slowed the pace. "Sorry. Just anxious to get you to myself."

Somehow she doubted that. "They won't bite, you know."

He looked down at her. "Who?"

"The women. They're just ordinary people who need help."

"If you say so."

"If you got to know them, you would understand their problems a little better."

"I don't want to get to know them."

They had reached the truck, and she let him open the door and help her inside. Topic closed for now. She had no desire to spoil the evening by arguing over the shelter. In the short time it took to reach Little Bush, they talked about the weather, the horses — safe stuff. At the coffee house he led her to a back booth that allowed more privacy.

Latte for her, coffee for him, he reverted back to the earlier subject. "Tell me you haven't changed your mind about keeping the shelter open."

Katie sat her cup down. "Call me the typical woman, changing her mind, and then changing it back. I can't ignore the feeling that I'm where God wants me to be, so I'm not going to close the shelter. It's a challenge, but one I can't abandon." At this point, she didn't care about his reaction. Her mind was made up, and nothing he said would change it. "The house wouldn't sell without a new roof anyway."

He shoved his cup back, slopping coffee over the rim. "You can't be serious. What are you doing, waiting until you go bankrupt and lose your grandfather's land?"

"My land now," she corrected. "I know it seems insane, but the shelter is *me*, Warren. Women deserve a safe haven from abuse, and they deserve to have a chance to develop job skills and start over. Someone has to do it, and I want to be a part of that movement."

Warren reached to take her hands. "Listen to me. I met a woman. Her name isn't important, but it's enough to know that I fell for her, fell hard. I thought we would have a life together."

Katie heard the pain in his voice, and she felt tears forming. After all these weeks, he was opening up to her. "I'm listening."

"I trusted her. I'd have given her anything she wanted; she had no reason to treat me the way she did."

He released her hands and picked up his coffee cup. "She charged thousands on my credit cards, costing me a fortune. Once she had the material things, she drained me emotionally. She ran off with a man I'd considered my friend. I got a phone call from her in Belize warning me not to come after her. It was over."

Katie shook her head. She suspected as much, but he'd never said and she'd never asked. "I'm so sorry." This time she reached out for his hand, holding tight. "Women sometimes do hateful things, but not all women. You're a victim, much like the shelter women."

His eyes hardened. "I'm not a victim of anything other than stupidity."

She couldn't argue. Why would a man turn his credit card over to a woman he was dating? Warren appeared to have more savvy.

"I loved her. You know how I was in school, Katie, the nerd. She was the first woman to make me feel important. I had just started on Wall Street and was still learning the ropes. It was like I owned the world when I was with her, but then after several years she walked away. The nerd struck out again."

Katie leaned forward, her eyes locking with his. "Don't give her the satisfaction of ruining your life."

He nodded. "I know I have some serious hang-ups because of her, but I'm working on overcoming them. In the meantime, I need your patience. I feel something between us, Katie. I know you've felt it. I've tried to ignore it, tried to keep you at arm's length, but it isn't working. That's why I'm asking that you reconsider and close the shelter. Give us a chance. The shelter may be your calling, and it may be a worthy one, but it isn't my calling." His gaze held hers. "Won't you reconsider? Give us a chance to find solid footing?"

Her heart sank. Well, here it was — what she'd hoped and prayed for. A chance with a man. A few days earlier, she'd been so certain he was *the* man. The shelter was threatening him and undermining their future. What did she do now?

She did the only thing she could think to do. She made a promise that she knew she wouldn't, couldn't keep. "I'll reconsider, but Warren, the shelter is my life. I'd be lost without it."

"Is it more important than us?"

It was a question she wasn't prepared to answer because never in a million years had she expected this reaction.

They sat for another half hour, Katie drinking another latte and Warren an equal amount of coffee, before returning to the pickup. Warren was the ultimate suitor, attentive, polite, and tonight, affectionate. Katie felt her resolve weakening.

Shelters all over the USA would lend hope to the abused; Candlelight was only one in thousands.

But it was hers.

Then suddenly he took her into his arms and lowered his mouth to kiss her. Her fingers traced the outline of his rugged features, features she knew so well, or did she? Did she really see behind his mysterious façade? Her senses told her he was a man, a handsome complex man. She explored his high cheekbones, skin exposed to Wyoming's rough winters. As the kiss became deeper, she relaxed, threading her fingers through thick dark hair that faintly smelled of shampoo. Maybe this would work—this odd thing between them. Not love—not yet and not fully on her part, but a lingering hope that maybe, in time, she would be his healing source. This was not a relationship with absolutes. Only time would tell if it would survive its rocky course.

Later they passed Ben parked in front of the bank on traffic duty. As they drove by he pulled out and followed them down Main Street. At the city limits, Katy expected him to turn around and go back to Little Bush, but instead he kept following them at a distance, never closing the gap, but never falling behind, either.

Warren kept an eye on the rearview mirror. "What does the creep think he's doing?"

She flinched at the word "creep." Ben was anything but a creep, and she owed him a debt of gratitude she could never repay. "He's probably on traffic duty. I'm sure he doesn't spend all of his time stalking speeders."

Warren flipped the night visor on the mirror. "He better get off my tail." Warren increased his speed, whipping into a narrow lane. "Hold on. I'm going to lose this hotshot lawman."

"Hey!" The exclamation came out stronger than she intended, but Warren was whipping down a narrow road like a crazed gazelle. Katie braced her hand against the dash and held on.

"Warren! This is insane. Stop it! You're going to get a ticket." He'd be lucky if Ben didn't throw him behind bars. The speedometer registered sixty, sixty-five. Seventy. Seventy-five. Ben stayed on his tail. She had a sense both Warren and Ben enjoyed the contest — that they were egging the other one on.

Warren spared a glance in her direction. "You ever stop to think maybe lover boy is the one who tried to hassle you? Ever think of that, Katie? Well I have, and believe me, if he's responsible . . ."

The unspoken threat settled around her heart like a noose as the chase continued. She had thought of that — she didn't want to, but . . .

Katie, listen to you. You don't have a clue who was causing you trouble. You've suspected Neil Townsend, Ben, who else? Maybe it was one of them, or maybe it was someone you haven't even considered. Why not Meg? Why not Janet or Ruth? Or throw the cats and dogs in — Goldie and Fritz harassing you.

As quickly as the race began, it ended. Ben turned off on a side road, and the squad car disappeared. Katie sat back, mentally mopping perspiration off her brow. Men. They could be insane!

When they drove into the farm lot, Warren stopped the pickup and turned to face her.

"I'll take my good-night kiss here. I don't care for an audience."

"Neither do I." She gripped the door handle and got out. He'd had his kiss.

He rolled down his window. "It's not your job to save the world!"

The roofers arrived early in the morning, bringing chaos — pounding hammers, debris from the old roof, men running up and down ladders carrying bunches of shingles. Katie was thankful there wasn't a baby in the house, though one better show up soon, or the drama would suffer.

The women bore the noise well, with only occasional outbursts of hammer fatigue. Meg was stoic, determined not to bother anyone. The expectant mother was practically living in a fishbowl, every eye tuned on her.

Forty-eight hours later, a new roof covered the shelter, and the house warmed again. Katie spent a lot of time talking to God, thanking him for his blessings. She didn't know how she'd pay for the thing, but it was good to know there was something stronger than a tarp between her and the sky.

Thirty-Two

Christmas Day steadily drew closer and still no baby in the manger. The drama had been rehearsed so many times, excitement waned. The only missing prop was a baby. The women were on point, ready to make a hospital run day or night.

Any disturbance caught Katie's attention, and Fritz barking late one night woke her instantly. The dog's protective instincts rarely proved wrong. Slipping from a warm bed, Katie stepped into her slippers and then pulled on her housecoat. She knew the deal between her and Tottie—no one goes out at night alone, but she didn't intend to go outside. She'd just peek out the window and see what had the dog so upset.

Easing aside the lace sheer in the front room, she came face to face with a man peering back at her.

Yelping, she sprang back, heart hammering in her throat.

He rapped on the frosted pane.

Did intruders announce themselves? No. Slowly easing the curtain back, Katie recognized Ben.

Whirling, she marched to the front door, undid the chain, hit the safety lock, then the door lock. When she opened the screen, she was prepared to throttle him. Was he nuts? Creeping around the premises at this time of night? If Tottie had heard him, he'd be quickstepping buckshot right now.

"Ben O'Keefe! Have you lost your mind?"

"No." His voice held a sheepish note.

"What are you doing here?" Suspicion replaced her fear. Why would Ben be sneaking around like a common criminal, unless . . . Her eyes narrowed.

"Now don't get your bustle in a knot. I can explain."

"You'd better."

"I was checking the roof."

"In the dark?"

He held up a flashlight. "Fritz saw the light and started barking."

His tone was hard to discern. Was he sheepish because she caught him? Embarrassed? Or surprised he'd been busted?

"Why were you checking the roof?"

"I planned to get out here earlier in the day, but something came up. I'd gone to bed, and then woke up remembering that I wanted to check the men's work."

"Ben." That was about as lame an excuse as Katie had ever heard. "They're reputable roofers."

"I didn't say they weren't. I just thought I'd do you a favor and check the work."

"It couldn't wait until morning?"

He shrugged. "I suppose it could, but I'd just lie there and think about it all night, so I figured I might as well check it out, then go home and get some sleep."

"You're lucky you're not spitting buckshot."

"I know. Sorry. I considered calling, but I knew you'd be asleep, and I saw no reason to disturb the whole household in order for me to walk around the house a couple of times and

271 / LORI COPELAND

make sure the roofers got the gutters back on right. So shoot me."

"I reserve the privilege."

"Stupid move," he agreed. "Night."

She shut the door, slid the lock, then the safety lock and the chain.

If it were *anybody* but Ben, she'd call the sheriff.

❃

Katie woke December 22 and looked at the clock: 12:30 a.m. She lay staring into the dark, trying to decide what woke her. She sniffed the air. Coffee. She smelled coffee. Someone was in the kitchen.

Throwing off the covers, she swung her legs over the side of the bed and fumbled for her slippers. She grabbed her robe on her way out of the bedroom, slipping it on as she descended the stairs.

Meg was seated at the table wearing a pained expression, a cup of coffee before her. She glanced up when Katie entered. "Did I wake you? Sorry."

"No. I smelled coffee and wanted a cup." She sized up Meg's intermitted winces. "Lightening pains again?"

Meg took a deep breath and closed her eyes. "I don't think so."

Katie frowned. "Are you having pains?"

She nodded. "I couldn't sleep, and while I don't feel exactly like I did the time before, something isn't right."

Katie shot to her feet. "Sit right there. I'm going to get Tottie."

By the time she roused Tottie, the other women were downstairs. The verdict was unanimous: a baby was on its way.

Pandemonium broke out as the women scrambled to their rooms to dress. Ruth grabbed the bag Meg had packed for the event. Janet and Katie ushered the young woman out to the waiting jeep, and Janet made Katie promise to call the moment the child was born.

Thirty-Three

Forty-eight hours later, Tottie fussed over the newborn like a mother hen. "Careful—put the blanket over her head. It's snowing again."

Meg protectively drew her daughter to her chest. "Will snow hurt her? Should I ask the doctor to let us stay until it's over?" The anxious mother glanced at Katie. "I can't do this!"

Katie gently took her arm and urged her into the jeep. "Snow won't hurt Chrissy, and you *can* do this. You're going to be a wonderful mother." Meg's natural instinct had already kicked in. Admittedly though, she had much to learn about newborns, and Katie would be learning right along with her.

This should be your baby. Your biological clock is ticking, ticking, ticking.

You can't let a clock determine your future. When the time is right ...

Tottie climbed into the farm truck, complaining. "I hope the old heater's working. My feet can't take much more of this cold."

"It was working earlier," Katie called. She climbed behind the jeep's steering wheel. "The only thing we have to worry about is getting this baby home." She grinned at Meg.

Katie started the motor. Meg and her baby were coming home for Christmas. Life was good.

Meg adjusted the blanket over the baby's head. "I don't know anything about babies. What if I do something wrong?"

Katie reached over and patted her hand. "You know more than you think you do. And you're not alone. You have us. We're a family. Don't worry. You'll do fine."

Funny, she could hand out assurance to others and have so little herself. She knew that keeping the shelter open was the right decision, but it was difficult to not give into worry and indecision. *I'm trying, Lord. Don't give up on me.*

Mother and child went straight to bed upon arriving home. For once the old house gave off rosy warmth. Outside snow flew against the new roof, but inside, Christmas Eve day reflected the spirit of the season. A tree that touched the ceiling conquered the living area, dressed in gold tinsel, bright red ornaments, and strings of popcorn. Janet volunteered her services for cookie duty in the kitchen while Ruth unpacked Meg's overnight bag. A small changing station filled with necessities sat beside the infant's cradle.

Katie surveyed the team with pride, knowing that she had given these women a place where they could feel safe and be themselves. The spirit of Christmas was alive and well at Candlelight. In the late afternoon, the women gathered for dinner, a festive soup with a name Katie could never pronounce and a recipe handed down from Tottie's ancestors, and warm bread freshly baked.

The baby had slept through the afternoon, and Meg was starting to relax. Pride warred with panic on the young mother's face when she cradled the newborn in her arms. Did Mary have much the same fears when she held her firstborn that night so long ago? Probably. Some things never change. Katie realized that she was looking forward to the humble nativity play. She'd invited Warren to come, but he had begged off, saying he had business that would last well into the evening. Katie saw through the thinly veiled excuse, but she hadn't argued.

She joined Ruth in the living room to help prepare for the evening drama. A manger now sat where the sofa used to be. A shiny star hung suspended from the upper right corner of the living room. Goldie and Fritz, drafted to portray sheep, sat on their haunches and tried to scratch off sets of corduroy horns (the only available material in the house) taped to their heads.

Janet and Ruth donned bed sheets and tied bailing twine at their waists to become passable shepherds. "Do you think Meg feels up to this?" Janet adjusted her sheet robe, fidgeting with the folds.

Ruth bent to help. "She says she does. She says she's feeling good."

Behind the cradle, a sixty-watt lamp, sans shade, illuminated the reenactment of the Savior's birth.

Katie put the finishing touches on the manger and prepared to don her costume, a king bearing myrrh, gold, and frankincense when she heard a knock on the back door. When she answered, Warren stood before her holding a huge red poinsettia—one of the largest she had ever seen.

"Merry Christmas!"

Astonishment and elation shot through Katie. She pulled him inside. "What happened to your business meeting?"

He shrugged out of his heavy jacket coated with snow. "I finished early, and I never miss a command performance." He leaned to brush his mouth across her cheek.

In spite of her invitation, she had very little hope he'd spend Christmas Eve at the shelter.

Katie carried the poinsettia to the living room and sat it next to the manger. It looked good, right somehow, next to the cradle, and held a special significance for Katie this snowy night of miracles.

Warren took center front in a folding chair positioned for his viewing pleasure. Katie hurriedly changed. House lights lowered. Soft music began to play.

Action.

Meg, carrying the infant, appeared in the doorway with Joseph, aka Tottie, on her left side. Joseph and Mary slowly walked to the manger where Meg knelt, gently placing the child in the cradle.

A CD of Mannheim Steamroller sprinkled "Silent Night" in the background.

To the left, two shepherds, Ruth and Janet, watched their flocks resplendent in corduroy horns. Goldie sat on her haunches, tongue lolling to one side, and eyed Warren. Katie prayed the friendly pet wouldn't lunge and make a scene. The canine loved attention.

Janet stepped aside and reached for a pulley. Amid squeaks, a large star hoisted to center attention.

Katie, a magnificent king, made her appearance dressed in a gold sheet with a cardboard sequined crown around her head. She towered above petite Mary when she offered gifts: first gold, then frankincense, then myrrh.

Goldie's eyes pivoted to the colorful jars.

"Easy, boy," Katie whispered, knowing the dog's propensity for curiosity.

Woof.

Inside the cradle, the baby stirred.

Katie knelt on the third presentation, myrrh, and bowed her head.

Woof.

A couple more minutes, Goldie. Hold on.

The music swelled magnificently, the "Carol of the Bells."

The infant started awake and then released a series of *waaa waaas* when the powerful tune was amplified in the small theater arena.

Goldie's eyes switched from Meg to the baby, from the baby to Warren, then back to Meg. Her tongue hung lower, salvia dripping on the stage. Her wagging backside knocked the manger cockeyed. Other thin props toppled like dominoes.

Waaa, waaa, waaa!

Meg caved. She reached for the infant at the same time Goldie lunged. Katie yelped, dropping her staff. "Goldie! Sit!"

Waaa, waaa, waaa!

Ruth made a grab for the dog, but the canine escaped the trap and thrust her head into the cradle, nosing the source of the crying.

Tottie poked the end of her staff at the dog, but Goldie refused to move. She sniffed and licked.

Waaa, waaa!

Meg batted the dog aside and clutched the child protectively to her chest. "Get!"

Goldie then turned on Warren. With a bounding leap, she landed in the rancher's lap, licking his nose and burrowing her searching snout into Warren's coat pocket.

Chairs overturned and staffs fell to the floor as "Carol of the Bells" crescendoed throughout the room.

Chaos battled bedlam.

When the last music strain died away, Katie had subdued the dog and banished her to the outdoors. Slipping the lock, she returned to the living room. The scene that met her eyes was one of shambles. Toppled manger. Poinsettia upturned on its side, blooms trampled. The shepherds sitting on a folding chair, dazed. Meg had whisked the infant to safety, and the look on Tottie's face was nothing less than despair.

Silence filled the room.

Then Katie heard slow clapping.

Her eyes flew to the source, and she saw Warren standing in the doorway applauding the performance.

For a moment she wanted to cry. All of the hard work, all the late night practices. Ruined.

Instead, she burst into laughter.

Seconds later, one by one the others followed. Janet, Ruth, Warren, and eventually Tottie joined in.

They laughed, each round getting stronger until they held their sides, tears rolling from the corners of their eyes.

When Katie found her voice, she shoved her askew crown back from her forehead and announced between snickered gasps, "And, ladies and gentleman, this completes tonight's performance." She curtsied. "The women of Candlelight

Shelter thank you for coming and invite you for cookies and punch in the kitchen area."

Then she folded over a chair and collapsed in a storm of laughter.

Thirty-Four

Calm restored, the women tried to salvage the remains of the manger. Goldie and Fritz were allowed back inside to gobble down a special treat—chicken-flavored dog biscuits. Goldie was forgiven for her part of the fiasco, although the women agreed she'd never make it in the movies. The joyful spirit of Christmas reigned throughout the old house as the women and guest consumed cups of cold eggnog and sugary treats provided by Ruth and Tottie.

Katie started in to the living room to change the CD when Warren snagged her around the waist. "Caught you!"

Grinning, she allowed the capture, aware of the mistletoe dangling overhead.

Drawing her close, Warren kissed her. Color warmed her cheeks when she returned his ardor. His reservations seemed to have melted like spring snow, and she dared hope his attitude toward the shelter was changing.

The women clapped when the kiss went on longer than necessary. Katie wondered *how* long it would go on, but Tottie interrupted the embrace when she bumped them apart on her way through to the kitchen.

Flushed, Katie stepped back but not before Warren captured her hand and held on tightly.

When the doorbell rang around nine, Warren had still refused to release her hand. Together they opened the door and found the sheriff standing in a near blizzard.

Katie's smile widened. "Ben! Merry Christmas!" Her eyes scanned his familiar form. For some crazy, completely irrational reason, she was happy to see him.

Ben eyes appraised the festive atmosphere, women's soft laughter, carols playing in the background. Katie knew it didn't take a wise man to know a party was in progress.

The sheriff removed his hat. "Sorry to bother you." He shuffled an envelope between his fingers. "I wanted to deliver this on my way to Susan's."

Katie focused on the envelope, smiling when he handed it to her. "Your sister is having a family dinner tonight?"

"Yes, she is."

"I didn't know sheriffs were so domesticated." Warren smile didn't reach his eyes. "Working late?"

Katie noticed Ben didn't rise to the bait. "No. I was asked to deliver this tonight."

Warren drew Katie closer to his side. "You should take more time to enjoy life, Sheriff. It'll be over before you know it."

Katie tore open the envelope, her eyes skimming the brief note.

Katie,

    A few of us in town decided that in lieu of exchanging gifts this year, we'd like to fix the shelter roof.

    God bless you and the work you're doing.

Ben

At least fifty signatures accompanied the sheriff's. Speechless, Katie stared at the gift.

Ben cleared his throat. "There should be over thirty-five hundred dollars there—unless I miscounted."

Warren's smile faded. "Katie has put a new roof on the shelter. The money isn't needed."

Katie located her voice. "Yes, it is! I mean, I can pay off the loan with no interest." She stared at the windfall, and then burst into tears. "Thank you, God!" Katie lunged and threw herself into Ben's arms. "Thank *you!*" she whispered against the warmth of his cleanly shaven neck. "You can't possibly know what this means to me."

She'd barely been able to sleep nights for thinking of Grandpops and how he'd be so disappointed in her if he knew she'd mortgaged the house. There'd been no other way, but now Ben had worked a miracle. She knew that he was responsible for this, knew without a doubt, and she could never, ever repay his vote of confidence.

His arms closed briefly around her and for a second, he held her. She settled into his arms, aware of the stiff collar on his crisp shirt, the smell of cold air and Dial soap.

Warren reached out and drew Katie back into his arm. "Thank you, Ben. Inform the town that Katie appreciates the gift."

Giving Ben a parting smile, Katie settled beside Warren. "Please. Come inside and have a cup of eggnog. Tottie and Ruth have baked goodies—"

"Another time, thanks." Ben settled his hat on his head. "I was due at my sister's half hour ago, and the weather is getting pretty nasty."

As he turned and walked away, Katie left Warren's side. "Merry Christmas!"

Ben lifted a hand of acknowledgment and continued on to his car. Snow fell in wet sheets from a brooding sky.

Katie lifted a hand and caught a flake, her earlier festive mood diminished. Loneliness swept her. She missed Grandpops and Grandmoms. She missed childhood innocence. She missed Ben's friendly banter. And worse, she was starting to doubt herself, exactly the way her guests had been taken in by the men they loved. Had she become an enabler because of one old gypsy that evening so many years ago? She told herself that God and only God guided her life, but was she practicing her belief?

Hugging her waist, she closed the door. *Why so melancholy? Wasn't this a magical night? Wasn't everything coming to a satisfying culmination? A new roof accepted the snow. Warren was coming around quickly now. Why this sudden feeling of incompleteness, the sense that new beginnings were a sham and the worst was yet to come?*

Wrapping his arm around her waist, Warren drew Katie deeper into the shelter's warmth. "Why the glum face?"

"Oh, I guess in a way I feel sorry—and guilty about the way I've treated Ben. He's been so ... I wish ..."

He finished her incomplete thought. "You wish that Warren would take you for a ride and show you the Christmas lights."

It wasn't exactly *all* she wished, but the suggestion partially restored her festive mood. "I do. I'll tell Tottie where we're going and get my coat."

He steered her to the hall closet. "You're a big girl, and we won't be gone long. Tottie will figure out that we wanted some privacy."

Privacy. Was God opening a whole new world for her, a world of Warren, maybe a new family life? In time she could help him adjust to the shelter and her purpose.

He took her coat from the closet and helped her into it. She reached for her cell phone and stuck it in her coat pocket as they went out the door.

Light spilled from the shelter windows. Inside music and laughter and new life thrived. For the briefest of moments, Ben flashed through Katie's mind. He was on his way to his sister's tonight. Family responsibility. Did he long for his own family? He could have one if he chose. She shouldn't feel responsible for his singleness. Many women in town would walk on hot coals to date Ben. Marry Ben. Have Ben's red-headed, freckle-faced, adorable babies.

Sighing, Katie rested her head on Warren's shoulder as they drove out of the barn lot.

"Warm enough?"

She nodded. Everything was good except for the nagging sense that something was terribly wrong.

Thirty-Five

The wipers whacked to keep up with the falling snow as the pickup rolled down the empty highway. Few motorists chose to brave the slippery roads. Why was it so important to view the lights tonight? When the headlights caught the shadow of Devils Tower silhouetted against the snowy landscape, Katie recalled N. Scott Momday's words, which she had studied in high school: "A dark mist lay over the Black Hills, and the land was like iron ... There are things in nature that engender an awful quiet in the heart of man; Devils Tower is one of them."

"The sight of the Tower never ceases to impress me," she said.

"It is awesome. Can you imagine what ran through people's minds when they came across the rock?"

Katie had spent her junior year volunteering for the park system, and she knew the Kiowa legend by heart.

Eight children played near the rock one day, seven sisters and their brother. Suddenly the boy was struck dumb; he trembled and began to run upon his hands and feet. His fingers became claws, and his body was covered with fur. Terrified, the sisters ran, and the bear ran after them. They came to the stump of a great tree, and the tree spoke to them. It beckoned them to climb upon it, and as they did so it began to rise into the air. The bear appeared and lunged to kill them, but they were just beyond its reach. It reared against the tree and scored the bark all around with its sharp claws. The seven sisters were borne into the sky, and they became the stars of the Big Dipper.

Each time she'd retold the story, she'd been met by wide tourist eyes, eyes that pivoted to reassess the national monument that rose 867 feet from its base. Tonight the Tower looked sinister in the falling snow.

The tourist site was closed. Darkness lay over the Black Hills in hushed reverence.

"We're going to see the lights from the Tower?" Katie laughed. "How do you plan to climb it? Unfortunately I left my rock climbing gear at home."

Warren grinned down at her. "I'm a hometown boy, remember? I know a place where we can see the lights, and it has nothing to do with the Tower being open."

The truck wound along snowy asphalt. When Katie started to doubt there was a way to view local lights other than the Tower road, Warren turned onto a dirt road. Ah, yes. She had forgotten it was here. The road climbed gradually, following the curve of a hill. The ascent was slow and treacherous and proved a challenge even for a four-wheel drive. Halfway up, Warren eased to the side and cut the engine. The vantage point was good. Katie relaxed. She would have never attempted the climb, but men are predators, hunters seeking a challenge.

Settling closer into Warren's arms, her eyes drank in the breathtaking beauty.

"Heaven must be like this."

"You think?" He gently turned her and kissed her lips.

She settled more deeply into his affection, his security.

Warren's voice was so soft she had to strain to hear him. "You've always known that you weren't going to close the shelter, haven't you?"

She closed her eyes, relieved that he knew her so well. "I want *us,* Warren, but the shelter's been my work for so long that I can't close it."

And honestly. She didn't want to spoil the evening by rehashing the subject. Couldn't he just leave it alone?

"You've got a loving nature, Katie. Maybe that's what draws me to you."

He kissed her again and something fluttered. Love, the everafter kind? Or was it a preconceived notion? Once she'd been so sure. Now she wasn't.

When their lips parted, he said. "Let's get out."

"Out?" Katie recoiled. It was cold up here, blizzard conditions. Not fit for man or beast, Grandpops would say. She'd stay in the cab, thanks.

"I think I'll stay put."

"Stay put? A little snow won't hurt you. Let's take a walk; it's so pretty up here."

A chill raced through her. Warren's tone had changed — ever so slightly, but she noticed it. The request was more an order than an invitation. Suddenly she was aware of the isolation, the seclusion. "No, it's too cold. You get out and I'll wait here."

He opened the door and got out, snow enveloping him.

"Nut," she muttered. "It's freezing out there."

He moved around the hood of the pickup and maneu-vered to her side of the truck, losing his footing a couple of times. The door suddenly opened. "Get out."

She shrank back, icy air stealing her breath. "What's wrong?"

"You're the problem. Get out."

Warren's hand snaked into the cab, grasped her arm, and hauled her partway out. She grabbed the doorframe, holding tight until he pried her fingers loose.

"I said get *out*."

Katie fell on her hands and knees in the snow.

Warren grabbed her shoulder, yanking her upright. "Come on. Move!"

Fear, all consuming, filled her. He caught her arm, drag-ging her toward the steep incline. She tried to hold back and fought to break free, but his grip was too strong. Her breath came in ragged gasps, her hands and face stinging from the howling wind. She slipped. He jerked her upright and forced her closer to the precipice. They were exposed to the ele-ments here, no sheltering trees, nothing to break the wintry explosion.

Katie wrenched free, whirling to escape, but Warren was on her in an instant.

"No, you don't. You brought this on yourself. Don't fight me, Katie. I'm bigger and stronger than you."

For the first time in her life, Katie felt small, insignificant to his height.

Warren hauled her against him, and the hatred in his voice rendered her speechless. "You're like all women. Sure you'll help abused women, help them to abandon their men who support and take care of them. Kick the guy in the teeth, right? Watch him suffer?"

"No, it's not like that. I'm not like that." *Help me, God. He's clearly lost his mind!*

The wind tore at her, threatening to hurl her off the exposed trail. Still Warren forced her on, dragging her even higher up the incline. Suddenly he released her and she stumbled. Regaining her balance, she confronted him, instinctively knowing it would be suicide to show fear.

"Why are you doing this? What have I done to you?"

"You know what you've done." His lips drew back in a snarl. "You're a fool, Katie. I gave you every chance to avoid this."

"I don't understand. What are you talking about?" She stalled for time. She could break through to him, turn him away from this cold rage focused on her. Why hadn't she acknowledged his erratic behavior earlier? He'd shown signs, signs she'd chosen to ignore. She was no wiser than the shelter victims.

"Don't play the innocent. I told you. I know women. You're all alike, greedy, grasping, not interested in anyone or anything except yourselves."

Katie struggled to stand erect against the wind-driven snow. "Stop this nonsense. Let's go back to the truck, talk about this." Why was she trying to reason with a madman? The steel glint in his tone terrified her.

"There's nothing to talk about. You and your God. Always prattling about his plan for your life. Let me clue you in, Katie. He doesn't *have* a plan for your life. He doesn't care about you. If there is a God, he doesn't care about your niggling problems. You're on your own, just like the rest of us, so don't give me any junk about how God wants you to keep that shelter open. You're keeping it open because *you* want to, and how I feel or what I want doesn't mean a thing to you."

How could she have been so foolish? This was the man she had wanted to marry? The one she believed God had sent? He was right about one thing, it was her fault she was standing on this snowy hilltop pleading for ... what? Her life?

"You. It's been *you* terrorizing me." Comprehension flooded her. How had she been so blind? How could he have run such a fright campaign and not been discovered?

He laughed. "And you called me to rescue you. How dumb could you be, Katie? You deserved what you got. Wise up, sweetheart. Women are like leeches, sucking the blood out of men. Well, this man isn't going to be taken for another ride."

The blizzard formed a blinding curtain. Katie was trapped in the storm's fury with a deranged mind, and there was a good chance she wasn't going to walk away alive. No one knew where she was. Warren hadn't given her a chance to tell Tottie or the other women. Katie realized he had intended this moment from the time he walked in the door that night.

The snow's reflection sharpened his features, carved of ice. She met his eyes and what she saw horrified her. She backed away slowly, sliding one foot behind the other in a vain attempt to escape the drop-off.

He reached out and snagged her arm. "You're not going anywhere."

She whirled but he lunged, shoving her closer to the edge of the ridge. Scuffling, Katie managed to regain her balance. For one split second, she stared into the face of a killer. "Don't do this. By all that is holy, *don't* do this."

He danced playfully, reaching out to nudge her closer and closer. "Scared, Katie? I've been scared. It's not fun, huh?" He shoved her, and then caught her arm seconds before she fell.

"Stop this!"

"Oh, poor little Katie. Where's your womenfolk? Shouldn't they be here to save you from a big bad ole man?" He reached out with a foot, easing her closer to the precipice.

Katie sidestepped his boot, but suddenly the ground gave way. For an instant, their eyes met before she toppled over the edge.

Warren hit the snow on his stomach, extending a hand. By now she was hanging by a thread on a loose bough.

"I can't ... reach you," she pleaded. Her fingers flayed air.

He scooted closer, bending more, reaching to grab her. Fingers brushed, and then suddenly the bough snapped.

Katie tumbled down, down, down.

Lying perfectly still, Warren listened to the snow and darkness envelope her screams.

"Poor baby." Finally, he leaned forward. "Merry Christmas. Broad."

Thirty-Six

Hours passed. No, she had fallen over the cliff only minutes ago, or was it hours? Disoriented, Katie tried to focus. She was on a ledge. Elation filled her. She was alive! She'd found footing. Elation turned to stark dismay. So what? She was perched on a razor-thin ledge with an indeterminable drop beneath her.

No way out.

"No way out, no way out, no way out!" shrieked the howling wind.

Even if she managed to cling to the ledge, she'd quickly die of exposure. Temperatures had to be in the low thirties and dropping. Her coat was heavy, but not heavy enough.

Sometimes what a person wants is under her nose all along. Tottie's words rang in her ears.

Ben, not Warren. Did it take a hundred-foot drop to oblivion to jar her thick senses?

Ben had been in her life for so long, she'd ceased to notice him. *Others knew his worth, but you, Katie, you set your eyes on the superficial, the adventurous; not without God, but not with him either.*

In that tent on the carnival ground, you took your eye off God.

And now you are paying for your mistakes.

Not for a moment did she think God had a vendetta against her. He'd given her choices, and she'd been so certain her choices had been his leading. Why else would he have allowed her to dream? What she wouldn't admit, but now knew with certainty, flooded her. Even with her belief in God, she had put stock in a carnival gypsy's ramblings. Shame flooded her. *Oh God. I'm so very sorry. If only I had listened to my heart instead of meaningless predictions. If only I hadn't taken my eye off of you—just that one moment, and I slipped.*

Sinking to the shelf, Katie huddled, tears rolling down her cheeks. Shelter, she had to find shelter, but there was none. She scooted, pressing her back to the thin wall. The wind had shifted, blowing north. A crevasse, narrow but wide enough to provide a break from the driving snow, offered protection, but not enough. She'd die here on this ledge, and no one would ever find her.

Katie heard the faint snap of dead branches. Someone was coming down the incline. Warren? To finish what he'd started?

Her cell phone rang.

Fumbling in her pocket, she hit the on button. "Hello."

"Katie?" Ben's voice came over the line, cutting in and out with the poor signal.

"Yeah?"

"Where are you?"

"Here."

"Where!"

It hit her. *Her cell phone.* Dear God, forgive a fool! Sitting up straighter, she babbled through stiff lips. "Oh Ben! I'm on a ledge!"

"On a what?"

"A ledge—I fell over an embankment." Her voice caught. "I managed to grab a branch and swing onto a shelf, but I think Warren's coming down the hill to find me ..."

No questions about Warren. No demanded explanations on why she had fallen over a cliff or why Warren was on his way down the hillside. *Thank you, my dear, sweet Ben.* Maybe he knew—maybe he'd known all along that Warren was a rat.

"*Exactly* where are you?"

Exactly? Think, Katie. Where are you? She remembered turning off on a dirt road and the treacherous incline.

"Dirt road," she managed through lips anesthetized with cold. "About ... half mile from the monument ... easy to miss. Have to watch carefully. On the right ..."

"Dirt road on the right about a half mile from the Tower?"

"I think so—I don't think they use the road much any-more—" The cell phone bleeped. Call ended. Katie's confusion bloomed. Sleep. That's what she needed. She huddled deeper into the crevice, her eyes drifting shut. It wasn't as cold now. *Thank you, God. It isn't as cold.*

Why wasn't it so cold?

Katie threw up her hands and shrugged, giggling. "Maybe spring has sprung!" Spring with its warm breezes and pasque-flowers carpeting the foothills. Larkspur, penstemons, and blue flag on the prairies.

Eight children were playing at the foot of the rock. Seven sisters and their brother.

You're hallucinating, Katie.

They were stars now. Big Dipper stars. She snickered. Maybe it wasn't God's plan for her to marry at all; maybe he intended her to be a big ole star ...

❦

Ben phoned for backup. He needed help, and he needed it fast. Katie sounded confused. She'd been exposed to the cold for too long. His mind went over the hazards of exposure. The body could be fooled into thinking it was warm and start shedding coats and other garments, speeding up the time of death. And if she was on a narrow ledge, she could get confused and walk off it to her death.

Ruby answered, and Ben filled her in on details. "Have an ambulance and emergency equipment standing by. We have someone over the side. I'll call with the location as soon as I have it."

"Someone over the side on a night like this? These crazy climbers."

He didn't explain.

"I need backup. Ruby? Patch me through to Candlelight Shelter." Seconds later Tottie came on the line.

"You were right," Ben said.

"I *knew* it. I've suspected that man was up to no good when I saw him take Katie without telling anyone. Where is she?"

"She's okay, Tottie. Relax. I'll bring her home as soon as I can. Gotta go." He clicked off. *God, help me keep that promise.*

Ben hit the siren, and the squad car flew down the highway throwing a wide slough of mud and slush. He located the dirt road and the tire tracks half hidden by blowing snow. One set going in, but nothing coming out.

What was he looking at here? Assault? Attempted murder? Was Warren Tate now making his way down the hillside to finish Katie off? He would assume that he could take his time, that no one would be looking for Katie, and nothing indicated that Tate meant her any harm. He couldn't survive the elements.

Halfway up the road, Ben spotted Warren's vehicle. Pulling in behind the truck, Ben braked and looked the situation over. The vehicle didn't appear to be occupied. He eased his nine millimeter automatic out of the holster and opened his car door. Nothing moved. Cautiously he approached Warren's pickup. A quick look inside revealed his suspicion; the truck was empty. Ben played light over the ground, spotting the faint outline of footsteps. Two people had walked away from the pickup. No one had come back. The headlights were on.

Warren had brought Katie out here for what? To harm her? Silence her? Whatever his intentions, something had gone wrong.

Thank you, God, that she had managed to get on that ledge. But if Ben didn't find Katie soon, it wouldn't matter. She wouldn't last long in this storm. If only he hadn't wasted so much time arguing with Tottie—wasted time that could cost Katie her life.

"She's in trouble, Ben. I feel it in my bones."

"I can't intrude on her and Warren's date," he'd argued.

"You can and you will. Something's wrong, Ben. Bad wrong. You go up there. Now."

A muscle worked tightly in his jaw. *Stay cool. You can't help Katie unless you focus.* His instinct was to go after the miscreant and deal with him man to man, though Tate wasn't a man. He was a coward, a simpering coward who badgered helpless women. Heat built inside Ben, and he clamped his jaw tighter and made a second call to dispatch to give his location.

Help arrived, one, then two cars. In the distance, a siren's wail filled the stormy night.

Deputies exited cars and approached Ben. "What have we got?" Ralph Parker studied the scene. Ralph had been with Ben twelve years, and there was none better at his job.

"Woman over the side." Ben pulled on a heavy down jacket and zipped it. "She's on a ledge somewhere down there. I'm going over."

"Are you sure?" Ralph frowned. "Why not wait until the emergency crews get here? The firemen will have better equipment than we have."

"Not on your life. Katie Addison's down there."

"Katie?" Both newcomers turned to focus on the steep incline.

Pulling on gloves, Ben snapped, "Find Warren Tate; he'll be able to give you the specifics. He's in the area. Get the others on it. You stay here in case I need you. I'll go after Katie."

"Is she okay?"

"Yeah." Ben turned to study the incline. "She's more than okay."

Brows lifted. "How can you know?" Bill asked.

He shot the man an impatient look. "I just talked to her on her cell phone."

Bill Hanks lifted his hat and scratched his head. "Of course. He just talked to her on her cell phone. Why didn't we think of that?"

"Ben, listen." Ralph latched onto his arm. "You can't go down there. Man alive, you don't have a chance of finding her in these conditions. Wait until help arrives."

"I'm going down when I locate the spot she went over. You know that." He strapped on a safety harness and tightened the straps. "It can't be too far from Tate's truck."

After a tense minute, the deputy nodded. "We'll have your back. If you need us, call, but be careful."

Ben followed the tracks, losing them more than once, but eventually they led to the spot on the rim of a steep cliff where it was evident someone had shuffled. He gaped at the sharp drop-off. Bad enough in good weather, it would be almost impossible to descend now that it was snow-covered and dark. Still, he didn't have a choice. Katie was down there some-where. He'd talked to her. She was alive, and he had to find her and get her out of there while she still had a chance.

Ben worked his way down the slippery incline, rope in hand. Twice he paused to dial Katie's cell phone, but the ring switched to voice mail. Where was she? There could be a hundred and one places she could have fallen. How could he expect to find her?

God, I don't ask you for much, but this time I'm asking you for a lot. Lead me to her, Lord. She might not need me, but I need her.

The soles of his boots slipped and slid. He caught hold of the rope to steady his descent. Distant sirens grew closer. Help was on its way, but help would be useless if he couldn't pinpoint her location, and if he didn't, and soon, they'd both die of exposure.

He flicked the flashlight beam over the hillsides and yelled, "Katie! Can you see the light?"

Light? Katie stirred. *Yeah, I can see the light. It's so pretty!* She reached out, drawn to the distant dancing, mellow beam filled with swirling white flakes. Could she touch it? There would be warmth inside the light, blessed warmth.

Grandpops suddenly appeared, holding out his hand. "Come on, Katie girl! You're going to like it up here."

"I'm coming." She reached out, groping the air, yet she didn't think that she actually reached out because her hands were too cold to move. Her senses reached out.

"Katie! Look around you. I'm shining the light. Can you see it?"

Katie stirred. "Ben? What are you doing here? Grandpops didn't say anything about you."

She struggled to open heavy lids. Vision slowly cleared, and she saw a bobble of light on a distant hillside. Light. Pretty, pretty light in the falling snow. *It looks like something out of painter Jesse Barnes's portraits, warm light spilling onto pristine snow.*

"Katie! Answer me!"

Cranky, cranky. Ben was certainly out of sorts this evening. She stirred, rising up on her forearm to focus on the beam.

"Can you see the light?"

"I see it!" Sheesh. She curled into a fetal position. Sleepy ... so incredibly sleepy.

Thirty-Seven

Ben played the lightbeam over the hillside. How far down could she have fallen? She could be hidden by an overhang. Despair filled him. How could he possibly find her in time? *God, help me! I have to find her.* He swept the beam of light down the incline one more time and something caught his attention. A foot. A woman's booted foot. Katie? *It has to be her.* But Warren Tate was out here somewhere. Could he have fallen too?

Moving slowly Ben eased his way down the glazed slope. He slipped, dislodging a stone that plunged over the edge. Pausing, he held his breath. "Katie? It's me, Ben. I'm coming. Wait for me."

Silence. He inched his way down, one step at a time. The wind tore at him, trying to peel him off the mountain. Finally the ledge was one step away. The light picked out Katie, curled in a fetal position.

He'd found her. *Thank you, God.*

She was still, so still. He dropped and crawled onto the narrow strip of rock, knelt and searched for a pulse. His heart jumped when he found a narrow thread of life. He fumbled for his cell phone, praying he could get a signal. He couldn't.

Shifting, he held the phone over his head, searching. Finally he got one bar.

Ben sagged with relief when Ralph answered. "I've got her. Look for my light. I'll need some help getting her out of here."

"We're with you, buddy. Got ropes and climbing gear, and we're on our way."

Ben ended the call and crawled back to Katie, pulling her close, trying to provide life-giving warmth. "Hang on. I've got you."

As soon as she was safe, Ben was going to find Warren Tate, find out exactly what had taken place out here, and if he was responsible. Violence wouldn't help. He was an officer of the law. He'd find Tate, turn him over to the authorities, and let justice take its course, no matter how badly he'd like to break the creep's neck.

Right now he had one single wish. That Tate was still alive to get what he had coming to him. One petition he didn't ask of God.

❄

Heaven was hushed. Katie figured there would be more fanfare when a child of God came home, but it appeared that stiff sheets and rubber-soled shoes were more popular than angelic hoopla.

"Katie. Open your eyes for me."

"I don't want to." For the first time in hours she felt good. Warm. No icy fingers or stiff limbs.

Tottie's voice barked the command. "Open your eyes, Katherine."

Oh, all right. She worked at it. First one heavy lid, then the other barely cracked. "What?"

"Oh, thank God." *Was that Ruth's voice? Was she here?*

Katie forced both eyes open. Ruth, Tottie, and Janet towered above her with anxious faces. "What?" she mumbled.

Tottie's worried face swam before her. "I'll get the nurse."

Ben? Where's Ben? Sweet Ben. Oh. Poor Ben. He was dead too? What happened to everybody? Tragic accident?

Ever so slowly the room focused, and Katie's mind started to clear. Her gaze roamed the sterile room. Hospital. She was in a hospital bed. Half-rising, she croaked, "Janet, Meg, Ruth? You shouldn't be here."

Janet gently eased her back to the pillow. "You've had an accident, but you're going to be fine."

"But you should be at the shelter . . ."

"We snuck in the back way. We were careful."

"Did I wreck the jeep?" Katie's hand came up to touch her head. "What day is this—Christmas Eve, isn't it?"

"Christmas Day," Ruth supplied as she smoothed the sheet. "You've been through quite a night."

Tottie returned, trailed by a nurse. By the time Katie's vitals were checked and the nurse gave her an encouraging smile, she'd heard the story of how Ben had found and rescued her from the ledge.

"Warren?" Katie prayed that he hadn't gotten away with his brutal rampage.

"Sitting in the county jail." Tottie's sharp retort didn't surprise Katie. "And I hope he'll stay there. Warren Tate isn't the man we thought him to be. I had my suspicions he was pulling the wool over our eyes, but I didn't want to upset you with my fears." Tottie smoothed Katie's hair off her forehead. "This is hard to hear, but you'll have to know sometime. Warren has been the one terrorizing you. It's been him all along."

"I know, he told me, right before he knocked me off balance and I fell over the cliff." Why would Warren want to hurt her? What had she ever done to him to make him hate her? Protecting abused women? He was sick, terribly sick; the man needed professional help.

Tottie shook her head. "He hates women, all women, Katie. That girlfriend of his did a number on him, but the trouble started long ago. According to Ben, he moved back here to evade charges being filed against him in New York for misappropriating funds. It was only a matter of time before the authorities caught up with him."

"But why did he want to hurt me?"

"Because you represented everything he hated, women in particular."

"He was so helpful in the beginning—moving the horses, helping with the budget. Why would he help me when he was hostile toward women?"

Janet shrugged. "Who knows the minds of the deranged? When I first met my husband, he was a perfect gentleman. Later he turned into Godzilla." She sat on the edge of the bed. "Listen, be glad that you've found out before you married the man. A woman can be closed-minded when love is at stake."

Katie grasped Janet's hand, reality sinking in. Warren had almost killed her. Her recent reservations had been right, and yet she had continued to encourage the relationship. Was she so desperate to marry and have children that she blindly closed her eyes when God repeatedly gave her clues to Warren's true nature—his moodiness, his lack of human compassion for the shelter women, wanting her to close the shelter down, his controlling nature, and the way he resented her friendship with Ben? She knew the signs of an abuser. Why had she so willfully ignored them?

Her only excuse was love, the pursuit of love and what began as a true desire to follow God's leading. There was only one hitch. She had been obsessed with Warren, controlling ways and all. She wasn't the only woman caught by this snare. But if she lived long enough, and God gave her the opportunities, there'd be far fewer women victimized by abusers like him.

"Katie." Janet spoke and Katie opened her eyes. "Don't blame yourself. Every day women awake to the reality that they're in an abusive relationship, but it's easier to get into the situation than to get out of it. They don't realize what they've gotten themselves into until it's too late. I understand he was abusive to his former girlfriend too."

Hot tears rolled down Katie's cheeks. "I was obsessed with him."

Janet laughed, not unkindly, but with war-torn misery. "We *all* thought we were in love, Katie. That's why we stuck it out for so long. It's not easy to give up on someone you love, someone who when the battering is over is on his knees vowing to change, to do better. And since that's what we so desperately want, we try again. And again. And again until it gets to be a habit, and we're in too deep to find our way out."

Katie didn't need glasses to see the physical scars on Janet's face or the deeper ones stamped on her heart.

A soft knock sounded, and Katie's eyes switched to the doorway. Her heart double-timed. Ben, sans hat, framed the opening, holding a large latte. Her eyes locked with his and an emotionally charged current passed between them.

"Am I disturbing you?"

Tottie seized the moment. "Glad you've come, Ben — we were just on our way out. Would you mind keeping Katie company for a while?"

Oh, Tottie. How obvious! Katie swallowed against a dry throat. "Come in, Ben."

The women melted from the room leaving her and the sheriff to verbally shoot it out. Katie guessed that Ben would undoubtedly gloat that Warren turned out to be a snake. Katie wasn't sure where to start. Maybe with an apology and admitting that she was blinded by a gypsy's wild ramblings. Then she could add to that her unwavering belief that God would send the right soul mate at the right time.

Pride warred with repentance, but the scale tilted to repentance. God had sent the right one, years ago, only she had been too blind to notice him.

Awaking to see what she should have seen all along was a humbling experience.

Ben quietly set the coffee on her nightstand and took a seat next to the bed. "How's it going?"

Katie eyed the latte. "Is that for me, I hope?"

"Your doctor said you could have it."

Closing her eyes, she inhaled the fragrant caffeine. "I could kiss you."

The old Ben would have jumped at the invitation. This sober Ben merely shook his head. "You and your coffee. How's the recovery going?"

"Fine, I think." The fingers on her right hand were frostbitten, and she had sore ribs, various bruises, and scratches. But all in all, she'd survived the incident with no far-reaching consequences — unless you counted her heart hanging in shreds.

"I understand that I owe you my life."

He shrugged. "God didn't need you yet." He flashed a grin. A week ago the familiar gesture would have caused little more than a passing glance. This morning, Katie fixed on the charming way one corner of his mouth lifted slightly more than the other, the crisp, professional uniform, and the way he wore it like he commanded it. His eyes searched and held hers with no hint of subterfuge — clear, honest, and direct.

She reached for his hand. "Can you forgive me for being so wrong?"

Her words brought heightened color to his cheeks. Ben, blushing? No. *Yes*, he was blushing.

"We all have our blind spots."

"What about stupidity?"

"That too." He eased closer, gently lacing his fingers through her bandaged ones. "Men like Warren — while I want to say are a dime a dozen, that's not quite true. There are plenty of good men out there, Katie. Honorable, hard working, self-sacrificing husbands and fathers who make the world turn. The Warrens of the world are there, but in their twisted and distorted views they try to make up for some imagined injustice done to them in their lives."

"I know that, but Ben, after all I've been through in my personal life and what I've seen in the lives of the women who end up at the shelter, I of all people should have seen the warning signs. I'm so ashamed that I didn't."

"You opened your heart to a man, there's nothing shameful about that. You open your heart to everyone."

"And that bothers you." It sure bothered Warren.

"No, I like that about you. You're open and accepting, maybe too much so sometimes, but I wouldn't want you any different. If God hadn't made people like you, I'd hate to think of where we'd be. You make the world a better place. You and others like you make a difference."

"He was the one causing all the trouble. All the noises and weird happenings. Did he confess to that? The incidents weren't all my imagination?"

"No, he wanted you to close the shelter. He contends he didn't plan to hurt you; he just wanted the shelter closed." Ben's hand tightened on hers. "He could so easily have—"

She placed her good hand on his. "But he didn't. Tell me more. I knew I wasn't imagining all those incidents that concerned me."

He answered her remaining questions about noises in the night and the owl (simple and laughable, Warren had bragged). The burned-out security light Warren didn't mention, but the reason why the dogs never barked was easy. On his nocturnal visits, Warren carried pork chop bones in his coat pockets. Goldie was a fool for fresh meat. Every baffling incident was accounted for.

"So you were telling the truth when I caught you sneaking around the backyard that night?"

"I wasn't *sneaking*. I was checking the roof."

She patted him lovingly.

His gaze softened. "Warren thought he could frighten you into closing the shelter, first by mind games—like the crumpled flowers in your mailbox. But when you didn't take the hint, he decided he'd try a softer approach, to talk you out of it. But the more you held on, the more desperate he became.

He wanted the shelter closed and all your attention focused on him. He's one sick dude, Katie."

"So he wasn't attracted to me."

He shrugged. "He was a fool."

"Will he get help?"

Ben nodded. "Considering the New York state warrant on him, my guess is he'll spend a good long time in prison. He will be a very old man before he can cause another woman trouble." He grinned. "There is a ray of hope in this: the town's now aware of the shelter's financial situation, and I think you're going to see donations pick up again. The people here love you, Katie. They don't want to lose you or the shelter. You should be in good shape within a few months."

Katie clung to his fingers, realizing what a true find he was and what a fool she had been. Could he forgive her? She'd even suspected him of harassing her. She summoned her courage, forming words of contrition.

"I haven't been very nice to you, Ben. I'm so sorry."

He winked. "No, you haven't. Where's all that goodness of heart we're talking about?"

She touched her chest, her eyes locked with his. "Here. Right here. Can we continue our friendship? Take time to explore each other, only on different terms now. I'd like a chance to know you, Ben. Know the man, Ben, and not the boy."

"I'm not a boy any longer, Katie."

"I know." Boy, did she know.

Silence closed around them. Finally he lifted his eyes. "Sorry. I don't want to continue down this path. You'll always have a place in my heart, but it's time to concede that what we have doesn't work."

"Oh, Ben, can't we try? This incident has opened my eyes. God has taught me so much about love and what's important and what's not."

He got up and bent to kiss her forehead. This red-headed, hazel-eyed angel had won her heart, and now he was leaving for good. "You're one terrific lady, but from now on, I'm going to concentrate on my future."

Katie blinked back hot tears. Well, what did she expect? Undying love from a man she'd ignored all these years? Ben wanted to put the past behind him and look to the future.

And he couldn't have made it plainer that future did not include her.

Thirty-Eight

Katie woke to a blizzard in progress outside her bedroom window. Closing her eyes, she pulled the sheet over her head. The doctor had released her yesterday with the warning to rest for several days, but this morning she was going to dress and drive into town for a latte, storm or no storm. After the week she'd spent, lattes were a little repayment for the turmoil in her life. Besides, she no longer had to explain expenditures to Warren; he had bigger problems than Katie Addison's lack of financial savvy.

Throwing off covers, Katie got out of bed and headed for the shower. Later, wearing ratty sweats and a ball cap, she found the women in the kitchen gathered around Meg and the baby. Since Chrissy arrived, focus at the shelter had changed from the wants and needs of five women to hovering over this little scrap of humanity. A good baby, she seldom cried, but she seldom needed to. Her every need was met immediately if not sooner.

Katie paused to join in the admiration and reassure Meg that Chrissy was the most beautiful baby in Little Bush and likely the entire world. Meg beamed at the praise. She was a far cry from the hesitant, fearful young woman who had arrived at Candlelight, her belongings clutched in a paper grocery sack.

Katie reached for a coffee cup. "Guess the weather will delay your departure?"

One positive thing had come out of the past hectic week. Meg's grandmother offered to take Meg and the baby into her home. In fact, she was so eager to help, she'd sent money for the plane fare. However, Meg's noon flight to Omaha appeared unlikely to happen that day. Snow pelted the window, and the wind howled around the eaves. Katie was even more grateful for the new roof. She planned to stop by the bank and repay the bank loan when she went for the latte.

Meg tickled the baby under her chin. "Yeah, I guess you'll have to put up with us a few more days."

Katie touched a finger to Chrissy's pug nose. "That's really going to be a problem."

The new mother grinned. "I'll have to leave soon before you guys spoil her rotten."

Tottie sat a bowl of oatmeal in front of Katie. "Too late for that. This old house will be far too quiet when you're gone."

"That's for sure." Ruth leaned over to stroke the baby's silken cheek. She held the baby almost as much as Meg. "She's made Christmas for us this year."

Katie knew Ruth was thinking of her own daughter. If there was any way to do it, they had to help Ruth get custody of that child. Maybe Ben could suggest something. She squelched the thought. Ben wasn't around anymore.

Janet carried her cup of coffee to the table and sat down. "Keep in touch with us, Meg, please. As soon as I can get resettled, I'll send you my address. I want to be an honorary aunt to this little girl."

Meg's smile was one-hundred-watt brilliant. "I'd like that. Being here has changed my life. You guys were there when I really needed someone, and I'll never forget that you cared enough to go to the hospital with me. I ... I love you."

"We love you." Tottie moved back to the kitchen sink. "A pox on this weather."

Katie reached for a day-old paper. "Why, Tottie, I thought you *loved* snow." Silently snickering, Katie waited for the explosion.

"God's sense of humor." Tottie rinsed a dish and set in the drainer. "I have to go to the store for milk."

Katie glanced up. "There's three gallons in the refrigerator."

"Three gallons spoiled. Did you smell it when you bought it?" Tottie shifted to the refrigerator.

Katie shook her head. "You can't smell milk. It's not like in the old days when you could take the cap off the bottle and take a whiff. Besides, I checked the expiration dates." Didn't she? One could only hope.

Tottie waved an uncapped jug under her nose. "It's spoiled. Taste it."

Katie shied away. "Why would I want to taste spoiled milk?"

"How a dairy would have spoiled milk this time of year ..." Tottie muttered all the way to the sink to dump the evidence.

"Better not pour it out," Janet said. "The store will replace it."

Tottie caught the stream and recapped the plastic jug. "I'll head into town so I can get back before the temperatures plummet. It's supposed to drop to zero tonight."

Lowering the paper, Katie stared at her. Tottie's driving abilities left something to be desired in good weather. She couldn't let the woman loose on snow-packed roads and besides—she was going for a latte. "I'll go."

"Don't be silly. You're just out of the hospital."

Other than the bandage on her right fingers and a few sore ribs, she'd never felt better. "I want a latte."

The housekeeper wagged her head. "You'd brave a blizzard for a cup of five-dollar coffee?"

"I don't *pay* five dollars—just three dollars and thirty-nine cents. And it's worth every cent."

"A dollar sixty-one back from a five?" Tottie dunked a skillet in sudsy water. "In my book, that's five dollars a shot."

"To each his own. For me, it's money well spent. Get your list ready, and as soon as I check on Sweet Tea—"

Janet interrupted. "Tottie, while you're out, you can check on that housecleaning job."

"What housecleaning job?" Katie asked.

"Don't argue—we can always use the extra money, and besides, it's a widow's house. The job shouldn't take me much more than a couple of hours a week." Tottie draped the dishcloth across the drying rack.

"The roads are slick," Katie argued. "Can't you call about the work, Tottie?"

"No, I can't call. I want to see what I'm getting into before I agree to clean once a week. Don't worry, the snowplow came by a few minutes ago. I'll be okay."

"But I'm going in anyway—"

Janet interrupted. "Go get your latte. You deserve some time to yourself."

The two women left the room before Katie could change their mind. If Tottie wanted to go running around the countryside in this weather, she'd go, and there wasn't anything Katie could do about it.

Katie checked on Sweet Tea and the other horses and assured the animals that she'd never felt better. She patted a mare's nose, quietly assessing the barn roof. "Good thing the weather's delayed your departure." The animals were now scheduled to be moved the first of next week. She sighed. "You're going to be missed as much as Meg," she assured the animals.

Sweet Tea nickered and accepted the sugar cube she offered. "Oh, you're staying." She ruffled the mare's nose. "Wild horses couldn't get you away from me."

When she returned to the house she found Meg alone, rocking Chrissy. "Has Tottie left already?"

"Twenty minutes ago. There's taco soup simmering on the stove, and Tottie mentioned something about apple cobbler for dinner, so I don't think they'll be gone long." She put the baby over her shoulder and gently patted her back. "Can you hold Chrissy while I take a shower?"

"Sure." Katie peeled out of her coat, warmed her hands before the fire, and then took the infant.

"I'll hurry."

Katie buried her nose in the baby's neck, soaking up the newborn infant smell. She suddenly lifted her head. "Meg, do you think you'll be happy living with your grandmother? You know you're more than welcome to stay here and look for work in Little Bush. You can stay as long as you want."

The young woman grinned. "Oh, Katie, going to Grandma's is the best thing that could happen to me. My Grammy is a churchgoing woman who lives what she believes. She'll be good to me and Chrissy. I didn't think she'd want me after the mistakes I've made, but Grammy told me that she loves me and she needs me. No one has needed me for a long time."

Katie smiled. Grammys were like that, and Meg would be all right. Candlelight had made a difference in her life, and her grandmother would continue the work. Warren had been wrong about so many things, but primarily about these women.

"That's great, Meg. I'm so happy for you."

An hour and a half later, Katie hurried to the jeep, wind-driven snow stinging her face. The warmth of the shelter called to her as she climbed into the cold vehicle and started the engine. Maybe Tottie was right. Coffee wasn't really that important. Katie conceded the housekeeper's point when she backed the jeep down the snowy, steep incline. The windshield wipers could barely keep up with the falling snow.

Snow drifted along fence posts and familiar landmarks. Once she reached the county road, Katie thought conditions would likely improve. Her predictions proved valid. Trucks with blades threw a wide shield of ice packed snow. She spotted the farm truck coming at her and beeped. Tottie flew past waving.

The drive was uneventful except for an occasional slide that she righted easily. She passed Ben's office, and her heart did a familiar spasm. She'd driven past the same office for years and never looked, but today all she could think about was the man sitting behind the desk.

He'd stopped by the hospital a couple of times, once with a detective to interview her about her relationship with Warren and the events leading up to her fall, the second only briefly to drop off a paper for her to sign. She'd had to go over all of the harassment and the frightening incidents. As she reviewed her encounters with the detective, she'd felt even more foolish not to have noticed the clues, like Warren's attitude toward women and the way he avoided the shelter. Having Clara in his house had driven him to distraction, but in Katie's innocence, she had chalked it up to the politician's personality. Not even the most optimistic person could expect Warren and Clara to be compatible.

Ben had looked good on his visits, with his wind-kissed cheeks and tousled reddish hair. Why had it taken all these years for her to recognize what a truly great guy he was? So great that during one of his visits a nurse had invited him to a New Year's Eve party and he'd accepted.

That would be tonight, him and her, toasting sparkling beverages to usher in the new year.

Happy New Year to you, Katie. Because of your thickheadedness, you will be sitting at home toasting with milk.

Ah, Katie, you never were good picking the odds.

True, Grandpops. Odds were I should have married a hometown boy and lived happily, if not boringly, ever after. Now she was on the downhill side of thirty (on a greased sled) with no prospects in sight. Marrying a hometown boy turned sheriff didn't sound the least boring, but a girl couldn't marry a man who refused to date her. There were some pretty hard-nosed rules to this ever-after stuff.

But Katie had given up on men. She was through trying to second-guess God. She'd just grow old, spout coarse hairs out of her chin, and hot flash her way to eternity. Drinking lattes.

What in your life has made you give up, Katie Addison? And whom have you given up on?

The last thought grabbed her attention. Who indeed. God? She would never give up on God. Gypsies, yes, but never on God.

A squad car pulled up when she was leaving the coffee shop later. Bill Parker, one of Ben's deputies, got out.

"Hey, Katie. Glad to see you up and around. You had us pretty worried for awhile."

"Thanks, Bill. Happy New Year."

He touched the brim of his hat. "The same. You got big plans?"

Oh yeah. Really big ones. Changing diapers and making milk toasts.

"Plan to spend a quiet one this year." She smiled.

The deputy walked on, and Katie slid behind the wheel and started the engine.

Bill suddenly shot out of the café. Katie watched as he jumped into the squad car and flipped on his emergency beacon. Rolling down his window, he called, "My CB's acting up. Can you tell Ben we got an emergency at the high school?"

"Sure—"

With siren screaming, the deputy screeched off.

Katie's heart sang. *Tell Ben they have an emergency.* Perfect timing. She could wish him a Happy New Year free of ulterior motive. Well, almost free.

She veered out of the drive and drove to the sheriff's office. Ben's car wasn't in his parking space. She exited the jeep and entered the cinder block building. The dispatcher looked up.

"Ben around, Ruby?"

"Think he's at the high school."

Rats. He'd already gotten the message.

"You going that way?"

Katie turned. "I can. Why?"

"Tell Ben when he's through at the school, the Barclays are having another marital spat. He needs to get out there as soon as he can."

Nodding, Katie closed the door and jogged back to the jeep, hope renewed. Minutes later she pulled up beside Ben's squad car parked at the entrance to the high school gym. The car was empty and the school dark.

Katie sat for a moment, lost in memories. She and Ben had graduated here. He'd been right there in plain sight all of these years. Katie remembered the childish Valentines they'd exchanged and the football and basketball games they'd attended. After a minute she pecked on the horn, then hit it with a resounding blast to get his attention.

Ben opened the door, dressed in a black tux, and held up a sign that read: *Come inside?* Katie's heart shot to her throat. He looked ... fantastic. He had a date with that nurse tonight.

She didn't have a sign to object, but she wouldn't have anyway. All she wanted was to walk into his arms. He opened the door wider and called, "Come on, Katie! You have to see this."

Oh, I see this clearly. You, looking better than a pizza banquet to a starving woman. Stretching the truth, she'd say, "Have a wonderful time at the party tonight." She would smile and wish him a Happy New Year. How far could her graciousness extend to the man she suddenly knew was Mr. Right? A man who was now ready to move on without her?

He pitched the sign aside. "Are you coming or not? It's cold out there!"

"I'm coming!" *Fool. You're going, but you shouldn't. Help me, God, to extend the courtesy this man deserves. With love so pent up inside me, I'm terrified it will spill over and I'll make a bigger fool of myself.*

Oh. He probably needed his tie adjusted. That's what he wanted. His cummerbund tightened? Maybe advice. Was his cologne too strong, not strong enough? Did he look okay?

And she in her Piccadilly world would straighten his tie, adjust his cummerbund, and make an honest assessment of his cologne—though he'd smell good no matter what. *I can only take so much, Lord.*

Sarcasm, Katie? Aren't you the culprit, not Ben?

Crawling out of the jeep, Katie yanked the hood of her coat over her ball cap and trudged to the gym entrance. Ben's tux made her sweats stand out like a hen in a stockyard.

"Grandma was old," he teased when she took her time stomping snow off her boots.

"I thought you threw away all your signs."

"I did—except for one. Stop grousing and get in here."

"Don't hurry me," she warned, on the verge of tears now. She swallowed the lump crowding her throat. *God, is this fair? Punish me some other way, but not like this, here with him so close I can smell his aftershave, yet planets apart.* "Ruby said to tell you the Barclays are into it again, and you need to get out there as soon as you can."

"Already have it covered."

Katie trailed Ben through the dimly lit building. *Katie, say something nice, compliment him on his looks because he looks smashing.* And tall. Funny, she was three inches taller but the difference wasn't all that noticeable. "You look nice."

He turned to glance over his shoulder. "Yeah, you too."

Her hand flew to her ball cap, and she thought about the sweats with a Chrissy burp on the shoulder. Yeah, she looked Kate Moss ravishing.

"What happened? Kids break in?"

"No, looks like the work of adults."

"Adults. Why would adults want to damage the school when they pay taxes for the building?"

"If I could read people's minds, my job would be a lot easier." The soles of his high sheen black dress shoes clicked on the polished hallway.

Katie's scuffed boots hardly made a decent squeak.

They reached the gym door, and he leaned to pick up something off a nearby table. She caught a glimpse of a corsage—white gardenias. He turned back, his tone softening. "Katie Addison, you're going to shoot me, and I admit this is an underhanded way to take you to your prom, but would you do me the honor of the first dance?"

Katie's jaw dropped when he bent and pinned the flower to her coat lapel.

"Ben ..."

"I know what you're thinking. What is that lovesick fool up to now? There's no prom—that was twenty years ago. This is New Year's Eve, and he's too old—we're both too old for a prom."

Her chin rose. "I wasn't thinking that."

"If the next words out of your mouth are 'go fly a kite' so help me—"

"No!" Her hand flew to cover his lips—sweet kissable lips. "Ben . . ." The scent of gardenias—and him, made her heady. "What have you done? How did you accomplish this?"

"Simple. Tottie and her crew decorated the gym. Ruby sent Bill to get you. Janet's going to take the milk home. By the way, the milk wasn't bad. That's the only excuse Tottie could think of to get out of the house. But since you insisted on going for coffee, they invented the housekeeping story. The town just wanted something to do on New Year's Eve, so I invited them to our prom."

He turned, opening the double set of gym doors. Inside party streamers, balloons, and banners hung suspended from rafters. Familiar faces swum before her: Tottie, Janet, Ruth, Meg, Mary Hoskins, a teacher or two she recognized, the principal, and former schoolmates, all townspeople she'd known and loved most of her life. In the center of the gym, a large crystal ball slowly rotated, scattering tiny stars across the gymnasium walls.

Ben reached for her hand. "Your prom, Katie. Twenty years late, but if we're going to start over, I can't think of a better night for new beginnings."

Katie sagged against him, and his arm protectively closed around her. Bending close, he whispered, "I've been meaning to correct my confusing statement—the one I said when you asked if we could continue our friendship."

Katie nodded. "The one where you said no, that you were going to move on?"

"That one." His arm tightened possessively. "I'm not willing to continue as is. But I'm more than willing to start over, and this time we know our mistakes and won't repeat them."

"Oh, Ben." She turned to kiss him, the way Mr. Right should be kissed, and should have been kissed years ago. His grip tightened as the crystal ball bathed them in sparkling light. Clapping broke out, and the Platters began to sing "The Great Pretender." Couples moved to the gym floor and the celebration began.

"I don't know what to say," Katie whispered when she caught her breath.

Ben's gaze softened to a silent plea. "Just say you're willing to start over."

"I'm so willing," she said.

"Good, I would hate to throw you in jail until you came around to my way of thinking." He kissed her long and thoroughly, and then pulled her onto the gym floor. "Come with me. I want you beside me when I tell Ruth the news."

"What news? Her daughter? Does it have something to do with her daughter?"

"You'll see. Come with me." They approached Ruth, who turned from the punch bowl smiling. Immediately the smile faded. "What? Has something happened—" Her face drained of color. "My husband—he knows where I am?"

"No." Katie reached out to support her. She glanced at Ben. "At least I don't think so. Ben?"

"Ruth, come over here." He led her to the sidelines, and Katie followed. *Oh, please Lord. The night is so perfect. Please don't let what Ben is about to say spoil it.* Ruth turned when they reached the row of folding chairs, eyes bright with unshed tears.

Pulling her gently into a seat, Ben said quietly, "A fax came in late this morning concerning your husband. I'm sorry, Ruth. He's been diagnosed with pancreatic cancer. It's terminal."

Ruth caught her breath and tears rolled from the corners of her eyes. Katie reached out to put a comforting hand on her shoulder.

"How long?"

"The doctors say he won't leave the hospital. You're free to pick up your daughter. She's staying with his parents, but they've asked that you be notified. They feel she should be with her mother."

Ruth burst into tears, burying her face in her hands. Katie glanced at Ben, and she knew that love shone brightly in her eyes. He couldn't have given Ruth a more precious but bittersweet gift. Janet and Tottie came to sit with Ruth, and Ben led Katie to the gym floor.

Katie gazed into his beautiful hazel eyes. "I love you."

"For what? I just had to do one of the hardest jobs in the world. Tell someone her husband is dying."

"I know, and Ruth still has feelings for him. But now she'll have her daughter back. She can rebuild her life." Katie suddenly remembered she was wearing ratty sweats and a ball cap. "Ben! This is my prom!"

"You look beautiful." His voice rose to a shout. "You're beautiful, Katie Addison. And I love you!"

Commotion at the front door interrupted their conversation. Two men wearing dark sunglasses commanded the doorway, arms piled high with week-late Christmas gifts. Katie recognized the newcomers as Clara's people. She hurriedly moved to meet the newcomers. "May I help you?"

"Katie Addison?"

"Yes."

In a monotone, the man indicated the boxes and explained. "Clara Townsend sends her Christmas wishes to the shelter."

Katie stared at the pile of gaily wrapped foil packages.

"There's fifty more in the trunk and backseat," the second man said.

Clara. The ice queen!

"Senator Townsend sent this personal note." The first man handed her a beautiful, foil-embossed envelope smelling faintly of cigarette smoke. Katie opened it, and her eyes misted when she read the handwritten message. "Merry Christmas to my shelter family. May God's blessing be upon you." Enclosed was a check for twenty-five thousand dollars. Katie's eyes teared. *Well, I guess there's more than one kind of simple white sari in this world.*

Ben stepped closer, his arm encircling Katie's waist. "Enough there to possibly buy those horses, if you're still in the market?"

"The horses?" Katie's mind whirled. "I can't—the owner wants them back."

"She does, but from what I hear, she loves those animals. But when I call and tell her what they've done for the shelter women, the therapy they provide, and shoot her a fair offer, she might see the wisdom of leaving the horses right where they are."

Katie stepped into his arms with every intention of remaining there the rest of her life. Color flooded her cheeks, and the sudden image of the plaque hanging over Grandpops's desk flashed through her mind. *I believe.* The gypsy made a lucky guess, but Grandpops hit the nail on the head. Katie wished he could be here today to witness this miracle.

She whispered a silent pledge to her Maker, her Redeemer—but most of all, her friend. "I'll never take my eye off you again."

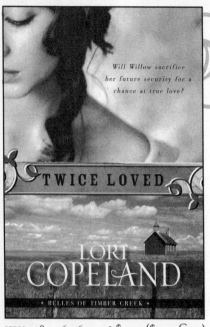

Monday Morning Faith

Lori Copeland

Dear Mom and Pop,

Two days ago we all spent the afternoon in palm trees. One of the village dogs broke his leash and treed the whole community. The dog is mean, but I have managed to form a cautious relationship with him by feeding him scraps from our table, and jelly beans ... I hope candy doesn't hurt a dog; it hasn't hurt this dog, I can assure you.

I know you're wondering about Sam ... I love him with all my heart, but sometimes love isn't enough.

Love always,
Johanna

Librarian Johanna Holland likes her simple life in Saginaw, Michigan. So why is she standing in the middle of the New Guinea Jungle? Johanna is simply aghast at the lack of hot showers and ... well ... clothing! She is positive the mission field is most certainly not God's plan for her life, but will that mean letting go of the man she loves? Warm and whimsical, *Monday Morning Faith* will take you on a spiritual journey filled with depth and humor.

Softcover: 978-0-310-26349-2

Simple Gifts

Lori Copeland

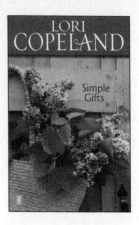

Can anything else go wrong? Marlene Queens goes home to Parnass Springs, Missouri, to put her late Aunt Beth's house on the market and settle the estate. But once she's back home, Marlene suddenly finds herself in over her head. Her Aunt Ingrid grows more demanding by the day. Marlene discovers her childhood sweetheart is now the local vet and the town's acting mayor. And when a group of citizens want to put up a statue in memory of Marlene's father — the parent who always embarrassed her as a child — Marlene is unwillingly swept into a firestorm of controversy.

As one thing leads to another, Marlene sees her entire life being rearranged before her eyes. Parnass Springs may never be the same. Marlene fears that the secret she's kept for years may be revealed. Can God work a miracle so she can finally have the future she's longed for?

Softcover: 978-0-310-26350-6

Pick up a copy today at your favorite bookstore!